MW00579760

Rustic HEARTS

AMBER KELLY

Copyright © 2019 by Amber Kelly

ISBN: 978-1-7336899-2-2

All rights reserved.

No part of this book may be reproduced or transmitted in any form or by any means, electronic or mechanical, including photocopying, recording, or by any information storage and retrieval systems without written permission from the author, except for the use of brief quotations in a book review.

This book is a work of fiction. Names, characters, places, and incidents either are products of the author's imagination or are used fictitiously. Any resemblance to actual persons, living or dead, events, or locales is entirely coincidental.

Cover Design: Sommer Stein, *Perfect Pear Creative Covers*
Cover Image: Michaela Mangum, *Michaela Mangum Photography*
Editor: Jovana Shirley, *Unforeseen Editing*
Proofreader: Judy Zweifel, *Judy's Proofreading*
Formatter: *Champagne Book Design*

To Momma, who taught me from the beginning that I am enough.

Rustic
HEARTS

Prologue

SOPHIE
Twelve Years Old

"WHY DO WE HAVE TO LEAVE NOW?" I ASK DROWSILY as Momma frantically throws my belongings into my pink suitcase at the edge of my bed.

"Because we need to be gone before your father gets home tomorrow. I already explained this to you."

"I still don't understand. What did he do that was so bad?"

"You're too young for all the details, Sophia. I will tell you one day, but for now, we have to get our things and get out of here if we're going to catch our flight to New York. You've always wanted to go to New York, right? That's why I chose it."

I have always wanted to go to New York City. Ever since I became obsessed with *Big City Girl*, which was a television program that came on Friday nights and followed the lives of a glamorous group of friends living in the Big Apple. They were all beautiful, wealthy, in college, and having the time of their lives. I wanted to be Sinclair Alcott one day. I didn't think that day would be today.

"When are we coming back? School starts in two weeks, and Blackberry's foal is due anytime now. I have to be back in time to help. She's my horse."

Momma stops her progress and finally looks at me. The manic excitement is draining from her face.

"I'm not sure when we will be back," she says a little more calmly. "You might be going to school in New York for a while."

What? I might want to visit New York one day, but this is home. The ranch, my horse, Daddy, and all my friends are here.

"I don't want to go to school there. I want to go to school here in Poplar Falls."

Her face falls at my declaration. "We can discuss this later. Here, get up and get your coat and shoes on. *Now*, young lady."

I begrudgingly do as I was told. I know my mother well enough to know that arguing with her when she is in this state is futile. I'll just have to call Daddy as soon as I'm able and get him to calm her down. He's the only one who has ever been able to talk her down, and he'll convince her to come back home.

"Stop sulking, Sophia," she says as she wraps her arm around me in the back of the taxi as we drive away from our farmhouse. "You're going to love this new adventure of ours. I promise."

I turn and look out the back windshield at the barn as we drive down the long driveway. I sure hope Blackberry holds on a little longer. I don't want her to wonder where I am when her baby is born. She'll think I abandoned her. I would never leave her or my daddy and my best friend, Dallas. They're my absolute favorite people. Technically, Blackberry is not a person, but she loves like one.

I do my best to hold back tears as the barn fades off into the distance.

Momma continues to try to convince me of the fun we're going to have.

"We will find an apartment in the city, close to Central Park. There are lots of animals in the park and horse-drawn carriages. You'll be able to see horses every day. I'll get a job and work during the day, we'll enroll you in a fabulous school, and in the evenings, I can audition for Broadway. It might take me a little while to get back into performance shape, but I will, and you can take ballet classes and voice lessons. It's going to be an amazing adventure. You'll see."

Excitement oozes from her pores as she squeezes me into her side.

There is no use in trying to reason with her when she gets like this, so I nod and play along for now.

"Sure, Momma, it'll be amazing."

I hope Daddy sees my note soon.

One

"STALL THEM UNTIL I GET THERE. OFFER THEM COFFEE AND doughnuts or a margarita or ten. Whatever it takes to keep their asses in those seats," I instruct my assistant, Charlotte, as I frantically try to hail a cab.

The electricity to my building was cut while I was in the middle of washing my hair this morning. A construction worker on the building site at the corner had dug in an area that he wasn't supposed to and cut our main power line. I got out of the shower, tried to get myself dressed appropriately in the dark, and towel-dried my long blonde hair as best I could. Then, I threw it up in an unflattering top knot and ran out the door, only to find the elevator was in slow motion, running on the backup generator. This left me with the option of waiting a long while for an elevator packed full of frustrated occupants or to take the stairs down the ten flights to the lobby. I opted for the stairs—bad choice. Ten flights down on my sky-high Manolos was a dangerous undertaking, and it took forever, so now, I'm facing rush-hour traffic in Midtown Manhattan on an unusually warm September day, heading to meet with what will undoubtedly be some pretty put-out business associates when I finally make it in.

I arrive at my office off 36th Street and run as fast as I can to the conference room with Charlotte on my heels.

Charlotte and I have been friends since we were in middle school. She was the first person I met when Mom and I arrived in New York over twenty years ago. Why my mother placed me in a private Catholic school is beyond me—I had been raised Baptist—but I'm so glad she did. I would have been lost without Charlotte and her blonde pixie cut and no-nonsense attitude.

Right now, however, she is a tad frantic. Like a little fairy flitting around me.

"The gentleman's name is Marcus Stedman. He's the general manager of the Park Avenue store, and the lady's name is …"

"Gail Caldwell, the head buyer for all of the Maple and Park department stores. I know who she is." I snatch the folders she just dug from her briefcase and pass her my coat and bag as we hurry down the hall.

"They've had coffee and doughnuts, and I entertained them with stories from my SoulCycle class. Thank God you're here because I don't think they want to hear about last night's disaster of a date, and I'm running out of interesting material."

Dear Lord. If I'm able to save this deal, it will be a miracle.

I stop in the hallway leading to the conference room and take a moment to compose myself. "How do I look?"

"Like a wet puppy who ran all the way here from Chelsea."

"Perfect, just the look I was going for. How do I smell?"

Charlotte leans in and wrinkles her nose in disgust. "Like an old gym bag."

Awesome.

She reaches in her briefcase, grabs a bottle, and liberally spritzes me.

"Ugh, what was that?"

"Perfume. It'll help."

"Perfect. Now, I smell like a sweaty flower."

"There's nothing you can do about it. They aren't here to sniff you anyway. Go." She shoves me toward the door. "They're here to pitch to you, not the other way around."

I turn back to her and say in a small voice, "Tell me we deserve this."

"You deserve this, Sophie," she confirms.

"We," I correct her. "We deserve this."

She smiles a pleased smile. "We deserve this. Now, go get 'em."

I smooth the front of my dress and take a deep, calming breath before I open the door and walk in.

All eyes turn to me as I make my way to the head of the conference table and introduce myself. "Hello, Gail, Marcus. I'm Sophia Lancaster." I clear my throat and continue, "But you can call me Sophie. Please accept my sincere apology for keeping you waiting. There was an unavoidable hiccup at my building this morning that delayed me."

Marcus shifts to extend his hand to me. Annoyance clear in his expression.

Gail offers her hand next with a genuine smile. "It happens. I'm afraid we're going to have to jump right into business though. We have another meeting in an hour."

"Of course."

She taps on the laptop in front of her, and the screen of the television on the opposite wall illuminates with a PowerPoint presentation.

"As you know, Maple and Park is interested in a partnership. We would like for you to design a few exclusive pieces to be sold only in our stores and online through our website."

A small thrill shoots through me at the thought of my jewelry designs being sold in one of Park Avenue's trendiest department stores.

"When you say exclusive pieces, that means, we can't sell other designs to other partners or on our website, correct?"

She looks up and smiles warmly. I'm obviously new to all of this.

"No, you are only obligated to keep the pieces we approve exclusive to Maple and Park. You can continue to design and sell anything else privately or through any other retail outlets."

I give her an appreciative nod as Marcus takes over.

"We want new designs. Something no one else has seen or worn before. We've outlined what we're looking for to help you. Simple.

Elegant. We'll start small with a few pendants, rings, and bracelets. Test the market. If those do well, we can revisit our contract and extend to·earrings and brooches. We want to launch the line before the holiday season, so that gives you a couple of weeks to get with our art department and get samples in."

"Okay, I can get some sketches together fairly quickly. Do you have projected sales? As of now, our newly purchased warehouse is being renovated and equipped to begin assembly, and I think we'll be up and running within the month. My staff is still minimal, but we're interviewing. Depending on the volume—"

He puts his hand in the air to halt my rambling. "We realize you're a start-up. We're buying the designs, and the customers will know and appreciate they are custom pieces. So, at first, we'll need a small amount for display and for purchase at our two locations. Online orders can be made to order."

Relief replaces the tension that was strumming through my body.

I started designing quirky jewelry pieces while I was a student at New York School of Design. I would sketch out each unique piece, then buy the materials, and make them by hand in my apartment at night. I sold a few of them at the Williamsburg open market in Brooklyn on weekends, and that led to me opening an online Etsy shop. It was a way to make easy money while finishing my degree. Sales were steady enough, and I was pleased to be creating something. Then, one day this past June, my world exploded when *the* Judy Winston wore one of my brooches to the Tony Awards. She won for Best Actress in a Musical and was photographed with her award, wearing my piece front and center on her gown. She later that night told an E! News interviewer that she had purchased it from my online site. The next day, orders started pouring in—hundreds and hundreds of orders. There was no way I could fulfill the volume from my living room. That was when Stanhope stepped in. Stanhope Marshall is one of the most successful businessmen in Manhattan, and he just so happens to be married to my mother, Vivian. He came to me with a proposition, and just like that, I had my first investor in Sophia Doreen Designs, LLC.

It's been a whirlwind ever since. Now, I have a sleek office in an uptown building owned by Stanhope; twelve full-time employees, including Charlotte; and a warehouse in the Fashion District that is being converted into a workshop as we speak. I'm about to close my first major deal to have my line in a real-life brick-and-mortar store. Exciting doesn't begin to describe this feeling.

After we hash out costs and crunch numbers, they stand to leave with a signed contract in hand.

"Thank you for your time, Sophie. I think this is going to be a profitable relationship for both our companies. I love your designs and think they will fit perfectly with the Maple and Park brand." Gail squeezes my hand before they enter the elevator.

Marcus gives me a quick wink as the doors slide shut, and I release the breath I've been holding since I walked into the meeting.

Charlotte comes bounding out from behind her desk and skids to a halt in front of me. "Well?" Her eyes, full of nervous anticipation, expectantly stare into mine.

"We did it," I whisper through a huge grin.

"Oh my," she squeals as we both start jumping up and down. "I knew you would nail it. In spite of the wet doughnut on your head and your sweaty pits."

"Thanks. We need to celebrate."

"Okay, I'll call and get us a table at Marea for seven p.m. Just us?"

"And my parents. I'm going to call Stanhope now and tell him the good news. I know Mom will want to rush right over."

Two

SOPHIE

FOUR HOURS LATER, CHARLOTTE AND I WALK INTO MAREA ON Central Park South. The hostess spots us immediately and motions for us to follow her to a quiet table in the back where my mother and stepfather are already seated with a bottle of red wine breathing. Stanhope stands when he sees us approaching. He's a towering man with silver hair and kind eyes, dressed in an expensive, custom gray business suit. He reminds me of Michael Douglas, and my mother is very much his Catherine Zeta-Jones, more than a decade younger and a classic beauty. Once we are seated, he motions for the waiter to pour the wine.

"Darling, I can't tell you how proud Stan and I are of you. I always knew you were destined to light this city on fire."

My mother has always been my biggest cheerleader. I know she was disappointed when I showed zero interest in the performing arts. Her greatest desire was to be an actress, and she wanted so badly to pass that passion on to me. She named me for Sophia Loren after all.

Mom was a dancer and vocalist. Those talents—along with her long, dark hair, ice-blue eyes, and svelte figure—got her cast in a handful of background roles in a few off-Broadway musicals through the years, but she never quite achieved the level of stardom she'd dreamed of reaching.

Once she knew it wasn't in the cards for her, she set her sights on her little girl becoming the next Kristin Chenoweth. Unfortunately,

I had been born with two left feet and without the ability to carry a tune.

I tried dance lessons and voice lessons from some of the most renowned instructors in New York, but she finally had to accept that her daughter was a theater dud.

One thing I have always been good at, however, is drawings. So, she decided to help me hone those skills, and she and Stanhope paid for fashion design school. I think she was hoping I would be the next Kate Spade or Vera Wang, but the way she is beaming at me at this moment tells me that she would be thrilled if I were to become the next Harry Winston instead.

"Yes, Maple and Park, that is quite impressive. You must be extremely excited," Stanhope says with pride in his voice as well.

"I am—and a bit nervous. I hope they like the designs I present to them and, more importantly, that their customers like and purchase them."

"Oh, nonsense. Stop biting your bottom lip," my mother says as she swats at my face. "Everyone is going to love them." She brings her hand to her chest, and her voice catches with emotion as she adds, "And with Judy wearing one of your brooches at the Tonys—*the* Tony Awards—that's just incredible. That buzz will make you the go-to designer for jewels for galas and events for the rest of this year's award season. You need to make sure that you send a few unique pieces to a couple of A-list stylists for free as well."

"Now, now, Viv, I'm sure Sophie knows what she is doing. We don't need to meddle." Stanhope placatingly pats her hand as he delivers the blow.

My mother is the master meddler. Especially when it comes to my life. I'm the only thirty-two-year-old I know whose mother still hovers like she did when I was a child.

"Of course she does, but there is no harm in a few helpful suggestions, now is there, darling?"

"Not at all, Mom."

The waiter arrives to take our orders and opens another bottle of wine.

"Charlotte, how is that brother of yours doing? Is he still at Harvard?"

"Yes, ma'am. He has one more year of law school."

"Your parents must be so proud. Does he plan to move back to New York after graduation?"

"I'm not sure. He seems to love the Boston area."

"Boston is a lovely town, but Manhattan is the place to be for any bright, up-and-coming corporate attorney. You should give him Stanhope's contact information. Perhaps Stan could make a few beneficial introductions for him."

Charlotte gives me a pointed look as she answers, "Sure thing, Mrs. Marshall. I'll pass that along next time we talk."

"Mom," I warn, "we've talked about this. Alex and I are not getting back together."

"Never say never, darling."

"Never. There, I said it."

"Oh, Sophia, I don't know why you insist on being alone. A strong, independent woman does not, by definition, have to be a single woman. I want you to be as happy as I was when I met Stan. Being his wife is my greatest joy. Can't a mother want that for her daughter?"

What she means is, she wants me to find a wealthy man with a prestigious name and let being his wife be my greatest joy. I know my mother loves Stanhope, but I also know that love would not be enough to keep her joyous forever should he wake up penniless one day.

"Mom, I don't need a husband to have joy. I'm very happy. If the right relationship comes along, great. If not, that's okay too."

"Speaking of, I gave your number to my friend Lydia. Her son, Lawrence, recently bought an uptown loft near your office, and she thought maybe you two could meet for drinks or dinner or something one evening."

"Mom, you didn't," I groan.

"He's handsome and successful and just a sweetheart. He picked her up from the club the other day in his new McLaren, and he offered to take us both to lunch. Such a gentleman and a real estate mogul. He has purchased and flipped an impressive number of properties in SoHo and Tribeca and is doing a renovation in the Hamptons. That boy is going places."

I roll my eyes in Charlotte's direction.

"Can't you meet him for drinks? He moved here all the way from Atlanta, and he doesn't know that many people in the city. He could use a friend if nothing else."

"Viv, don't push."

Stanhope gives me a sympathetic look. We both know that once my mother gets an idea in her head, come hell or high water, she will connive and scheme until she gets her way. It's better just to give in than to fight it.

"Fine. If he calls, I'll be happy to meet him out. As a friend."

At that, she beams her gorgeous hundred-watt smile at me.

Charlotte chuckles and then coughs out, "Sucker," under her breath.

I am indeed a sucker when it comes to my mother.

We finish our meals, and Stanhope orders one of every dessert they have on the menu along with a bottle of their best champagne.

We toast to the future, and for the first time, I feel like I've found my niche in this world. I've always felt a little like an outsider here. It's been twenty years since we landed in Manhattan, and it has taken me all this time to feel like I belong. I'm not the Colorado imposter anymore. I'm a true New Yorker, a businesswoman, and my career is just taking off. I can't wait to see what comes next.

Three

SOPHIE

THE LAST FEW WEEKS HAVE BEEN A WHIRLWIND OF ACTIVITY. Gail and Marcus approved the set of sketches I'd sent over, and my line launched in the stores two days ago. Just in time for the holiday sales push. According to Gail, end of September, first of October is the ideal shopping period to maximize holiday sales.

It was a more significant success than I could have imagined. Maple and Park almost instantly sold out of all the in-stock pieces at both locations and placed a double order for next month.

Our manufacturing shop was completed late last week, and our staff has been working nonstop to replenish Maple and Park's stock and to fulfill their online orders.

At this rate, we'll be able to break even this year. That's a remarkable feat for a first-year start-up.

Stanhope is more than pleased with the return on his investment, and he has other partners who are ready to invest if I need that cash flow in the future. For now, however, I'm content to continue at the pace we are growing and see how it goes.

I just finished my last conference call with a raw material supplier and have a few minutes to freshen myself up before Lawrence—Mom's fix-up—picks me up for our blind date.

I don't date often. It's not that I don't want to date; it's just easier not to. After Alex and I broke up when he moved to Cambridge for law school, I went out with a few guys from class and even joined an online dating service, but the last few guys I met online were less than honest on their profiles. One flat-out used a different name, photo, and bio. When he showed up at the coffee shop we had agreed to meet at, he was at least two decades older than he had listed. It's hard being single in this day and age. No one is who they present themselves to be on social media.

Lawrence picks me up from the office at six p.m., and we head around the corner to one of my favorite casual bar restaurants for happy hour and dinner.

Mom was right. He is beautiful, tall with dark hair that he pulls back off his face into a tasteful man bun. His cheekbones are high and his jaw chiseled. He has full lips and gorgeous caramel-colored eyes. I actually think Mom might have done the impossible and set me up with someone with potential. That is, until about halfway through dinner.

"So, Sophia, how is it that someone as stunning as you is still single?" he asks nonchalantly as he twirls the stem of his wineglass.

"Just haven't met the right guy, I suppose. Not that I haven't been a little too preoccupied to look for him."

"I bet you wouldn't have to look too hard. I'm sure a long line of men would be at your door, if given a chance. I'll be honest, the way your mother persisted, I half-expected a middle-aged spinster, not a beautiful, smart, sexy woman."

I take a sip of my wine and let his compliment pour over me like warm honey. "Thank you. You're not hard on the eyes yourself, and yes, my mother is very persistent when she wants something. Although I would bet it took a lot more persuading for you to agree to this date than it did for me."

He quirks one eyebrow in question. "What makes you say that?"

I lean in and lower my voice to just above a whisper. "Because, Mr. Newberry, I dare say you have spent much more time tonight gazing into our waiter's eyes than you have mine."

He sinks back in his chair and gives me a sexy grin. Then, he shrugs. "Still not a hardship to spend the evening with you, Miss Lancaster."

I raise my glass. "To the beginning of a beautiful friendship."

"Indeed."

He winks and clinks his glass with mine.

After dinner, we move to the bar and end up closing the place down. I call myself an Uber, and Lawrence takes our waiter, Jose, back to his apartment.

All in all, not the worst date I've ever been on.

My phone rings as I make it home.

I grab it from my purse and answer, "Hi, Mom. Hold on a second. I'm just unlocking my door."

Once I'm inside, I pick back up.

"So, how did the date go? Or is it still going? Is he there?" she asks hopefully.

"No, it's just me. He got a better offer."

"What do you mean, he got a better offer?"

"I mean, our date ended when he picked up another one at the bar."

"What? He didn't!" She gasps, appalled by the possibility.

"Oh, he did," I confirm.

"That's just not done. I'm calling Lydia this instant."

"Mom, Lawrence is into men. He left with our server."

"He just left you and went off with someone else in the middle of your date? How rude," she stammers, offended on my behalf.

"It wasn't the middle; it was the end. Did you hear the part about him being gay, Mom?"

"Yes. Damn it, all the pretty ones are nowadays."

"Yeah, they are," I agree because, well, they are.

"Are you sure he's not just bi-curious?"

"Mom!"

"Just asking."

"No. And how do you even know what bi-curious is?"

"Please, I grew up in the seventies. We were all about free love."

Ew. I do not want to hear anything about my mother and free love.

"I'm sorry, darling. Lydia never mentioned he was unavailable in that way. Oh my, she must not know."

"It's fine. It was actually one of the better dates I'd been on lately."

"Oh, honey. That's just sad."

We both burst into laughter because she's not wrong.

"I want you to be happy, baby. Married to a handsome man who treats you like a princess."

"I am happy, Mom. And I know you are jonesing to be a grandmother but—"

"What? No, I'm way too young to be a grandmother. My mother is a grandmother. Not me."

"If you marry me off and I start popping out babies, what do you think that's going to make you?"

"Nina. I'll be Nina."

"Did you just make that up?"

"Yes. Don't you think it sounds so much more sophisticated than grandmother?"

There really isn't a posh alternative to the title *grandmother*. When I was little, I called my grandparents Maw Maw and Paw Paw and Gram and Pop. None of those would do for Vivian Marshall.

"Not really. But don't worry. I don't plan to make you use either title anytime soon."

I yawn.

"It's late. I'll let you get your beauty sleep, darling. I'm sorry about the Lawrence thing."

"It's okay, Mom. I think I made a new friend, and in my book, that's a pretty good way to spend an evening."

"Good night, my onliest only."

"Good night, Mom."

Four

SOPHIE

"YOU HAVE A CALL ON LINE ONE. SOMEONE NAMED DOE. Who the hell names their child Doe?"

My chest seizes as Charlotte's voice comes through the intercom.

"It's my aunt Doreen. My father's older sister. I used to call her Aunt Doe when I was little."

"Oh," she says in surprise. "You want me to get rid of her?"

I haven't spoken to anyone in my father's family since I was a kid. They're practically strangers now. Just faded memories.

Something must have happened for her to reach out now.

Momentary fear hits me. *What if it's Daddy?*

"No, I'll take it. Just give me a minute and send her through."

"Okay, I'll give you two."

I take a few deep breaths and give myself a quick pep talk before the line rings, and I answer, "Hello?"

"Sophie," she says my name on a small sob.

"Hi, Aunt Doe."

"How are you, baby girl?"

"Not a baby girl anymore. It's been a long time. What can I do for you?"

"I know. Too long. I'm hoping to remedy that though. We need you to come home, sweetheart."

Home. For so many years, all I wanted to do was go home. But now, this is home. New York is home.

"I'm assuming you mean Colorado."

"Yes. Your grandma Lancaster passed away this morning. It would mean a lot to Pop and us if you could come home for the service."

My grandma was a huge part of my childhood. I loved her with all my heart. She taught me how to bake cookies and braid my hair.

Grief hits me. Unexpected pain. I mourned the loss of my family a long time ago. I thought I was past it.

"I don't know, Aunt Doe," I whisper over the line.

"Sophie, it's time to come home and face your father and work this out. Don't you think?"

"Why should I go to him? He knows where I am. He's always known where I am. Not once in all these years has he come looking for me."

"It has to be you, sweetheart. He's a stubborn, old coot. He wants to see you, Sophie. He doesn't know how to reach out."

I snort. "Of course he does. He's a grown man. A grown man with a happy family from what I've been told."

"A grown man with an incomplete family and a broken heart."

I sniffle across the line. I don't believe a word she's saying.

"A broken heart? He threw us away. He threw me away because of them. He wanted them instead of us."

"Oh, Sophie, honey, you only know the part of the story you were told, but it's not the whole story."

"Really? What am I missing, Aunt Doe? Because, from where I'm sitting, it looks like my mother caught him having an affair with one of the ranch hands' sisters, and when she confronted him, he told her to get out. Then, he proceeded to marry the woman, the two of them raised her niece and nephew, and he forgot all about us. Am I right so far?"

"That's not the whole story or the entire truth."

"You know what? It doesn't even matter anymore. I'm okay now.

I'm no longer the shattered twelve-year-old, waiting for him to call or show up. He's had twenty years to clear up anything that he needed to. Twenty years of missed birthdays and holidays and school events and graduations. He's missed my entire life."

"I know he has. And that is a regret he will have to live with for the rest of his days. But, sweetheart, I don't want something to happen to him or to you and for the two of you to never have the conversation you need to have. Besides, Pop and Aunt Ria and I are getting old, and we want to see our girl. At least once more. Come home for Gram's funeral. Please, Sophia."

She's laying it on thick. Exactly the way I remember her.

"I'll think about it."

"That's all I ask. The service is scheduled for next weekend. We'll have the will reading after, and Gram's attorney asked for you to be present for that as well. Book a flight and call me. You can stay here at the house. I've missed you so much."

"I've missed you too."

And I have. I forgot just how much until I heard her voice again.

I hang up and then sit and stare at the phone. Hurt that I thought I was well past starts to prick at my heart.

When my mother stole away with me in the middle of the night all those years ago, I knew my daddy would come for me. Even once we got to New York, I waited for him. Every day. But he never came.

After about a year of me asking to call him and begging to go home, Mom broke the news that he was marrying someone else and that he was moving a new family into our home and didn't want us anymore. I couldn't believe it. I didn't believe it for a very long time. But he never came, so I accepted it and boxed up all that hurt and all those memories of my life in Colorado, placed them in a compartment in my heart, cemented it closed, and tried not to think of him or the ranch ever again.

I hear a soft knock, and then Charlotte's head peeks around the door to my office.

"Are you okay?"

I swipe at the tears falling down my cheeks and nod. "I'm fine. Just assaulted by a bunch of memories that I've been trying to forget since I was twelve. I guess the wounds are just as fresh. Stupid."

"It's not stupid." She comes and sits in the chair across from me. "What made her call all of a sudden?"

"My gram died."

"Oh, Sophie, I'm so sorry."

I shrug. "She died, and I never got to tell her how much I loved her and how much I appreciated all she had done for me when I was little. I should've called her. I just didn't. I don't even know why."

Just because Daddy didn't want me anymore didn't mean I had to shut everyone out. I guess it just made it easier to pretend as if none of them existed.

"I'm sure she knew, and I'm sure she loved you too."

"Aunt Doreen wants me to come home for the funeral and the will reading."

She folds her hands and places them on the desk close to mine. "Maybe you should," she says carefully.

I look up at her. "You think so?"

"Yeah, I mean, what's the worst that could happen? You find that your dear ole dad has this great family and life and doesn't want to have anything to do with you? You already think that, so what?" She shrugs.

"You think I want to witness it?"

"No, but what if you're wrong, Soph? What if he misses you and has all these years? What if he wants to be a part of your life? Don't you think it's worth a shot? You walk around, acting like you don't need anyone, especially a man in your life. You sabotage every single relationship. Just like you did with Alex. You freaked out on him when he applied to college. Like he was abandoning you. He wanted you to consider moving with him or doing the long-distance thing for a while, but you jumped ship the moment he mentioned Boston and wouldn't allow him to explain."

I sit there and absorb what she said in silence.

"I get it. I do. And if you were single because you wanted to be, fine, but you are because you're scared of needing a man or loving one too much and being let down again. You make every single guy in your life pay for what your dad did, and that's not fair. Until you face it head-on, you're always going to fear being loved. I don't want that for you. I mean, the worst that could happen is, he doesn't want you. But maybe, just maybe, what you find in Colorado will surprise you. You owe it to yourself to find out."

"What about work? We're just starting to get busy."

"I think I can hold down the fort for a few days."

Honestly, in the age of laptops, iPhones, Messenger, and FaceTime, it's not like you have to be physically present in your office anymore to keep a business running smoothly. We live in a world where you can run it from just about anywhere.

The truth is, I am scared. Scared to be rejected again.

It's time to be brave.

I decide before I can talk myself out of it. "Okay. I'll do it. It's a couple of days. I can do anything for a couple of days. Will you book me a flight to Denver, and can you make a reservation with the car service? An SUV if they have one available. I'll have to be driven out to Poplar Falls. It's about two hours from the airport."

"You got it." She stands and heads for the door. Then, she stops and turns back for a moment. "I'm proud of you."

"Don't be proud of me yet. I still have to get on the plane."

Five

SOPHIE

"**Y**OU'RE WHAT!" MY MOTHER'S PANICKED VOICE SHRIEKS across the line as I corral my luggage out of the taxi and into the airport.

"It's just for a few days, Mom. I want to pay my respects and see Pop."

I knew she was going to be upset about me going to Poplar Falls, and that's why I waited until the last possible second to tell her.

"This is a bad idea, Sophia," she says nervously.

"Maybe so, but I'm about to board the plane, so for better or worse, I'm going."

"You don't have to. You can turn around right now. I'll send you a car myself."

She sounds even more distressed than I expected.

"It'll be fine, Mom. I'm a big girl now, and you don't have to protect me anymore. If it's too uncomfortable or unpleasant, I'll come back early. It's not like they're going to hog-tie me and refuse to let me leave."

I try to ease her mind, but she doesn't laugh.

"I just don't understand why you have to go. You haven't seen your grandmother in over twenty years. It's not like you were close anymore. Sending a condolence card would suffice."

"Mom …"

"Just the thought of you being around that woman and those children turns my stomach."

At her admission, I drop some of my annoyance. I know how crushed she was when word got back to us that Daddy had remarried so quickly after their divorce—and to the other woman, no less. The last thing I want to do is hurt her.

"Trust me, I'm not looking forward to meeting them either, but this trip isn't about them. I want to see Aunt Doreen and Aunt Ria, Emmett, and Pop."

"And your father," she whispers over the line.

"And my father," I admit.

She sighs, and there is a long pause.

"Mom, you still there?"

"Yes, darling. Promise me something before you go."

"Anything."

"No matter what happens while you're there, promise me you'll come back."

I laugh at her request. "Of course I'll come back, silly. I live here. My apartment, my office, my friends, you and Stanhope—my entire life is in New York. Nothing could keep me from coming home."

I hear her sniffle, and I know that she's crying.

"Mom, don't you think you're being a little overdramatic? There's no reason to be so upset. It's a quick trip. A vacation. I'll be there and back before you know it." I dig in my bag for my ID and ticket as I near the head of the security line. "I have to go. I'm about to go through the TSA check. I'll call you when I land in Denver."

"All right, Sophia. Have a safe flight. Remember you're my onliest only."

"Bye, Mom. Love you." I hang up just as I pass my ID to the scowling agent. "Sorry about that. I have a nervous Nelly for a mother."

He grunts at me as he passes back my card.

Okay, I guess we aren't in the talkative mood today.

Once I'm through to my gate, I pull out my Kindle. Time to get lost in my latest obsession—historical romance—for a while, so I don't overthink this trip.

At the Denver airport, I head to baggage claim to grab my luggage before making my way to the information desk to inquire about my car service.

Just as I pluck my bag from the carousel, I hear a deep voice calling my name, "Sophia Lancaster!"

I turn to see a man standing there with his hands in the pockets of his well-worn jeans. He's wearing a baseball cap on his head, pulled low over his blue eyes. Tendrils of dark hair are escaping at his nape. His tanned arms are barely contained by his rolled-up shirtsleeves. He's a very impressive sight indeed, except for the annoyed scowl he's wearing.

I shake myself from my staring and slowly approach him.

"I'm sorry, do I know you?" I ask.

"Are you Sophia?"

"Yes," I answer hesitantly.

"I'm your ride," he announces matter-of-factly.

I look around, confused. He's definitely not a driver for the service we usually hire. Their uniforms consist of black ties and jackets, not flannel and dusty boots. Maybe there's another Sophia he's supposed to meet.

"I think you have the wrong girl. I'm Sophia Lancaster, but I'm not expecting a ride. I have a car service picking me up."

He walks over and firmly takes my bag from my hand. "Lancaster. Yep. You're the one I'm here for." He turns and starts walking toward the exit.

"Wait. That's mine."

I hurry after him as he rushes toward a parking deck, dodging cars arriving to pick up other passengers.

"No time to wait, sweetheart. Rush-hour traffic is about to hit, and we want to be on the other side of Denver when it does," he calls behind him.

We make it to a large gray Chevy truck, and he tosses my bag over the tailgate as I skid to a halt behind him.

"I'm sorry, but I'm not getting into your truck. I have no idea who you are. Please give me back my bag before I call for security," I rasp out as I try to catch my breath.

At that, he smiles a little half grin and walks toward me. I start backing up as he approaches.

"Name's Braxton. Doreen sent me to get you. The ranch isn't that easy to find in the dark, and GPS isn't much help. So, if you don't mind getting your ass in the truck, we can get on the road and make it back before Emmett scoffs down supper and leaves us nothing but scraps."

Braxton. The new wife's nephew. *Why would Aunt Doreen send Braxton to get me?* He and his sister are the ones who replaced me.

I stand there, rooted in my spot.

I knew I would eventually meet him and his sister, Elowyn. I went over the scenario in my head a thousand times. I'd be introduced to my father's new family, and I'd be polite but distant. Then, I'd do everything I could to avoid them the rest of my stay.

Here I am, caught off guard at our first meeting, and I can't seem to get my practiced mask in place.

There's no way I can ride two hours in a confined space with him.

"I'd prefer to try to make it on my own."

He lets out an unamused chuckle and shakes his head. "Look, Princess, I'm not thrilled about this either. I have work to do, but it's important to Doreen, and that makes it important to me. She just lost her mother."

At that, I deflate a little. I realize I seem like a petulant child at the moment, so I give in. *How bad could it be?* "All right, fine."

I walk over as he unlocks the passenger door and swings it wide for me. I climb up and slide into the seat.

"You're welcome, Princess," he says sarcastically as he shuts the door and rounds the truck.

This is going to be the longest road trip of my life.

I take my earbuds from my purse and stick them into my ears as I close my eyes. I'll let Norah Jones sing me all the way to Poplar Falls without sparing a single word or glance at my companion.

Six

SOPHIE

I FEEL A GENTLE SHAKE TO MY SHOULDER THAT JOLTS ME AWAKE. I remove the earbuds and stretch my stiff, aching limbs like a cat. I must have fallen asleep shortly after we left the Denver city limits because the last thing I remember is the buildings fading off into the sunset.

"We're almost there," he informs me as my eyes start to adjust to the twilight sky.

Up ahead in the distance, I see the familiar, old iron gate that leads to my childhood home. I sit up and focus on the top where the words *Rustic Peak Ranch* welcome us, and a sliver of nervous energy runs down my spine.

"It looks exactly the same as I remember," I utter with bewilderment as we approach the massive entryway.

"Yeah, Jefferson isn't much into change," he agrees.

My daddy, Jefferson Lancaster, has run the daily operation of Rustic Peak Ranch since Pop put him in charge when I was about ten years old. Not that Pop actually took much of a step back. He was still up with the sun and working the ranch every morning like clockwork. He just handed off all the management responsibility and ranch-hand oversight to Daddy.

"Sounds about right," I whisper into the cab.

"He's excited to see you, ya know. Nervous but excited."

"Daddy? Excited?" I ask in disbelief.

"Well, as excited as he gets." He shrugs.

"I don't know what he does or doesn't do anymore. For all I know, he gets as giddy as a schoolgirl now. We're strangers."

"Yeah, well, maybe you finally coming to visit can change that."

"Finally?" I turn in my seat to look at him. "What the hell is that supposed to mean?"

"Means it's about time you made a trip home to see him."

"No one asked your opinion. And my relationship with my father is none of your business. Besides, he's the parent. If anyone should've been flying to see anyone, it should've been him."

"Right."

The truck pulls through the gate, and the retort I was about to deliver falls from my mind as I take in the beauty before me.

The long, pear-tree-lined driveway stretches out before us. I reach over and roll the window down, and the sweet brown-sugar smell of chrysanthemums drifts in on the breeze and wraps around us. The crunch of the gravel under the tires brings a flood of memories back to me as I watch the dust settle on the windshield.

Me sitting on Daddy's lap as he let me steer the old tractor. Riding bikes to town with Dallas and taking Blackberry out for her evening run. Me and Pop walking to the pond out behind the stables with fishing poles in hand. Gram and me taking our evening walks. So many happy times spent on this long, winding driveway. Memories I had long-ago filed away in that closed compartment in my heart.

A gasp escapes me when the house comes into sight. I've been trying to remember exactly what it looked like. The four-story white farmhouse with a huge wraparound porch is a shade past needing fresh paint, but it is still stunning. Regal. The centerpiece of the ranch. The heart. I can still picture Gram at the table, peeling apples, and Aunt Doreen sitting on the front porch, snapping beans. So different from the Fifth Avenue lifestyle I was thrust into in the city.

"It's like time stopped," I state as we draw closer.

But it hasn't. It just moved on without me. New people moved in, life continued, and now, Gram is gone.

As soon as the truck stops in front of the house and Braxton puts it in park, the front door swings open, and out bounds my aunts and Pop and Emmett. Emmett is one of Daddy's best friends and has been working the ranch alongside him since before I was born. I grew up calling him Uncle Em. He is as much a part of the family as anyone.

As I open the door and jump down, Aunt Doreen comes running down the steps and throws her arms around me. "Oh my, Sophie. Let me get a look at you."

"Hi, Aunt Doe."

She pulls back and looks me over from head to toe.

Aunt Doreen is tall and soft around the edges. Her blonde hair is cut shorter than I remember and laced with white. Her kind blue eyes are set in fine lines now, but she's still so lovely. I must have inherited my hair, eye, and complexion coloring from my father's side.

"You're a woman. All grown up and so beautiful."

Her eyes fill with tears, and Aunt Ria comes up and shoos her away.

"Oh, don't start the waterworks, or you'll have us all blubbering." Then, she wraps me in a bear hug of her own.

Aunt Ria has always been what I call a robust lady. Big, round, loud, and strong as an ox. Dallas and I were terrified of her and her switches when we were little. I can remember spending many days hiding from her among the hay bales in the barn.

"You're a sight for sore eyes, girl."

"So are you, Aunt Ria."

A throat clears, and I look up over her shoulder. There stands my daddy on the porch with his arm around a pretty woman who's wearing a timid smile.

Jefferson Lancaster is a presence, standing at over six feet tall with broad shoulders. His dark hair has turned a distinguished salt and pepper, and so has his mustache.

"Hi, Daddy."

He looks intently at me for a moment, like he's not quite sure if

26

it's actually me. Then, he nods his head and barks out, "Everyone give Sophie a little breathing room, will you? She just got here, and I'm sure she's tired after a long day of travel."

The pretty lady under his arm breaks away and makes her way to me. "Hello, Sophie. I'm Madeline."

I look down at her outstretched hand. I pause for a moment before my manners override my hesitation, and I take it.

"We're so happy you're here. Everyone has been waiting on pins and needles for you to arrive."

She motions for a girl, who looks to be in her early twenties, to come over.

"You've met my nephew, Brax, and this is his sister, my niece, Elowyn."

She looks very much like her aunt's twin. Long black hair, thin frame, and large brown eyes.

"It's nice to meet you, Sophie," she says as her aunt pulls her in front of me.

"Same to you," I clip.

Her face falls a little at my tone.

"Elowyn can't wait to hear all about living in New York. She's been obsessed with fashion and celebrities since she could walk and talk. I think she might have been the most excited when we found out you were coming."

I give her a tight smile, and she beams back at me.

I'm overwhelmed at this moment with this little family reunion and introduction. Not sure how to act, I look up at my father. He can see the plea on my face.

"Are you hungry?" he asks.

"A little, I guess, and I could use the ladies' room."

"Oh, of course. Look at us, making a fuss when you have to be ready to freshen up and eat. Let's get you inside." Aunt Doreen guides me up the steps to the house. "Brax, can you bring her things in, dear?" she asks as she shuffles me in.

"Yes, ma'am," he calls.

I walk into the foyer, and the first thing I notice is a portrait of Daddy, Madeline, Braxton, and Elowyn where one of him, Mom, and me used to hang. I stop in front of it. Aunt Doreen stops with me, and her chattering goes silent.

She gently tugs my elbow to get my attention. "Let me show you to the bathroom." She nudges.

"I know where it is. Unless that's been moved and replaced too?"

She lets out a heavy sigh. "No. Still right where it used to be."

"Thank you."

Seven

SOPHIE

I BARRICADE MYSELF IN THE BATHROOM FOR WAY TOO LONG. A MINI breakdown is had. I didn't realize how enormous the flood of emotions would be when they finally washed over me, memories crashing over me like waves. This place was my home. This house was where I learned how to walk and talk. I learned to ride my bike on the driveway out front, and I fell from my horse and broke my left arm when she was spooked by a rattlesnake out by the big barn. It's where Dallas and I played and where she kissed Myer Wilson—a boy we had both been crushing on since third grade—during a cutthroat game of Truth or Dare. I didn't speak to her for three whole days after that.

This ranch is where I learned to milk a cow, how to saddle and brush my own mare. I was my daddy's shadow, following him all day long as he worked this ranch. I woke up with him before the sun every day. During the school year, I would help him feed the cows, horses, and chickens before I caught the bus. On summer days, I would spend hours helping him and Emmett mend fences and build new coops. This is where I picked up a charcoal pencil for the first time and started drawing. I would sketch the landscape or the house and barn and present the masterpieces to Gram. She would proudly display them all on the refrigerator door. This place is where I became me.

I wash my hands and look up into the mirror above the sink. I brush my carefully curled hair behind one shoulder with my perfectly manicured fingers. My makeup is flawless. I'm a far cry from the tomboy who used to climb trees and shovel stalls. That girl doesn't exist anymore, except for in my dreams. My armor is securely in place.

A small knock at the door startles me.

"You okay in there, Sophie Doe?" Aunt Doreen's muffled voice comes from the other side. Concern evident in her question.

"Yes, I'll be out in just a minute," I call back.

I take one last look in the mirror and take a deep breath. I have come this far, no reason to chicken out now.

"You're not a little girl anymore. You can put on your big-girl socks and handle your feelings. Be brave." I give myself the small pep talk, and then I open the door and walk to the living room.

Everyone is awkwardly standing around, waiting for me.

Madeline is the first to speak, "You want supper, Sophie?"

I ate on the plane a few hours ago, but I could eat again.

I shrug in response.

She claps her hands together. "Perfect. We'll get you settled in, and then we'll have supper on the picnic table out back. It's such a nice night."

I see my suitcase sitting at the end of the couch, so I pick it up. "I'll change and come help with dinner."

I turn from the room and walk through the archway leading to the hall where the downstairs bedrooms are located. I make it a few steps when Aunt Doreen races up behind me.

I reach the last door on the right, and as I open the door, I hear her voice. "Sophie, you're staying in my room, sweetheart."

The door swings open to my childhood bedroom, and I'm assaulted by every shade of purple known to man. The walls are pale lavender, and the bedding is a bold, royal hue. Polka-dotted throw pillows are strewed about the floor. There is a vanity in the corner where my desk used to be, and it is covered in makeup and hair products. Stuffed animals are crowded in the reading nook below the large bay windows that look out into the backyard.

I stop and stare.

My heart drops.

All my things are gone. Not that I honestly expected it to be the same as it was when I left. Did I?

Maybe I hoped it would be. That my daddy had kept my things the way they were when I left as a shrine and that, from time to time, he would open the door and sit on my bed and miss me the way I missed him.

"This is Elle's bedroom now," she says hesitantly as she falls in behind me.

"I can see that."

I swallow back the tears and turn back toward the living room.

"I think maybe I should go," I say as I keep my head down and march back down the hall.

"Go? Go where?" she asks as I squeeze past her.

"I can get a room at a hotel in town. I'm only going to be here a few days anyway." I try to sound nonchalant as I look to escape.

"Oh no, Sophie. You don't have to do that."

I raise my head as I make it back into the room with the others. All eyes are on me. I find my daddy standing in the entryway between the living room and kitchen with his arms folded across his chest. He doesn't say anything. He just looks at me with disapproving eyes.

"This was a mistake. I shouldn't have come here. Obviously, there isn't any room for me here anymore."

That's when I feel a tear slide down my cheek, and I swipe at it as embarrassment fills me.

Daddy clears his throat. "Doreen is staying in Ria's room with her. They stay up half the night, watching that Netstick thingy, and she falls asleep in there most of the time anyway."

"He means, Netflix. We are watching *The Crown*. It's so good," Aunt Ria interjects.

He cuts his eyes to her and then rolls them. I guess he's not a fan of Netflix. Or the British monarchy. Probably both.

"It's true. We're late-night binge-watchers. I've fixed my room up

31

nicely for you. It's quiet up there. You will be glad to be on the third floor when these loud rascals get up and stomp around that kitchen at four a.m.," Aunt Doreen adds.

I turn to face her. "Please," I choke on a whisper, "can you drive me into town?"

"Honey, there's only one hotel in town and then the bed-and-breakfast on Route 3. Both are going to be full because of the Apple Festival next week."

"This is your home as much as it is anyone's." Daddy's voice booms across the room. "Elle was afraid of the dark when she was little. She wanted to be down here, close to us, when she woke up scared at night. She took your room. Not your place in this family," he says all matter-of-factly. Embarrassing me further by making my tears seem ridiculous.

"Okay." I nod my head at Aunt Doreen in defeat and head to the stairs without looking back at everyone.

"It's the first door on the right off of the landing on the third floor. It has its own bathroom," she calls after me.

As I pass the front door, Braxton walks in from the porch and catches my eyes.

He gives me a concerned look for a split second, and then he walks fully in and past me without saying a word.

Great. The last thing I wanted was for the evil step-whatever to see me this upset.

Why did I let Charlotte talk me into this trip?

Eight

BRAXTON

PRINCESS SOPHIA NEVER CAME DOWN TO DINNER LAST NIGHT. She locked herself in her room and claimed jet lag when Elle went to fetch her. It was a shit move. Aunt Madeline and Doreen and Ria had worked hard all damn day, preparing for her arrival. They'd baked bread from scratch and peeled apples for homemade pies. Elle had fluttered around as they worked, asking them all kinds of questions about the prodigal daughter. She was as excited as they were.

Then, Sophia snubbed them.

We all sat around the table that they had prepared outside with the fancy linens. Lights strung up in the tree limbs, eating our fancy feast and looking at each other like assholes, everyone melancholy and no one saying anything.

This afternoon, when she finally graced us with her presence at lunch, the woman barely ate a thing and was rude when Elle tried to talk to her about New York City.

Elle's face fell, and I had to take my sandwich to the porch to eat before I put Miss Haughty Ass in her place. I promised Doreen I'd be nice. I'm a man of my word, but I'm afraid if I have to spend too much time with her, it will be a promise I break. No one treats my sister like she's beneath them.

After lunch, Emmett and I head to the stables and set to cleaning the horse stalls and filling them with fresh hay. Aunt Madeline has a new class of youngsters coming in the morning to start riding lessons.

"What do you think of our Sophie?" he asks once we are working.

I wipe the sweat from my brow and let out a sneer. "Not much, to tell you the truth. Seems to me like a spoiled brat who likes to walk around, making assumptions and judging everyone."

He cuts his eyes to me. "I don't know about all that. I think it was probably a bit jarring for her to be back after all these years, seeing how much things have changed around here."

"Right. Nothing ever changes around here," I tease him.

"You're right, but I bet it didn't look that way to her."

Maybe not. Still doesn't give her the right to come to our home and stomp all over our hospitality.

"She sure grew up to be a beautiful woman. Of course, she always was a pretty little thing. Even when she was just a tomboy in overalls with wild blonde curls, bare feet, and dirty hands and knees," he muses.

"Can't imagine her getting her hands dirty now."

And I can't. She might break a nail or something.

"Now, who's making assumptions?" He gives me a disappointed look.

"Just sayin', with those fancy clothes and that superior attitude, no way she would fit in here."

"She's got Lancaster blood flowing through her veins. That means, she's tethered to this land. Those clothes and shoes of hers don't change that. She has a rustic heart beating in her chest, just like we do."

I release an amused breath. "Right."

"What exactly is it about her that irritates you so much, Brax?"

It's a fair question. *Why does she bother me so much?*

"She came here with a chip on her shoulder and an agenda."

"She came here because her grandmother passed, and she wants to pay her respects."

"Yeah, that's the excuse, not the real reason. If she gave two shits about Gram, she would've visited her while she was still alive."

"The roads from here to New York City run both ways, son, and lest we forget, she was a child when her parents divorced. It wasn't her responsibility to come to us. We failed her. All of us."

He gets a far-off look in his eyes like he is revisiting somewhere in the past that I'm not privy to.

"Whatever. She's an adult now, and she has been for a while. She has a parent alive and well here, and she acts like he doesn't exist. She'd rather be up in the big city with her rich stepdaddy than slumming it here, which suits me just fine. Just don't come here, riding into town like a damn princess, expecting everyone to bow at your feet, and stick your nose in the air to my aunts and sister, who have been nothing but kind and welcoming to you."

He stops and leans against his pitchfork as he gives me a steely look. "She was a daddy's girl. Loved him with all she had. She lost him and everything she ever knew without warning. She comes here and sees that everything about her home has changed and that everyone has a happy life that she's not a part of. How would you feel, walking into that?"

"Appreciative. That's how I'd feel."

"Son, you lost your mother and father. It was tragic and painful. But you grew up, knowing they loved you and that they didn't leave you on purpose. Sophie lost her daddy too, but unlike your parents, he had a choice. He made that choice, and for whatever reason, he didn't choose her. He chose to walk away. Not because he didn't want to be a father or couldn't be a father because he took you and Elle in and raised you. It was because he didn't want her. That's what it looks like to her anyway. It has to cut deep."

I take a minute to let his words set in and try to imagine if our parents had chosen to leave us. How much worse the pain would have been, being left on purpose.

"That doesn't sound like Jefferson."

I can't reconcile that the man I know, the man who raised me and taught me how to be a man, would walk away from his responsibility to his own flesh and blood that way. Something doesn't add up.

"No, it doesn't, and there's more to the story." He shares no further.

"Is he going to tell her what that is?"

"I sure hope so. He should have done it a long time ago. That brokenhearted girl hiding behind all that makeup and those fancy clothes deserves an explanation. It's been long enough. That's why Doreen arranged for her to come here because he was never going to face it if he wasn't pushed. Time to set the skeletons out of the closet."

He thrusts his fork in the pile and picks up another batch of hay. Then, he adds, "Would be awfully kind of you to cut her some slack while she's here."

"I'll try, Em."

"That's my boy."

"I said, try."

He shoots me a sideways smile. Between him asking and Aunt Doreen making me promise, I think my best line of defense is to avoid Miss Lancaster until she hightails it back to where she came from.

The sooner, the better.

Nine

"WELL, I'LL BE DAMNED. THE RUMORS ARE TRUE. Sophia Doreen Lancaster has finally returned to Poplar Falls."

I look from my perch on the front porch to see a gorgeous woman with long strawberry-blonde curls, tanned skin, and hazel eyes standing on the lawn. She's wearing cutoff jean shorts that barely cover her butt cheeks and a gray V-neck sweatshirt that says, *Classy, Sassy, and a Bit Smart-Assy.*

"Oh my God. Dallas Henderson, is that you?" I squeal as I jump to my feet and head down the steps to embrace my long-lost best friend.

Gone are the bright red Pippi Longstocking braids, freckles, and braces that I remember. The woman before me is stunning and a complete stranger.

"In the flesh. It's Dallas Stovall now." She steps back and gives me a once-over. "I barely recognize you though. What's with the get-up?"

I look down at my emerald-green silk drawstring pants and flowing, off-the-shoulder white linen blouse. The teal tips of my toes are peeking out of my strappy nude stiletto sandals.

"Sorry. My closet doesn't carry much cowgirl chic nowadays. It was this or a little black dress, I'm afraid."

She shakes her head at me and laughs.

I wait for her to get it all out before I ask, "You're married? Anybody I know?"

I reach back into my memories, try to place the last name Stovall to a face, and come up blank.

"Divorced. And, no, you don't know the jackass. He and his family breezed into town senior year. Long after you disappeared, the silver-tongued devil talked me into running off and getting married two seconds after we crossed the stage to get our diplomas. The biggest mistake I ever made."

I'm not the least bit surprised. Dallas was always a *fly by the seat of your pants* kind of girl. Even when we were little, she could talk me into the most ridiculous situations against my better judgment.

"Wow. Divorced. You're like a real-life grown-up."

"I can do you one better. I'm also a momma. I got myself a little six-year-old stud. He looks just like his daddy. Hopefully, he won't act like him. Or me, for that matter."

"A son. Really? Congratulations."

"Thanks. He's the one good thing that came from the whole situation, so I have no regrets. Well, maybe a few, but no need to dwell on the past. Right?"

I assume that is her not-so-subtle intro into asking about why I'm back in Poplar Falls.

I put my arm around her shoulders and lead us toward the porch. "Come sit with me a while. We have a lot of catching up to do. Do you have time?"

"Sure. I don't have to pick Beau up from school until later this afternoon, and I'm working the night shift at the tavern, so I'm all yours this morning."

I love this porch. It's large with a breakfast table on one side where Gram and Pop would have coffee every morning. Then, Aunt Doreen and I would sit on the wide steps and snap green beans from her garden all afternoon. At night, I'd curl up with my mother in the huge swing. We'd rock as she read me bedtime stories. I'd always fall asleep before the end, and Daddy would join us when he finished with the cows and carry me to bed.

"I'm sorry about Gram. She's sure going to be missed around here. I think the entire town is still reeling from the loss. She was kind of everyone's grandmother."

I let out a sigh as we take a seat in the swing. "I wish I had made it out to see her before it was too late." I take a deep breath. "I bet she thought I didn't love her."

"Ah, Sophie, she knew you loved her." She blows off my guilt.

"How could she? I hadn't spoken to her since I was a little girl."

"Do you think she loved you?" she asks.

I think about it for a minute. I let all the memories of her braiding my hair, teaching me how to garden, showing me how to can tomatoes, and helping me learn how to recite my ABCs and write my name wash over me.

"Yeah, she loved me." I don't know how, but I know it in my heart.

"See? She knew just like you know. You don't have to say it. Real love survives time and distance. It doesn't need to be constantly reassured. It just is. Besides, isn't she the one who always said that when we die, we finally know all the answers to the questions in life, and until then, it's a waste of time to keep asking why?"

She did. Gram's faith was strong. When we were younger, Dallas and I swore she could literally pray down a mountain if she wanted to.

"Yes, she sure did." I nod in agreement.

"Well then, that means she knows all now, right? So, she knows how you feel, and she wouldn't want you down here, grappling with nonsense guilt."

And just like that, the weight falls from my shoulders like Gram herself swatted it off.

Just then, Madeline opens the front door and peeks out. "Hey, Dallas. I didn't hear you drive up."

"Truck's in the shop again. I had Momma drop me off at the gate on her way to the bakery."

"Would you girls like some iced tea? I just made a fresh pitcher."

"Yes, ma'am," Dallas answers for us.

I give her a tight smile before she disappears back into the house.

"Uh-oh, did I feel tension?" Dallas asks.

"No. Not really. I don't really know her. Or anyone here, for that matter. It's awkward."

"Madeline is one of the kindest women I know. Everyone around here loves her. She was only twenty-two years old when she took Brax and Elle in after her sister and brother-in-law died in that car crash. Brax was thirteen, and Elle was just three years old. She didn't bat an eye. Just quit vet school, and she and Jefferson took them right in. She also runs an equestrian therapy program for children with disabilities. Parents bring their kids from all over the state to have her work with them. And she puts up with your old grump of a dad. She's practically a saint."

"Yeah, a saint. Who seduced a married man and stole him from his family," I mumble under my breath.

"What was that?"

"Nothing. Let's talk about you. Divorced. Boy mom. What happened? Tell me the rest."

"Well, after the wedding, Travis and I moved to Denver. He was a mechanic. Just one of those guys who was good with an engine, you know?"

I nod, and she keeps going, "Mom and Dad gave us some seed money as a wedding gift, and he opened a little garage in town. It did well. He did excellent work, and word started spreading. Travis and success did not mix well though. Fast-forward a few years, and he was working all the time. I barely saw him. And when he wasn't working, he was off somewhere, drinking and partying. All we did was fight. It's like he changed all of a sudden. His entire personality morphed."

She pauses for a moment.

"You know, there is a reason all the fairy tales they tell us as kids end with the wedding. Nobody wants to read about how hard it is to actually be married. Falling in love is the easy part, the fun part. It's staying in love that's hard. I finally got fed up, and I left him. Stayed at a girlfriend's house for about a week. Then, he came around with pretty flowers and pretty words, and I fell for his promises and went home. Then, he knocked me up. I'm fairly sure he thought that would keep me there. Before I knew it, he slipped back in his old ways. I stayed. I thought for sure when the baby came, things would be different. That is, until one day, the FBI came knocking on my front door. They sat me down and explained that my husband had been selling drugs and laundering the money through the garage."

I gasp, "No."

"Yep. I had no clue. I was so stupid." She shakes her head and continues, "After his arrest, they froze all our accounts and assets. We lost everything—the shop, the house, both our cars, and every penny we had in the bank. The government seized it all and sold it off to pay restitution. He went to prison, and I came home to Momma and Daddy with my tail between my legs and a baby in tow. They took us in, and we lived with them. They watched Beau for me while I worked at the diner during the day and at Butch's Tavern a few nights a week to save enough money to get us on our feet."

"So, where do you live now?"

"Dad and Uncle Jimbo turned one of the old grain silos on the farm into a house for us. It's cool as shit. Industrial and functional. We made it farmhouse chic."

I try to imagine what farmhouse chic looks like. I assume it's probably like the old converted warehouses in the city.

"Listen, Momma cooks, and I have built-in sitters, so there's no need to be in a hurry to leave. Right?"

"No need at all," I agree.

"So, you're all caught up on me. What's your story? I mean, you just take off and leave your very best friend in the whole wide world, never to be heard from again. I was devastated. You left me to face middle school alone. Not cool, dude. Not cool at all."

"I know. I'm sorry. It wasn't my choice. Mom just upped and moved us in the middle of the night. I thought it was one of her whims and that we'd be back in a day or two, but somehow, it turned into twenty years. Honestly, I kept waiting for Daddy to come and get me. It just didn't happen, and after a while, I stopped expecting him."

It sounds foolish. Here I am, a grown woman, trying to explain the fantasies of a little girl.

"I did the same thing. I'd walk the whole way out here all the time to see if you were back yet. Must have done it every day after school the entire first year. Gram was so used to it that she would have milk and cookies waiting when I got here. Finally, I just stopped coming by. I figured, if you ever showed back up, you would call me."

"I'm sorry I didn't call."

"It's fine. You're here now. Tell me all about New York. Is it as gray as it looks on TV?" She wrinkles her nose at the thought.

"Gray?"

"You know, all concrete and buildings. No trees or grass, no houses?"

"There are trees and grass. They're just in the parks. And as far as houses, most people live in condos or apartments."

She looks confused. "Do you like that? The only yard you get is in a park?"

"Well, sure. I have a great apartment in the city. It's got incredible views of the river, and there are so many great shops and restaurants within walking distance at the Chelsea Market. There is a subway line right around the corner. Which is super convenient. Plus, my office is just a short train or taxi ride."

"Hmm, maybe I can visit one day and see what all the fuss is about."

"I'd love that."

We hear someone approach from the side of the house.

And Dallas looks up and shouts, "Braxton Young, you'd better come over here and say hello to me."

Braxton rounds the corner and stops in front of the porch. He is covered in dirt and sweat. He removes his ball cap from his head and squeezes the content of the water bottle in his hand over his head, washing the sweat from his eyes. Then, he pulls his tee from his jeans and wipes his face dry.

"Ladies," he mumbles in greeting.

"Hey, sexy. You can remove the drenched T-shirt if you want. We don't mind," Dallas croons in his direction.

I elbow her in the side.

"Ouch. What?"

He shakes his head at her. Then, he stomps up the steps just as Madeline emerges with a pitcher of iced tea and glasses. He takes the tray from her hands.

"Thank you, Brax."

"You're welcome, Aunt Mads." He gives her a genuine smile and kisses her cheek.

She lovingly pats the side of his face and walks back into the house.

"Thanks, Mrs. L," Dallas yells through the screen door as she leaps from the swing and saunters over to Braxton. She arches her back and tosses her hair over her shoulder in a flirtatious manner. "Can I help?"

He gives her an exasperated look and shoves the tray into her hands. "I have to get back to the cattle."

"Oh, you're no fun." She snatches the tray, sets it on the table, and pours us each a glass.

Braxton looks over at me. Looks me up and down and comments, "Nice outfit."

I roll my eyes. "It's not like I have an evening gown on. I only packed a couple of outfits and a dress for Gram's service. I didn't have time to shop for appropriate ranch attire. Get the hell over it."

He looks me in the eye for the first time, and he grins.

Then, he puts his ball cap back on, pulls it over his eyes, and heads back toward the barn.

"Wow, you got a grin. That's more than he ever gives me. Stubborn ass."

"You like him, huh?"

She hands me a glass. "Every female with a pulse in a fifty-mile radius likes him. You do have eyes. I know you can see him."

I shrug. "He's attractive, I guess, but ..."

"You guess?" She looks at me like I've grown another head.

"He's a jerk. And I don't find assholes attractive."

She grins. "Well, that's part of his charm. Give it time. You'll see."

I wouldn't bet on it.

Ten

SOPHIE

DALLAS AND I SPEND THE REST OF THE AFTERNOON CATCHING up. It's strange how all the years and all the miles apart seem to just melt away. I thought I'd have to grovel for her forgiveness or that maybe we would be too different now and the friendship of the little girls we'd once been wouldn't translate into one for the adults we now are, but it's easy. I guess that's just how it goes with true friendship. No matter how long you're apart, you can pick back up the second you find your way back to each other. No anger. No resentment. No explanations or apologies needed.

I hate to see her drive away as I wave to Mrs. Henderson, who came by to pick her up. She felt like an ally in this hostile environment.

Okay, maybe not hostile per se, but I definitely feel like an outsider, and it's uncomfortable, to say the least.

My stomach growls, and I venture inside to find Aunt Doreen and Aunt Ria in the kitchen, kneading what looks like enough dough to make biscuits for the entire town.

"What are you two doing?"

"Starting supper," Aunt Ria answers.

I look at the clock above the stove, and it says 2:04 p.m.

"Isn't it awfully early for that? And how many people are you cooking for anyway?"

"The family and some of the staff. That's Jefferson and Madeline, Braxton and Elle, Pop, Emmett, the two of us, Walker and Silas, two of the boys who work for us … and you, dear. Those men get up and start working at the break of dawn, and they're starving by four p.m. That's when they end their day. So, we try to have supper on the table by four thirty p.m. sharp."

Dinner before five p.m.? That is unheard of where I come from.

"No one is home until well after six p.m. in the city. We don't even think about dinner until eight p.m. at the earliest."

"Eight p.m.?" Aunt Ria gasps in question.

They both laugh.

"That's bedtime around here. We're usually up and at it by four a.m. So, nine p.m. is a stretch for us. If we tried to feed those boys that late, there would be a riot," she informs.

"It's like you guys live on a different planet," I accuse.

"I seem to remember a little girl who woke with us and helped gather eggs to make breakfast well before it was time to catch her school bus," Aunt Doreen muses.

"Well, now, she is an adult who still gets up way too early to fight Midtown traffic, and coffee is usually her only breakfast."

"Sounds like you need more rest and better food to fuel your day, Sophia Doreen." Aunt Ria has her hands on her hips and is giving me her stern, disapproving look.

I forgot what it felt like to have her focus on me. It's quite intimidating.

"I'll get there. One day. I just opened my own jewelry design business a few months ago, and everything has been happening so fast."

"Life needs balance. It can't be all work. And the good Lord only gave us one body. We have to take care of it. You don't want to wear it out too early, do you?" Aunt Ria gently scolds, and they both turn their motherly stares on me.

This is laughable, coming from the two women who work harder than most people I know in Manhattan.

I start to argue, but my good manners override my tongue.

"No, ma'am," I quickly agree. I grab a banana from a bowl on the kitchen table and watch them continue to work. "Can I help?" I effectively change the subject.

Aunt Doreen's eyes light up at my offer, and she moves down the counter as Aunt Ria hands me an apron.

"What are we making?"

"Dumplings. Here, just knead it like this and then take and sprinkle a little flour on the counter. Pinch off about this much and place it in the center."

I watch as Aunt Doreen takes a batch the size of a softball and uses a rolling pin to roll it out in a thin sheet.

"Then, cut it into strips about this thick." She picks up a strip to show me. "And lay it over here." She places it on a pan to her right. "Got it?"

"Yes, ma'am."

The three of us work in peaceful silence until two pans are overloaded with dumplings. Then, we set to shredding the chicken, which was boiling in the large cast iron pots on the stove. Once that's done and the chicken and dumplings are back simmering in the stock, we start stripping the Silver Queen corn and shucking peas.

Back in New York, we have a small community garden for Chelsea residents, and I've had the best intentions of contributing to and taking advantage of the fresh vegetables, but I never seem to get around to it. If I'm not eating at restaurants or ordering takeout, the closest I come to fresh, homemade food is heating up steamed veggies in the microwave and baking a chicken breast for one. I forgot how much I enjoy being in the kitchen and how rewarding it feels to make food to feed your family with your own two hands.

Just as I finish the last of the peas and get up to discard the pods, the back door swings open, and Daddy walks into the kitchen.

"Ladies." He nods his head in our direction and scoots to the sink to fill a canteen with water. Then, he turns and leans against it. He focuses on me as he takes a drink. "You planning to join us for supper tonight?" he asks me.

"Yes," I answer him, but I keep my eyes on the bowl in my hands.

"Good. It was rude of you not to show up at the table last night after Madeline and your aunts prepared a meal and held supper just for you."

I lift my head and look him in the eyes as anger flares. "I didn't ask anyone to hold anything for me," I snap.

"I don't know how they do it up there in New York, but around here, when people go out of their way to accommodate you, you show a little appreciation."

I set the bowl down on the counter hard. "Are you going to try to parent me now, Jefferson? Teach me how to behave? Because, by my calculations, you're about two decades too late. I'm already grown, and you don't get to raise me now. I was tired and overwhelmed last night. I couldn't have eaten if I tried, especially with everyone looking at me like I was some kind of sideshow freak."

"No one thinks you're a freak, Sophie," Aunt Doreen interjects.

Daddy just looks at me for a few minutes and doesn't say a word. Then, he stands to his full height and says, "All right. See you gals at supper."

He takes his canteen and heads back out the door. That's it. I guess having a real and candid conversation about the last twenty years is off the table. I shouldn't have wasted my time coming here, thinking I might get any answers or the closure I need.

Sunday and my flight back to my real life can't come fast enough.

"He's not good with words. Never has been," Aunt Ria explains as she watches him retreat through the backyard.

"I need the words," I whisper into the kitchen.

She turns, looks at me, and nods. "You deserve them. Give him time. He'll come around."

"He's had a lot of time, Aunt Ria. Not sure I can give him much more."

With that, I take off the apron and head to my—*Aunt Doreen's* room to grab my sketchpad. Then, I poke my head back in and ask them if there is anywhere with decent shade besides the front porch.

"Yes, there's a huge boo-hoo tree in the backyard, and it gives great shade. Just grab a quilt out of the living room," Aunt Doreen answers over her shoulder as she washes a pan in the sink.

"Okay, thanks," I say as I start to head to the living room. Then, I stop. "Wait, what? What's a boo-hoo tree?" I ask in confusion.

"She means the weeping willow out back. She forgets what it's called sometimes," Aunt Ria answers from the pantry.

"Oh."

That makes a strange kind of sense.

She comes out with a jar of strawberry preserves and keeps explaining, "You should've seen us last week, trying to find the vet's office on Sweet Water Road in Cedar Ridge. That GPS thingy had us nearly in the next county until I called their number and realized they were on Sugar Creek Road."

That makes me giggle.

"I was close," Aunt Doreen mumbles.

"Close only counts in horseshoes and hand grenades. In a car with a puking pup, it just gets you lost and aggravated," she mumbles her gripe in my direction.

They're such a funny pair. Sometimes, I wish I had a sister. It's just been Mom and me my entire life. Who am I going to give shit to when I'm old and grumpy? At the rate I'm going, I'm going to be an old spinster, bickering with my cats.

I grab a blanket, head out in the yard to clear my head, and draw for a while before dinner.

Eleven

BRAXTON

JEFFERSON WAS IN A FOUL MOOD AS HE, EMMETT, AND I WORKED ON repairing the tractor that had a broken timing chain while hauling bales of hay yesterday.

He barely said a word the whole afternoon, and when he did, it was to bark an order at one of us. I can only guess that the princess's appearance is what has him so on edge. Of course, we start culling the cows for next season this week, and that could be weighing on him too.

I run up to my personal space above the barn to take a quick shower and wash the day's dirt off before heading to the main house for supper.

As I cross the yard toward the back door of the house, I notice a figure under one of the large trees.

Sophie is lying on her stomach with her bare feet kicked in the air. Her hair is pulled up in a sloppy knot thing on top of her head. One of the sleeves of her top has slid down her shoulder, and as she absent-mindedly reaches up to move it back in place, the pencil in her other hand moves furiously over the page of the book in front of her on the blanket.

She's humming as she draws. It's the most serene I've seen her since she arrived. Carefree even.

Her shirt rides up slightly, and I can see the beads of sweat pooling in the dip of her low back where it meets the hem of her pants. My gaze slides down further to her ass, and I notice how nice it looks in those ridiculous silk pants she's had on all damn day.

I shake my thoughts from her ass. It doesn't matter how perfect it looks. She is off-limits. And even if she weren't Jefferson's daughter, I would never touch a woman who looks at and treats my family and me like we're second-class citizens.

She must hear my approach because she startles and gasps, rolls to her back, and protectively raises her hands and feet.

"It's just me."

She lets out a relieved breath. "Sorry. Habit. People sneaking up on you in the park in the city isn't exactly a good thing. I get lost in my head sometimes, and I don't always pay enough attention to my surroundings," she offers in explanation. Then, she rolls back to her stomach and continues to draw.

She was almost polite.

I keep walking toward the house and stop to look back over my shoulder at her. "You spend a lot of time in the park by yourself?" I have no idea why I asked or why I care.

She looks up from her page and answers, "Yes. I can't breathe in my apartment sometimes. Like the walls are closing in on me or something. I crave the outdoors, fresh air, and sunshine. Charlotte thinks I must be claustrophobic or something." She shrugs.

"Charlotte?"

"My friend and assistant."

I nod. "I know the feeling—the need for wide-open spaces," I reply, and then I open the door and walk inside.

"Brax," Elle squeals the second my feet hit the kitchen floor. "Look!"

She pulls a piece of paper from her bag and excitedly shoves it an inch from my face as she starts talking in rapid-fire sentences, "Professor Madar thinks my essay on the benefits of organic farming to the local environment and economy is insightful and offers a great perspective on why ranchers in the area should consider co-opting parcels of their land to organic farmers. She thinks it's good enough to be published. She submitted it to the local paper and *The Denver Post!*"

I take the paper from her hands and get a closer look. "That's amazing, sis."

"I know!"

I look up, and she's beaming as she bounces up and down on the balls of her feet.

"This could help when I apply for funding for school."

It's great to see her so excited about something.

Since graduating from high school, she has struggled to find her passion. It was easy for me. All I ever wanted to do was follow in Jefferson's footsteps and become a rancher, but Elle is restless. She tried her hand at vet tech school and realized that her love of animals did not translate to the love of caring for them when they were sick or injured. Then, she tried beauty school and realized her love of makeup and hairstyling did not apply to mixing chemicals for perms and dealing with finicky clients. Now, she's trying her hand at writing and taking classes at the local community college. If it holds her interest, she hopes to enroll in the journalism program at the University of Denver next fall.

"I'll chill some sparkling wine to go with the cobbler I made for dessert," Doreen offers as she wipes a tear from her cheek.

I love how these women support Elle in everything she attempts.

"Really?" Elle asks with pride in her voice.

"Of course. We have to celebrate. It's not every day our niece gets published."

"Not published yet. Just submitted for publishing."

Doreen waves off the modesty. "Whatever. It's a big deal, and we're going to toast to you, my dear."

Elle turns back to me. "Do you think Sophie will read it?"

I see the hope in her eyes, and I don't want to crush her. She has developed a warped sort of hero worship for Jefferson's long-lost daughter ever since Doreen explained over breakfast last week that Sophie would be coming in from New York. Elle has always been fascinated with Sophie and that city. We haven't heard a word from the girl as long as we've lived here, but the aunts and Gram used to often tell stories of her as a child. Especially Gram. Elle was always enamored and had this fantasy in her head that Sophie would return and they would be fast friends and sisters.

"Maybe. If you ask her." I don't even sound convincing to myself.

"Of course she will," Doreen pipes up.

"I'm sure she'd love to read your article. Sophie knows her way around the subject, you know."

I can hear the pride in her voice as she talks about her niece.

"She does?" Elle asks.

"Oh, yes, she would help Gram plant and harvest the vegetable garden every year, and they grew their own herbs in flowerpots on the back porch. All organic. No pesticides. Sophie fed the chickens and the hogs every single day too. She'd gather eggs in the morning for break-fast, and Pop even taught her how to milk the dairy cows. She was quite the little farmer."

"Wow, really? She seems too sophisticated," Elle responds.

"Not at all. She's a rancher's child. It's in her nature to know her way around the animals and the land. You two should chat later."

"That would be awesome."

I hate that they think the kid Sophie used to be is the same as the woman who looked at me like I was some type of disease when I picked her up from the airport. I don't think any of that girl is left. I don't say it though. They'll eventually figure it out for themselves.

Twelve

SOPHIE

"SOPHIE, CAN YOU HELP ME WITH THESE?" AUNT DOREEN calls to me from the back deck.

I leave my sketchpad and pencil on the quilt and hurry to the door to relieve her of the basket she has in her hands.

"Thank you, sweetie. It's so lovely out that we thought we'd eat out here again this evening. We won't get too many more opportunities before the bitter cold blows in," she explains as she leads the way out to an extra-large picnic table under an old oak tree.

The basket is filled with colorful plates and silverware and napkins. She takes a checkered tablecloth, shakes it out, and spreads it over the wooden table. I set the basket on a bench, and we start setting the places. Aunt Ria joins us and loads the table with trivets and serving utensils. She places mason jars with fresh-cut sunflowers and candles in the center.

"Perfect," she declares as she lights the candles.

Braxton and Elle emerge next with covered pots. Braxton sets the chicken and dumplings on a trivet, and Elle follows with the creamed corn and peas. Madeline brings up the rear with pitchers of water and iced tea.

"Excuse me. I'm going to go freshen up real quick," I tell Aunt Doreen.

I grab the quilt and my supplies as I make my way to the house. I pass Daddy as I enter the back door.

"Sophie?" he questions as I race through the kitchen.

I look back to him. "I'll be out in a minute. Just putting my things away and washing up."

He looks relieved as he nods his head and continues out.

Once I drop everything in my room and use the bathroom, I return to the backyard.

"Sophie, flip the switch to the left of the door, please," Madeline calls to me.

I do as she asked, and the entire backyard illuminates with twinkling lights. They are strung all through the big oak trees. The sun is starting to set, and the sky is painted in gorgeous shades of pink and orange. The whole scene is magical, like stepping into a fairy garden.

I join them at the table and sit in the space left for me between Pop and Madeline across from Elle and Braxton. Pop picks up a spoon and slaps a massive pile of dumplings on my plate. Then, he loads me down with corn and peas.

My eyes widen as I look at all the food. "Um, I can't eat all that, Pop."

He side-eyes me. "We have to plump you up, little'n. Gram would have had a fit if she saw how slight you are."

I grimace. "I'm not slight."

"You ain't sturdy either," he notes.

"Sturdy?"

I hear a snicker and look up to see Braxton trying to suppress a laugh.

"Gram was always trying to fatten me up too. Like I was a calf they wanted to send to auction," Elle chimes in, and I look to see her smiling at me.

"Men like a woman with a little meat on her bones," Pop informs me.

"Oh, Dad, stop. Women don't like being told they're too skinny. You can't force-feed them," Aunt Ria interjects.

"Back me up here, Brax. Men prefer a soft woman with curves. Am I right?"

I bring my eyes back to Braxton, who is swallowing a big bite of dumplings.

He picks his glass up and washes it down. Then, he speaks, "Yes, sir. Curves are definitely appreciated," as he looks at Pop.

Then, he brings his attention to me and grins as he takes another bite. His blue eyes are dancing with amusement. He's teasing me. My stomach does a little flip as I realize I like it. Thank goodness the sun is going down and casting a pink haze across the yard, so no one notices the blush that I'm sure is tinting my face.

"How long are you here for, Sophie?" The question comes from a man at the far end of the table, who looks to be about my age.

I raise an eyebrow at him.

"Sorry, I'm Silas. I work here on the ranch. I live up the hill, near the county line, with my wife, Chloe. She's at her parents' house this week, waiting the birth of her sister's baby, or she'd have joined us."

"And I'm Walker." A deep voice booms from the guy to his left, startling me. He is large, and his brown coveralls barely fit, stretched across his massive chest. He has thick, dark hair that needs a trim and bushy eyebrows. He reminds me of a teddy bear.

"It's nice to meet you both," I reply.

I look around the table, and everyone's attention is now on me, so I continue, "I'm not sure how long I'll be in Poplar Falls. I know I'm staying through the weekend for Gram's service, and Aunt Doe asked me to stay for the reading of her will. I guess it depends on when all that's happening."

"It's great your job lets you travel with an uncertain schedule," Silas adds.

"It was easy to get approval since I'm my own boss."

"Really? That's great. What do you do?"

"She's a jewelry designer," Elle chimes in.

"Is that so?"

"Yes. I have a design studio and manufacturing site in the city."

"So, you make, like, necklaces and stuff?" Walker asks.

"Yep. I design specific pieces for people, and my team creates it from my sketches."

"So, it's special jewelry?"

I consider his question for a moment. "You could say that. Sometimes, a client asks for a particular thing or a replica of something I have sold before, but mostly, they just want something unique to them. A piece that commemorates an event or a place, maybe a moment in time or even a person."

"You can do that with a hunk of metal and some beads?" Silas asks the question, but I can tell he is curious and not being an ass.

"Absolutely. For instance, I made a hairpin for a client before I left. His wife had suddenly passed away last year, and his daughter is getting married in a few weeks. He wanted to have something special made for her, so it would feel like her mother was a part of it. His wife had loved hummingbirds, so I designed a lovely hummingbird hair comb made of silver and clear crystals. Then, I used a sapphire from one of her mother's rings for the bird's eye. That way, she has her something old, something new and something blue and a piece of her mother with her on her wedding day."

All eyes are on me as I finish my story.

"That's beautiful, Sophie." Aunt Doreen beams at me, and I return her smile.

Then, I hear a sniffle from across the table.

"It really is," Elle whispers. Probably thinking of her mother and her own wedding day.

Braxton has finished eating, and he's staring at me with an odd look.

I'm uncomfortable, being the center of everyone's attention.

"Thank you. I do love it. It pays the bills, and luckily, I can sketch from anywhere, so here I am."

"We hope to keep her for a little while," Aunt Ria says as she fills my glass with tea.

"Not too long. I do need to get home before my mother goes crazy."

"Vivian has had you all to herself for long enough. Time to share you with the rest of us," Pop says as he finds my hand under the table and squeezes.

I look over to Daddy. He hasn't said a word. He just keeps eating as Madeline adds seconds to his plate. When he notices me watching him, he looks up and purses his lips as if he wants to say something but can't find the words.

Maybe there is too much to say and too many years between us.

I pick up my fork and start eating. A little moan escapes me as the gravy from the dumplings hits my tongue.

Braxton snaps his eyes to mine, and I blush again.

"This is so good, Aunt Doe and Aunt Ria," I manage to choke out.

"It is."

The table at large agrees.

"Sophie helped," Aunt Doreen acknowledges with pride.

"Only a little, but I did enjoy it."

"You used to love helping Gram in the kitchen," Daddy adds.

"She loved every minute of it too," Pop adds.

"I remember," I reply softly, and he squeezes my hand once more.

After we all finish and dessert has been served, Emmett breaks out a bottle of wine.

"None for me," I say as I cover my glass.

"We're celebrating our Elle girl's paper. You have to have at least a sip," he says as he gives me a wink.

"I don't know. I'm kind of a lightweight with alcohol."

"One cup won't kill you," he murmurs conspiratorially and grins at me.

"Okay, one," I concede.

They all lift their glasses as Aunt Ria gushes about the essay Elle wrote. She beams with pride. It must have been nice, growing up with a large, supportive family who toasted your every achievement. All I had was my mom, and she was more a fan of my extracurricular activities. She never showed much interest in my grades, much less a single paper.

A tinge of jealousy rears its head, and I tamp it down. It's not Elle's fault my mother is so self-absorbed. It's not any of these people's fault. Mom is who she is.

So, I tuck in my irrational crazy and raise my glass with them as we congratulate the lucky girl who is Jefferson Lancaster's replacement daughter. Then, I excuse myself before I say anything to ruin the otherwise pleasant evening.

Thirteen

SOPHIE

I OPEN MY EYES AS THE DOOR TO MY ROOM CRACKS OPEN, AND LIGHT pours in from the hallway.

"You alive in there?" I hear Dallas's voice before my eyes can adjust, and I see her curls peek through the crack in the door.

I reach over and grab my phone on the nightstand. I look at the time. Eight a.m.

"Ugh, it's still early," I whine.

I stayed up late, reading, last night because I was having a hard time falling asleep without the sounds of the city. It's too quiet here.

"Early? Girl, it's practically the middle of the day. Get your lazy bones up and get dressed. We are going to town."

"For what?" I ask on a yawn.

"Lunch."

"Come back in four hours." I roll onto my stomach and cover my head with my pillow.

She grabs it and yanks. Then, she parks her ass on the bed beside me. "I'll starve to death by then. Now, get up. I want to introduce you to Beau."

"Fine, but only because you bribed me with the kid," I groan and sit up in a huff.

"You're cranky in the morning."

"And you're way too chipper. Now, go away, and I'll be down in a few minutes."

"All right, but you'd better not go back to sleep, or I'll return with a bucket of ice water," she says as she narrows her eyes and points her finger into my chest.

"You wouldn't dare."

"Oh, I'd dare," she threatens as she backs out of the door.

I scowl at her as I toss the pillow in her direction. I hear her laugh as she makes her way downstairs.

Twenty minutes later, I walk into the kitchen to find Dallas and Aunt Doreen chatting over a glass of orange juice.

"Good morning, Sophie. How did you sleep?" Aunt Doreen leans over and kisses my cheek.

"Good—once I was able to fall asleep. I don't know how you guys do it without a symphony of music blaring, sirens screaming, and horns honking."

"What's that?" Aunt Doreen asks.

"I'm used to the sounds of Manhattan traffic lulling me to sleep at night. Tree frogs and crickets aren't quite the same."

"Just leave the TV on an episode of *Cops* next time. That should do the trick," Dallas suggests.

"I'm sorry you missed breakfast. We didn't want to disturb you. There is bacon left in the oven, and I can scramble you some eggs if you'd like."

"That's okay. I'm stealing her for a while. We're going to Faye's," Dallas answers for me.

"How nice. Tell Faye I said hello." She turns to look me over. "Do you want to borrow a coat?"

I look down at the peacoat I'm wearing over my one-piece jumpsuit. "I have a coat on."

"It looks like snow today. You're probably going to need something a bit warmer."

"Snow?" I squeak.

Yesterday, it was warm and sunny. We ate dinner in the backyard, for goodness' sake.

"Welcome to October in Colorado. Sunshine one day and a blizzard the next," Dallas muses from the table.

I look outside at the overcast sky. "Should we be driving around in the snow?"

"Sure. We do it all the time. I have four-wheel drive. Besides, it's only calling for a light dusting this afternoon. We'll be fine."

After Aunt Doreen raids Madeline's closet to outfit me with a warmer coat and more appropriate footwear, I'm in the passenger's seat of Dallas's truck, and we're headed into town.

"Mom is meeting us at the diner with Beau. He was on the John Deere, helping Dad cut the grass when I left, and I couldn't bribe him off that thing. I swear, it's like it's a ride at Disney World or something. I hope he's as enthusiastic about the mower when he's a teenager."

I remember riding in front of Daddy on our mower when I was little. It was one of my favorite things.

"So, how did things go after I left yesterday?"

I shrug. "Okay, I guess."

"That good, huh?"

"It's just strange. I don't know any of the new ranch hands or new family members. My aunts are trying really hard to make me feel welcome, but Jefferson doesn't seem to want me here. He has said less than ten words to me, and all of them have been to let me know how rude he thinks I am."

"That's just Jefferson being Jefferson. Can't fault him for his personality."

"That's not how I remember him."

She glances at me as she turns into the parking lot of Faye's Diner. "He changed after you left. Turned into an old Grumpy Gus."

She parks in a spot up front marked *Employee of the Month.*

"You work here?"

"Yep. Don't be too impressed; there are only four of us. Faye, me, and Kim—the other waitress—and Andy, who cooks. So, I'm the Employee of the Month every third month."

We get out and head inside, and a little boy with blond hair, round-framed glasses, and a chocolate milk ring around his mouth shouts to us, "Over here, Mommy."

He's standing up in a booth, waving a green crayon in the air, and Dallas rushes over. She scoops him in her arms and starts smattering his face with kisses as he squirms in protest through his peals of laughter.

She sets him down, and he walks himself across the bench to make room.

"Beau, this is Mommy's friend, Miss Sophie."

He curiously eyes me as Mrs. Henderson slides over to make room for me next to her, across from Dallas and Beau.

"Hi, Miss Sophie," he greets me.

"Hi, Mr. Beau. It's sure nice to meet you."

He grins a snaggle-toothed grin at me and adjusts his glasses back into place. "I'm not a mister. I'm a little boy," he corrects me.

"Oh, pardon me. You look so grown up that I couldn't tell."

That wins me a huge smile.

We order food, and before it even arrives, Beau has wiggled his way under the booth and between me and Mrs. Henderson. He scoots up close to me, and we color together as he regales me with made-up stories about the pirates we are coloring on the diner's paper placemat, designed to entertain kids for a few minutes while their parents eat.

After we have finished eating, Mrs. Henderson wrangles him into his coat and mittens to take him to a birthday party.

I wave to him out the window in front of our booth. He keeps waving as he is buckled in.

"Thank goodness it's a party for one of Mom's friend's grand-daughters, so I don't have to go. I swear, that kid has a better social life than I do. It's a party or playdate or both every weekend," Dallas tells me as she blows kisses to him before they pull out of sight.

"He's adorable, Dallas."

"Thanks. He's the best thing I've ever done; that's for sure."

We pay our bill, and Kim brings us to-go cups of coffee.

"So, now what?"

"Now, we head to the shops in town, so I can buy a dress to wear to Gram's service tomorrow, and you can buy some real clothes."

"I have real clothes."

She rolls her eyes at me. "Girl, you have city clothes. You need jeans and sweaters and boots and coveralls."

"I'm not going to be here that long, Dal. I don't need to buy a bunch of clothes that I'll have to drag back to New York with me."

"Dad says that Dennis Phillips is handling Gram's estate. He is in Seattle, visiting his son's family, because his daughter-in-law gave birth to his second grandson a few weeks ago. That means, you'll be here for at least another couple of weeks before he can get home and schedule a will reading. Besides, you won't have to drag anything back with you because I'll be more than happy to take it off your hands when you leave."

A couple of weeks? I wasn't expecting to be here longer than a few more days.

"Weeks?"

"Yep."

She smiles huge, and I get the uneasy feeling that she and my aunts are in cahoots to keep me in Poplar Falls.

"I don't think I can stay for weeks."

"Sure you can. You can work from anywhere, remember?"

"I can, but I can't take advantage of Charlotte. Plus, I have an apartment, and my mom will lose her mind if I'm gone for that long."

"Well, I don't know who Charlotte is, but I assume she is an adult and will be just fine. Your apartment is just a building. It's not like it has to be fed and watered. And as far as your mom goes, again, she is an adult, and she will be just fine."

"Do you remember my mom?"

"Yes, and I know she can be a little high-strung, but you're a grown-ass woman. She can't make you come home until you're good and damn ready."

I balk. "A little high-strung? Obviously, your memory isn't that great."

"No, it is. I'm just saying, maybe it's time to put your foot down and set some boundaries for Mommy dearest."

"I'll think about it. I can call Charlotte and get her thoughts. She's my friend and my assistant. She helps me handle Mom."

"Sounds like a plan. Now, we shop."

Three hours later, and I'm the proud owner of a brand-new Colorado-appropriate wardrobe. I don't even know how it happened. Dallas just has a way of talking me into things. I guess that is one thing that hasn't changed since we were kids.

When we pull back up to the ranch, Daddy and Emmett are sitting on the porch, playing checkers, just like they did every Saturday afternoon when I was a kid.

Dallas and I grab all the bags out of the back of the truck and head up the steps.

Emmett watches us with an amused expression. "Good afternoon, ladies. Whatcha got there?" he asks.

"Real clothes for Sophie," Dallas answers before I can.

Daddy turns in his chair and eyes the bags in our arms. Then, he looks up at us. "Planning on staying awhile?" he asks.

I shrug. "I haven't made up my mind yet. Is it a problem if I do?"

"This is your home, Sophie. You're always welcome here. Stay forever if you want to."

"Okay. Thank you." I nod my head at him and open the door.

Dallas and Emmett beam at each other like they just witnessed the signing of the Treaty of Versailles.

If only it were that easy.

Fourteen

BRAXTON

I BACK THE TRUCK UP TO THE BARN AND LET DOWN THE TAILGATE, SO I can unload the twenty-pound bags of salt I picked up at the hardware store. Snow has already started to fall this year. It's not sticking yet, but with several elderly adults living and working on the ranch, it's a priority to keep the walkways and steps clear of any ice hazards.

As soon as I open the double door, I see Sophie's long blonde ponytail. She's making her way down the aisle of stalls, peeking in each one, speaking softly to the horses as she goes.

We have four stalls here in the main barn for the family's personal horses. They are separate from the stables, which is a little walk down the east side of the property, and house all the horses for Aunt Madeline's riding classes and therapy camps.

I stop and watch Sophie as she almost reverently reads the name tag on each stall until she reaches the fourth one and freezes.

"Huck," she says the name of the stallion aloud and then stands on her tiptoes to get a good look inside.

"Careful. He's temperamental."

She starts at my voice and turns to face me.

"You shouldn't sneak up on people like that," she scolds.

I drop the bag from my shoulder onto the barn floor. "Not sneaking. Working."

She looks sheepish as she asks, "Is this horse male or female?"

"Male."

She turns back to the stall and draws closer.

I walk toward her because the stubborn woman is not listening to my warning.

"Huckleberry," she whispers to herself.

I stop and watch as she lays her cheek against the door and closes her eyes.

"Is his momma still alive?"

Confused by her question, I ask, "His momma?"

"Blackberry was his mom, wasn't she? Is she still alive?"

"No. She died about two years ago."

I watch as something washes over her. Anger? No. Grief.

Tears dampen her lashes, and she swipes at them with her eyes still closed. I feel like I'm imposing on a private moment that I don't understand, but I don't want to leave her propped against that horse's stall.

"You mind moving back a few steps? I don't want him to kick the door and hurt you."

She opens her eyes as if realizing where she is again. She straightens and looks at me. "Why would he kick the door?"

"As I said, he's temperamental, and he doesn't take too kindly to strangers."

As if on cue, Huck whinnies and starts to buck against the door.

Sophie hops back and then starts to soothingly speak to the animal, "It's okay, Huckleberry. Did you hear us talking about your momma? I bet you miss her, don't you? I miss her too. She was my horse and my best friend."

Huck settles and pokes his head over the top of the door, and Sophie draws near again.

Odd. She doesn't seem the least bit afraid of the large animal.

She reaches up to run her fingers down the horse's long face. Then, she lays her cheek against his nose.

Huck doesn't react; he stands there and lets the human nuzzle him.

"I left her. I left her right when she was about to give birth to you. I bet she wondered where I went and what she had done wrong."

She wraps an arm up around the horse and holds on to his neck for a long while, and as much as I need to get the truck unloaded and start salting the sidewalks, I don't want to leave with her so close to the unruly animal.

After a while, she releases her hold. She reaches into the pocket of her coat and pulls out an apple. Huck sniffs the offering and then gently takes it from her open hand.

"Good boy," Sophie coos and gives him one more scratch on his nose before she turns and walks right past me toward the doors. "You're right. He's an ornery beast," she throws over her shoulder in my direction as she exits.

I stand there, looking the horse in the eye.

"What was that, Huck?" I ask as he stares me down.

All I get in return is an agitated snort. Then, he turns his back on me.

Damn horse.

I guess all the creatures on this ranch are enamored by Miss Sophia Lancaster.

Traitors.

"Want to come out to Fast Breaks with us tonight?" Elle asks Sophie as we finish up supper and start cleaning the table.

"Fast Breaks?"

"Yeah, it's the pool hall in town. Brax usually takes me on Saturday nights, being as Sunday mornings are the only ones he takes off."

She looks up at me in surprise. "You take a day off?"

"Yep. Madeline insists. Walker handles Sunday mornings."

Aunt Mad walks in at the sound of her name. "That's right. Your life can't be all work, Braxton. You have to actually live in between."

"You teach Jefferson to do that?" Sophie asks.

"I've tried. But it's hard to teach an old dog new tricks."

"I bet."

"Brax here is a different story. I still have a chance at convincing him that the ranch won't fall to pieces if he sleeps in one day a week."

She reaches up and pats my cheek. I appreciate the concern, but the truth is, I'd rather be up with the cattle than sleeping in. My eyes pop open at the same time every morning anyway; my internal alarm clock doesn't give a damn if it's Sunday or Monday.

"His wife will thank you one day," Elle agrees.

"That's my hope."

Elle hands a plate to Sophie, who is loading the dishwasher.

"So, you want to come with?"

"Rain check?"

"You sure? It's a lot of fun. Everyone in town usually ends up there by the end of the night."

"I think I'm just going to read a little and turn in early tonight. I didn't sleep much last night, and I don't want to be too tired for Gram's service tomorrow."

The service begins right after church tomorrow at First Baptist Church of Poplar Falls. Gram was a well-respected and active member of the congregation her entire life. She spent a good bit of her time trying to wrangle us all in the doors anytime they were open.

"That's probably a good idea, Elle. Gram would be mighty disappointed if we showed up haggard and hungover tomorrow," I agree with the plan of turning in early.

Elle twists her nose in consideration and then nods. "I'll call Sonia and tell her we decided to stay in tonight. How about we do a movie and popcorn instead?" she asks the room at large, but her hopeful eyes are directed toward Sophie.

"That's a great idea. I can whip up some homemade chocolate chip cookies too," Ria offers.

Sophie looks around at the expectant faces and hesitantly agrees, "Okay."

Elle claps. "Yay! We can have a pajama party. I'll go shower and change and meet you guys in the living room in half an hour." She makes her way to me. "What about you? Want to join us?"

I wrap her in my arms. "Nah, pajama parties aren't exactly my thing. I'll leave you girls to it."

I kiss the top of her head, and she scurries down the hall.

Sophie finishes loading the washer, and Ria begins to pull out the ingredients to make her cookies.

"Good night, ladies."

"Good night, Brax. I'll save you a few cookies for breakfast."

"Thank you, ma'am."

I head for the back door, and Sophie offers a quick, "Night."

I nod in response as I walk out on the deck. It's a chilly night. The snowfall only lasted a few hours, and the thin layer of white didn't stick around long once the sun peeked back out a couple of hours before sunset.

My phone chimes in my pocket, and I pull it out. It's a text from Lori, a girl I see from time to time, asking if I'm coming out tonight. I reply that I decided to stay in, and she offers to come and keep me company when she gets off work.

It looks like I'm set for the night.

I look back through the kitchen window at Ria pointing Sophie toward the mixer on the counter.

Jefferson and Emmett come around the side of the house, carrying trash bags, and Jefferson follows my line of sight.

"Guess it's a hen party in there tonight," he grumbles.

"Yep. Just you two and a house full of women, old man."

"Can we come and hang out with you and watch the game?"

"Sorry, I have plans."

"Traitor." He stomps off toward the garbage cans.

Emmett chuckles. "He can complain all he wants, but I know he loves having all his girls under one roof."

"Thank goodness it's a big roof."

"Ain't that the truth? Enjoy your night, Brax."

He slaps me on the back and follows Jefferson, and I head to my apartment to get ready for my guest.

Fifteen

SOPHIE

I STEP OUT ONTO THE FRONT PORCH WITH MY QUILT AND SKETCHPAD. It's five a.m., and the house is still silent. I guess Sundays really are the day of rest around here.

I tossed and turned all night, trying to decide what I was going to do about staying here until Gram's attorney returned. I could always go back to New York on Monday and fly back out here when he is ready, but that doesn't feel right. Nothing has been resolved since I arrived. If nothing else, I'm even more conflicted than before.

Madeline and her family were easier to hate from afar. Spending last night watching a scary movie with her and Elle and my aunts, laughing and filling up on junk food, was actually nice.

Who am I, and what have I done with the angry, bitter, jealous girl who stepped off that airplane?

Then, there is Braxton. I'm still not sure how I feel about him. He is either ignoring me or looking at me like I'm an alien who sprouted another head.

Sometime in the middle of the night, I decided to roll the dice and stay through the end of the month. I do want to spend more time with Pop and Aunt Doreen and Aunt Ria. Maybe Daddy and I will finally have a real conversation too. Perhaps not, but at least I'll know it's not because I ran away.

As soon as it's a decent hour, I'll call Charlotte and run my plan by her. I feel guilty for heaping so much responsibility on her plate, but

I'm sure she'll agree that it would be better for my head to be in the game when I return home. At least, I hope she feels that way.

I settle in on the swing and start to sketch a dragonfly pendant when I hear a door open. I peer around the side of the house and see two people standing on a landing at the top of a staircase to the right, above the barn doors.

It's Braxton and a brunette. Her back is to me, and she's looking up at him. He's in nothing but pajama pants, his feet are bare, and his hair is disheveled. The brunette reaches up and runs her fingers through it. It's nice hair. I've never really noticed before because he's always wearing that raggedy ball cap. He lays his hands on either side of her hips as she comes up onto her tiptoes and plants a kiss on his lips. He returns the kiss, and then he whispers something that makes her laugh before he releases her. She turns and trots down the steps. She gets into a red Mercedes convertible and drives away. Braxton stays on the landing and watches until her car is out of sight down the drive. Then, he turns and disappears back inside his door.

I stand up and walk to the side of the porch, so I can get a better view, and through the windows, I watch him move around. He walks out of sight and then comes back with a toothbrush hanging out of his mouth and a towel around his neck. He opens the door again, and I dodge behind a column and hold my breath, hoping he didn't see me.

A moment later, a small brown-and-white bulldog puppy rounds the side of the porch and gives a sharp bark, startling me.

"Shh," I say as I look down at the pup. "Please don't give me away," I plead in a whisper as it continues to yap its greeting.

I move closer to the beam and pray that Braxton doesn't hear it.

The excited puppy pees all over the porch as he jumps up at me, no doubt wanting to be picked up and petted.

It's the cutest thing.

After a few terrifying moments, I hear Braxton's deep voice from across the way. "Hawkeye, you done, boy?" His question is followed up by a loud whistle.

The puppy scampers off the porch and toward the barn.

I continue to hold my breath until I hear the door close once more, and then I let it out and bow over.

Jeez, why am I sneaking around, spying on him?

I return to the swing and finish my sketch before going in to shower and get ready for church.

Breakfast is potluck, prepared by the ladies at church and served before Sunday school. Aunt Doreen and Aunt Ria's contribution is a delicious blueberry, cream-cheese-stuffed French toast casserole.

The entire town has come out for Gram's service. Every pew is filled when Reverend Burr begins his sermon. He starts with a joke, saying that only Mrs. Betty Sue Lancaster could turn a Sunday service into a standing-room-only event.

After church, the family is given some private time with Gram. Pop stands by her casket and holds his hand on top of hers in silence for several long moments before Aunt Ria walks up and lays a white rose in with her. Then, one by one, everyone comes up and pays their final respects and hugs Pop. After everyone takes a turn, I approach slowly.

She looks like an angel. Her silver hair is arranged in a knot on top of her head, just as I remember her always wearing it. Her face is serene, and she has a hint of a smile on her lips, like she is finally in on the secret. The secret she preached to us all—that heaven is better than we could ever think or imagine, and she is already enjoying herself.

When I make my way to her side, Pop wraps an arm around me.

His solemn gaze never leaves Gram's face as he speaks to me, "She'd be so happy you are here, Sophia."

"I'm sorry I didn't come earlier," I tell him as a sob of regret escapes me.

"It's okay. Gram would be tickled, knowing that she had a part in bringing you back home."

He squeezes me in tighter, and I realize that I'm supporting him now.

Daddy comes along my left side, and he places a hand on my shoulder. The three of us stand there in silence for a beat.

Then, Daddy leans down and kisses her cheek. He whispers, "I'll see you when I get to where I'm going, Momma."

"Are we ready to begin, Mr. Lancaster?" the funeral director asks Pop.

A few minutes later, we are ushered out into the sanctuary with the others.

After a beautiful service filled with uplifting music and the town reminiscing about how Gram helped and served her community, people filing up one by one to tell stories of how she touched them in some profound way, we make our way to the cemetery where one last hymnal is sung and one last prayer is prayed. Then, she is lowered to her final resting place, and everyone starts to disperse.

I stay seated in the front row, and people start to mingle and offer condolences to the family. Several ladies head home to grab their prepared food, so they can beat us back to the ranch and set things up for the wake. As is customary, we will receive friends and family and every type of casserole known to man for the rest of the afternoon.

"It's what we do when people are hurting, and we have no idea what to say. We cook, and we feed them. It's how we take care of each other and show our love in times of loss," Dallas explains as my eyes grow bigger with each foil-wrapped porcelain dish that walks in the door.

I watch as Aunt Doreen tries to stuff another pie into the refrigerator.

"There's a lot of love in there," I muse.

"Yep, that was Gram," she agrees.

I feel little arms wrap around my legs and look down to see Beau staring up at me.

"You wanna play catch with me?" he asks sweetly.

"No, Beau, Miss Sophie has to stay inside with her guests," Dallas tells him as she tries to untangle us.

"But everybody is loud in here," he protests.

"It is kind of loud," I agree.

I bend down on one knee, so I'm face-to-face with him. "You know what? I'd love to play catch with you. Can I play in my dress, or do I need to go change?"

"You can play in your dress. The girls at school do it all the time."

"Well, okay. If they can do it, so can I." I stand and take him by his hand.

"Sophie, you don't have to," Dallas starts.

"I know, but I want to, and I think Gram would have wanted to, too, if she were here right now."

She nods, and we head outside. She grabs a baseball and a couple of mitts from the back of the truck. Then, the three of us stand out in the driveway, away from the parked cars, and start playing catch.

I keep pretending that every toss Beau sends my way is so fast that it actually hurts my gloved hand to catch it. I drop a few on purpose, and I miss a few. Beau giggles and runs after each attempt I make to throw it back at him while Dallas "coaches" me from the sideline.

I watch as he trots after a runaway ball, and I think to myself, *Gram would definitely be smiling at us playing catch at her wake.*

Sixteen

BRAXTON

"WHO IS THAT?"

I follow Myer's line of sight to where Dallas and Sophie are tossing a baseball around with Dallas's son, Beau.

"That's Sophia Lancaster," I inform him as I twist off the top to the cold beer in my hand.

Walker thought a wake was a good occasion to bring by a tub of iced-down beers and set up lawn chairs out by the barn. Which is where he, Silas, our buddy Myer, Payne—Dallas's brother—and I are currently hiding out from the crowd.

"No way. That is not the Sophia Lancaster I remember at all."

"Me neither," Payne adds.

"It's her," I confirm.

"Damn, she grew up just right. Is she single?" Myer asks.

I shrug. "She's not wearing a ring, and I haven't heard her mention a man. Not that I've been paying too much attention to anything she has to say."

"Why?" Myer turns his attention to me.

"Not interested, I guess."

He turns back to watch just as Sophie misses an easy catch and starts running after the ball in those ridiculous heels of hers while Beau shrieks with laughter.

"She could probably read me my rights, and I'd hang on every word," he declares as he tracks her every move.

"Stop ogling her like some creep," I order as I chuck the bottle top at his head.

"Ouch." He reaches up and rubs his forehead but doesn't take his eyes off Sophie's ass as she retrieves the ball and jogs back to Beau. "There's nothing wrong with looking." He brushes off my reprimand.

"Why do you care anyway? You got it for your sister?"

I look up, and Payne is wagging his eyebrows at me.

"First of all, she is not my sister, and secondly, Jefferson would rip my and either one of your dumbasses' balls off if we so much as laid a finger on her."

"She's what, thirty-one, thirty-two? It's not like she's a sixteen-year-old whose virginity he needs to protect."

I cut my eyes back to Payne. "You want to be the one to tell him that?"

He grins. "Hell no."

"That's what I thought. Besides, it might come in a pretty package, but that chick is one hundred percent high-maintenance headache. No, thank you."

Myer looks back at me.

"Pretty? Son, that woman"—Walker points in her direction just as she reaches down again to snatch up the ball, her firm breasts peeking from the top of the plunging neckline of her dress—"is sexy as hell and would be worth every bit of trouble."

"I said, stop ogling her," I demand with a little more force this time.

He throws his hands in the air. "Yes, sir. Eyes off your girl. Got it."

"She's not my girl," I growl.

Walker and Payne burst into laughter just as Dallas gallops up to our group.

"What's so funny?" she asks.

"Oh, we're just ribbing Braxton here over his fascination with—"

"Nothing," I cut Payne off with a hard look, which starts the laughter back up.

Dallas turns to me with a suspicious look.

"We're just making fun of Sophie trying to play ball in a dress and heels, is all."

She glances back toward her son and her friend and smiles. "Yeah, I guess it does look ridiculous, but isn't she sweet to play with him and get him out of that house full of somber adults?"

"I guess."

She looks up at me. "You don't like her very much, do you?"

"I don't really have an opinion of her either way, to tell you the truth."

Walker coughs.

She cuts her eyes to him and then quickly back to me. "You know, I never considered you a snob before, Braxton Young."

"Me?"

"Yes, you. You had your mind made up about her before she ever got off that plane. She walked onto this ranch with her head held high, and yes, maybe her defenses were up, but damn, she was an army of one, facing down a whole troop of people she barely remembered or didn't know at all. I'd think you would be a little more compassionate."

Her comment hits its mark, and she knows it because she gives me a victorious purse of her lips.

Then, she pulls up one of the chairs and parks herself next to Myer.

"Hey," he says as he smiles at her and offers her a frosty bottle from the tub.

She nods, and he pops the top off before handing it to her. She accepts, oblivious to his attention.

We all sit in the sun and watch as Sophie completely wears Beau out—or he wears her out.

He comes and hops up on Payne's lap before falling sound asleep.

Sophie timidly walks over and joins us.

"Hey, guys," she says, and Walker opens another lawn chair for her.

Myer stands, leans in, and offers her his hand. "Hey, Sophie. Remember me?"

She wrinkles her forehead in concentration and tries to place him.

"Myer Wilson." He quickly lets her off the hook.

Her eyes widen in surprise and then light up. "Myer? Oh my goodness. How are you?"

She lets go of his hand and wraps her arms around his neck. He hesitates for just a second as his eyes come to me, and then he hugs her right back.

"I'm good. How about you?" he asks as she lets him go and looks up at him.

"I'm shocked; that's how I am. You're a man now."

He flushes slightly at her announcement. "Yep."

"I mean, of course you're a man now. I just … it's strange. I have all these memories, and in them, everyone is stuck at twelve years old. It's startling to see how much everyone has changed."

He smiles at her. "I bet it is. We all grew up and changed together, so we didn't really notice. However, we've all definitely noticed how well you grew up."

She blushes at his statement.

"I mean, that you've grown up," he sputters.

Her red deepens.

"You know what I mean, right?" He looks around to us for help.

"I do," she murmurs.

I find that I'm not enjoying this little exchange in the least. So, I clear my throat.

"You want a beer?" I ask her.

"I'm not a fan of beer," she replies.

Walker fake gasps.

She grins at him. "Got any more moonshine?"

He hops up to his feet. "Now, there's a girl after my own heart," he says as he heads over to the cooler on his tailgate and grabs a jar.

A few hours later, the driveway is empty as everyone packs up and starts making their way back home.

"Thank you, Soph," Dallas says as she wraps her in a hug. "I think you're officially his new favorite person."

"He's pretty high up on my list too. Hopefully, he'll sleep well for you tonight," she replies.

"Speaking of which, I'd better get him home and in his pajamas."

"I'll load him in the truck." Payne stands and starts walking with his nephew in his arms.

"You want me to drive you guys home?" Myer offers.

"Why?" Dallas asks him.

"I haven't had anything to drink." He shrugs.

"Um, I only had one beer, but I guess so," she replies, puzzled.

"You can never be too careful. Payne can follow us in my truck," he says as he gets to his feet and rushes to open the passenger door for her.

Dallas waves as she hops in. Myer scurries over to the driver's side, and they drive away.

"Looks like I have to go too," Payne says as he grabs Myer's keys and follows.

Sophie looks over at me with her forehead wrinkled in confusion. "I thought Payne lived beside Dallas and his parents?" she asks.

"He does."

"Then, why didn't he drive them home?"

I chuckle. "I guess because he had a beer. Safer to let Myer drive them."

"But he's okay to drive Myer's truck?"

"It appears so."

She looks at me as it dawns on her. "Oh. Ohhh. Does Dallas know?"

"I don't know what you're talking about."

She narrows her eyes at me.

I ignore her look as I start folding chairs and toss them into the barn. She grabs the one she was sitting in and folds it up before following me.

She gets the heel of her shoe caught in a hole near the door and starts to buckle, and I reach out and grab her around the waist just as she begins to fold.

"Whoa," I say as I take her weight into my arms and steady her.

She lets out a little cry of pain as her ankle gives.

I quickly pick her up off her feet to keep her from twisting it further, and she wraps her arms around my neck as I take her off-balance.

She buries her face into me, and her hot breath slides down my neck, sending a shiver up my spine.

I hold her against me for a couple of beats, and then I rasp out, "You okay?"

She nods her head while still hiding her face.

"You sure?"

She looks up. "Just embarrassed," she admits.

"That's why you shouldn't be wearing those shoes out here. They might be sexy as hell, but you'll break your neck."

She sternly looks at me. "I'll have you know, I can run down ten flights of stairs and dodge traffic in these shoes without so much as stubbing my toe. It's the moonshine." She sticks her bottom lip out at me in defiance.

"You're probably right. Not the ridiculous shoes. It's the liquor to blame." I instinctively tighten my grip on her and focus my attention on her mouth.

She leans toward me, and just as I'm about to do something foolish, a throat clears behind me.

"Hi, Daddy," she says over my shoulder.

Shit.

I turn with her still in my arms to see Jefferson and Emmett standing behind us.

"I twisted my ankle, and Braxton caught me before I fell."

He nods his head. "You still falling?"

She gives him a quizzical look. "No."

"Then, maybe he should put you down."

"Oh," she says as if just realizing she still has her arms around me. She disengages from my neck and hops down.

"You okay? Does it hurt?" I ask as I steady her shoulders.

"No. It's good," she says as she wiggles her foot and puts all her weight on it. "Thanks."

"You're welcome."

She faces the other men and says her good nights before heading off in the direction of the main house.

I start loading chairs again.

"Thanks for watching out for her, Braxton. I appreciate it, son." He claps me on the back and walks off behind her.

Emmett grins at me and winks.

Fucking Emmett.

Seventeen

SOPHIE

I WALK INTO THE KITCHEN TO FIND EVERYONE GATHERED AROUND the table, eating breakfast. They're all bright-eyed and bushy-tailed.

Don't they realize it's too damn early for this level of awake?

I stumble over to the percolator and pour myself a huge cup of coffee.

"Any chance you have a carton of soy milk in here, Aunt Doe?" I ask as I shuffle to the refrigerator.

"Soy milk? What the hell is soy milk?" Daddy asks as he lowers his morning newspaper.

Who still gets a newspaper delivered?

"It's a healthier milk option that is derived from the soybean plant," I calmly point out.

He stares blankly at me as if I just said the stupidest thing he had ever heard. Surely, they've heard of soy milk before.

"Emmett, you ever tried to milk a soybean?" He raises an eyebrow as he asks the ridiculous question.

"Can't say that I have. Never came across one with a teat before," Emmett replies without looking up from his plate.

I hear a chuckle coming from the doorway and look over to see Braxton leaning against the frame.

"What are you laughing at?" My frustration is transferred from Daddy to him.

He shakes his head and walks fully into the kitchen where he begins to make a plate.

Daddy speaks back up, "You kids and all your food hang-ups. No carbs, all carbs, no fat, all fat, gluten-free, dairy-free, vegan—it's all a load of horseshit. If you eat what the good Lord provides, straight off the land, and then work hard, you don't have to worry about all that nonsense," he informs me as he shovels in a mouthful of bacon.

"That's just not true. Diabetes, heart disease, and gluten-sensitivity are real things, and you have to be proactive in your dietary choices. Especially if you don't want an ass as big as the broad side of a barn," I huff.

That gets Braxton's attention. His eyes shift down to the ridiculous Carhartt coveralls Dallas talked me into buying. Apparently, we are taking Beau four-wheeling at some point, and I need to be dressed for briars and gravel-slinging.

"Maybe if you had more real milk and bacon, you would fill out those new coveralls a little better," he states with a gleam in his eye.

He is trying to bait me. *Great.* I thought we had reached a sort of truce last night, but I guess it was just my imagination.

"I wasn't talking to you," I snap in return.

"I'm just making an observation."

"Thanks," I bite out.

"Look, sweetheart," Daddy interrupts our little spat, "Pop is seventy-eight years old, and he still works circles around the hired hands on this ranch. Most of who are a quarter of his age. He has been eating bacon from our pigs, eggs from our chickens, and drinking warm milk straight out of our cows' udders his entire life. All those issues you are talking about are a result of all the soda and the prepackaged, processed, sugar- and salt-laden crap your generation calls food. Now, put a couple of teaspoons of that real milk in your coffee and sit down and eat."

Without saying another word, I do as he said and sit at the table in a huff. It's like talking to a brick wall anyway.

After finishing eating, I grab my cell and head outside. The crisp, cold bite of the morning air helps to focus me as I dial the office.

Charlotte picks up on the second ring. "Sophia Doreen Designs. How may I direct your call?"

"Good morning, Charlotte. It's me."

"Sophie. I was about to call you. I just got off the phone with Gail. She is working on the new order, and she wants to double what they ordered last month. I talked to Justin in production, and he says it's absolutely doable. I need your okay, and we will move forward. Also, she'd like to get one more exclusive design. How do you feel about designing a watch?"

"A wristwatch? I've never thought about it."

"Yeah, she said a female watch with a chain band. Something different, elegant. Whatever you can come up with. They'd just like one to offer with the line and the Sophia Doreen name on it before Christmas. Apparently, watches are a hot-ticket item for men to gift their significant others, and she wants one that they can only get at Maple and Park. They'd like to start marketing the hell out of it ASAP."

"Okay, sure. I'll start working on some sketches right away."

"And what do you think about us offering the ink-quill bracelet in precious metals?"

"The copper one?"

"Yes. It's selling like hotcakes in the online store, and we thought maybe we could offer it in fourteen-karat yellow, white, and rose gold and perhaps a sterling silver along with the copper option?"

"Yeah, I think that piece would look good in any material."

"Perfect. I'll e-mail you over the price points to approve once Justin gets me the projected cost figures for each option. He's making samples as we speak."

"Oh, he is, is he?"

"I had a hunch you would be okay with it, and I wanted to have them priced out with samples we could photograph and upload to the website as soon as possible. The holiday crunch is almost upon us."

"I'm sorry I'm not there in the trenches with you."

"We have it covered. As long as you're still hammering out designs in between the family drama, we're all good. Speaking of which, how did the service go yesterday?"

"It was good. Exactly what Gram would have wanted."

"That's nice. Now, how was it for you though? You okay?"

"I think so. Making progress at making peace. Baby steps."

"Oh no, we've reverted to speaking in fragmented sentences. What's wrong?"

"Nothing's wrong. It's just … Daddy and I are still in this weird place, and Braxton is a pain in the ass most of the time. The women are all great though."

"Men, ick."

"Right? And the attorney who is handling Gram's estate is out of town, so it could be a couple more weeks before I can head home."

"Don't worry. We have the office covered. You take care of business there."

"Mom is going to lose her mind when I tell her."

"So, you plan to talk to her?"

Busted. I've been avoiding Mom's calls all week and letting them go to voice mail. Each one has been polite, but I can tell she is growing more and more frantic with each passing day.

"Eventually. I just haven't had it in me to deal with her this week. I'll call her this afternoon and let her know what's going on."

"Good. As much as the woman can drive me insane, I've felt kind of sorry for her the past couple of days. She showed up Friday to take me to lunch. Just me. It was awkward as hell."

"I'm so sorry, Charlotte. You're the best friend a girl could ask for, you know that?"

"I do, and you can thank me with an extra Christmas present this year."

"Done."

"Listen, don't let those men push you around, you hear me?

Remember who you are. You are Sophia fucking Lancaster, and if you start to forget that, you pick up the phone and call me. I'll remind you."

"Yes, ma'am."

"I have to go. I told Justin I would meet him for lunch."

"Oh, really?"

"Don't start. Go do cowgirl stuff and make sure you check your e-mail this evening. Love you."

"Love you more."

Eighteen

SOPHIE

AFTER A MORNING FILLED WITH A SIX-YEAR-OLD OUTRUNNING me on a four-wheeled death trap, Dallas and I head into town to check out the Apple Festival while Beau naps.

We grab a slice of warm apple strudel topped with homemade vanilla-bean ice cream from one of the vendor tables and head toward the coffee shop.

Downtown looks idyllic, like it's frozen in time. The same little shops and boutiques of my faded childhood memories line Main Street. Even the quaint gazebo still stands proud in the center of the lawn of Town Hall Square. Dallas and I used to spend long, lazy afternoons picnicking in that gazebo while Mom visited with Mrs. Henderson at the Bountiful Harvest Bread Company, a bakery Dallas's mom has owned and run forever.

"I swear, it feels like I'm walking on the set of a Hallmark Christmas movie," I muse as we pass a couple of dueling banjo players.

Dallas tosses a few dollars in their case. "Right?" She stops and looks around for a moment. "Who doesn't love a good Hallmark movie though?"

"Don't you wish there were more development around?"

"Like what?"

"I don't know. Restaurants, hotels, shops, bars, just … more things to do?" I ask because I truly want to know.

She thinks for a moment. "Not really. I mean, for the most part, we like cooking and eating at home with our families. We have Butch's Tavern and Fast Breaks pool hall when we want to drink and blow off a little steam or shoot a cutthroat game of billiards. They aren't fancy, but everyone knows each other, and you can get shitfaced without worrying someone will drag you off because we look out for each other. Plus, you always end up home safe and sound because either Butch calls your parents or your brother to come and get you or one of your neighbors drives you home. The schools are great. Beau is happy as a pig in mud on the farm with all the critters and his Pop-Pop. As far as stuff to do? We have the lake for boating and swimming, pastures for bonfires. We four-wheel, fish, hunt, ride horses, play cornhole and horseshoes, tube down the river. We have snowmobiles and an ice-skating rink when the lake freezes over. What exactly more do you think we need?"

"Museums? Theaters? Ballet?"

She wrinkles her nose. "We have the cinema plex and the drive-in theater. Miss Lucy still teaches dance at the old ballroom. But, honestly, Sophie, who enjoys walking around a museum or sitting through a dance recital all damn day? Those things are what middle school field trip nightmares are made of."

"I like ballet and opera, and I thoroughly enjoy Broadway."

She nods. "I guess those can be fun for some people, but I'd rather watch a good chick flick by the moonlight while eating a hot dog and chili fries."

"That does sound good."

"Plus, you can wear your stretchy leggings and a comfy sweatshirt instead of a girdle and high heels."

I giggle.

"Besides, Denver has all those things and great shopping, and it's only a day trip away. You don't have to live all the way up in New York to look at a bunch of dead folks on a canvas, you know. We can be just as sophisticated as you, and we do it on our terms without turning Poplar Falls into a bunch of crowded streets full of franchises."

"Touché."

Just as we reach the end of Main, Braxton and Emmett appear, carrying a table and a tent.

"Hey there, ladies," Emmett greets.

"Hi. What are you two studs doing down here?" Dallas asks.

"Doreen and Ria are setting up a table to sell their apple butter and fried apple pies for the church," he replies.

"You need any help?" I offer.

"You guys can grab the chairs in the back of the truck," he says as he nods toward the loading area.

I hand the remainder of my strudel off to Dallas to throw in the trash and lick the melting ice cream from the side of my hand.

Braxton's eyes follow my movement before he comments, "First, coveralls, and now eating with your fingers? Careful, Princess, people might confuse you with one of us."

"I wasn't eating with my fingers."

He smirks at me and walks off, following Emmett.

Ugh, he is infuriating.

"Hey, Braxton. I've been eating with my fingers. I could use a little help, licking myself clean," Dallas calls after him.

"Ew."

"What?" she asks me innocently as we grab the folding chairs from the back of the pickup.

"I hate how much you like him."

"Why? Honestly, what's not to like? You see those eyes and those lips and that five-o'clock shadow right? Plus, he's a good man, hardworking, loves his little sister, and dotes on her. He's the whole package."

"They stole my daddy, my life," I mumble the accusation under my breath as we start walking toward the setup.

She must have heard because she stops in front of me, and I almost collide with her back.

Then, she turns and lays into me gently. "No, they didn't. They were forced from their home, just like you were. Do you think for one

92

second they didn't wish they were at their own house with their own mom and dad? I know you are dealing with a lot of pain from what went down with Vivian and Jefferson, but don't lay blame where it's not supposed to be. They were just kids, Sophie. Just like you were."

Then, she turns back around and heads to where Emmett and Braxton are assembling the tent. I let what she said sink in for a minute, and I'm a little embarrassed by my words. She's right. They were kids. I might be envious that they had Daddy all those years, but they didn't steal him away. The only people I have a right to be angry with are Daddy and Madeline. I decide to try a little harder with Braxton and Elle.

We get the table set up and tent in place just as Aunt Doreen, Ria, and Madeline arrive with boxes full of mason jars filled with my aunts' homemade apple butter and a large insulated tote full of individually wrapped fried pies. I snatch one from the top, unwrap it, and take a bite.

Aunt Ria shoos us away. "You rascals go on now before you eat all our profits."

My eyes roll to the back of my head as I finish the delicious pie. I lift the wrapper to my lips and shake the excess cinnamon sugar that gathered there onto my tongue.

"What about the diabetes and heart disease you were going on about this morning?" Braxton asks as he watches me in amusement.

I finish chewing and wipe the back of my hand across my face.

Then, I stick my tongue out at him, and he laughs.

"I never said you couldn't enjoy a treat from time to time."

"Just not in your coffee?"

"If my coffee were a treat, then I couldn't have the pie. It's a compromise. The eighty-twenty rule. If I eat a salad for lunch, then I can have a steak for dinner. Or I have steak for both and find a way to work it off physically."

He comes in closer and whispers against my ear, "And what do you do to work off strudel and ice cream and pie for lunch? Physically?"

"Um, go for a run or something."

"Or something, huh?"

I look up at him, and his eyes are dancing as he teases me. I try to think of a smart retort, but before I can come up with anything, Dallas walks up.

"What are you two whispering about over here?"

"Sophie is just giving me a nutrition and physical education lesson."

"Yeah, right, says the guy who literally tosses around tractor tires for fun."

"I have to follow the eighty-twenty rule."

"I know; I know. That's what Myer says too. I'm more of a sixty-forty girl myself," she says as she stuffs the remainder of a pie in her mouth.

My eyes snap back to his, and he gives me a quick shrug.

"Well, look at that. We can agree on something," I muse.

"Yep, better grab a coat. It looks like hell might be freezing over tonight," he says with a grin.

Nineteen

SOPHIE

"SOPHIA?" MY MOM'S RELIEVED VOICE COMES OVER THE LINE. "Hi, Mom."

"I have been calling and calling you, and your line goes straight to voice mail. I've been so worried. Haven't you been getting my messages?"

"I'm sorry. My phone reception is so spotty up here in the mountains. Calls don't come through. Ask Charlotte. We've had the worst time trying to talk without getting cut off," I lie.

"It doesn't surprise me. You're basically stuck in the middle of nowhere. That town has always been in the dark ages."

"It's definitely a simplistic way of life down here."

"So, how have things been?"

I can hear the shakiness in her voice.

"Fine. More or less."

"Don't be vague, Sophia. Tell me how it's really going."

I sigh. My mother has always been able to tell when I'm evading her questions.

"It's fine, Mom. I don't know what else to tell you. Aunt Doreen and Aunt Ria are just as you remember them. Emmett is still hanging in there, and he is still crushing on Aunt Doreen. Pop is a little melancholy, but he just lost Gram, so that's expected. Dallas and I reconnected, and she is divorced and has a son. His name is Beau, and he is the cutest little boy. Blackberry is dead, but I got to meet her son, and I hope to ride him soon."

"Soon? Aren't you coming home tomorrow?"

I take a deep breath and brace myself for her freak-out.

"No. I'm staying through the end of the month."

Silence.

"Mom? You still there?"

"What did your father tell you?" she calmly asks.

That's not the reaction I was expecting. I guess she assumes that Daddy and I made up, and he talked me into staying.

"Not much," I grumble.

"You have to give me a chance, Sophia."

"A chance for what?" I ask, confused.

"To explain."

"Mom, you don't have to explain why I need to come home. I know I need to get back to the city, but Charlotte has everything covered at the office, and my houseplants are probably already dead. I'm getting plenty of time to design here. I think the fresh air and the peace and quiet have renewed me and gotten my creative juices flowing because I've filled two sketchbooks with new designs this week."

I stop babbling and wait for her to give me the thousand other reasons she has thought up. She gives me nothing.

"Mom? You still there?"

"Yes, darling, I'm still here. I just thought ..."

"What?"

"Nothing. Why are you staying until the end of the month?"

"The attorney handling Gram's estate is out of town and won't be back until then, and I just thought, instead of flying home just to have to turn around in a few weeks and fly back, I'd stay and spend a little more time with Dallas and my aunts."

"All right."

Hmm, that seemed a little too easy.

"Are you okay, Mom?"

"Of course I am. I just miss you, is all."

"I miss you too. And I promise to try to call and check in more often. By the time I settle down at night, it's so late in New York with the time difference."

"It doesn't matter how late you call. I'll always answer," she says, and I feel even guiltier for letting her calls go to voice mail.

"Then, I'll call before I go to bed at least a couple of times a week."

"Promise?"

"I promise. But I do have to go now. I love you."

"I love you too, my onliest only."

I disconnect. That wasn't as hard as I'd thought it was going to be.

I shove my phone into my back pocket and hop off the porch. It's like a weight has been lifted from my chest as I make my way to the barn.

I find Braxton with a rake and bucket, cleaning out the first stall. I swear, the man never stops working.

"Hey," I call as I approach.

He stops and looks over his shoulder at me. "Hey."

"Do you think it would be okay for me to brush down Huck? I want to build a little trust with him."

"I told you, he's temperamental."

"I've visited him every day this week, and he hasn't been the least bit aggressive with me. I think he's getting used to me. I thought maybe, if he gets comfortable enough, I might be able to saddle and ride him."

"You know how to ride?"

"I knew how to ride before I knew how to walk."

"You still ride?"

"Not as often as I'd like, but I'm a member of a riding club in Manhattan, and I help instruct the children during their summer camps."

That seems to appease him.

He chucks a heap of dirty hay into the bucket at his feet. "Suit yourself. Just be careful and move slowly with him. He hasn't been ridden often, and we don't saddle him much."

"I will." I start to walk off, and I change my mind. "Can I ask you a question?"

"I don't know. Can you?"

Grr.

"What's with the ball cap?" I ask as curiosity gets the best of me.

"What do you mean?"

"It's a Red Sox hat," I explain to him unnecessarily.

"Yeah, so?"

"Well, speaking as a New Yorker ... who is required to hate the Red Sox on principle alone ... how do you not get your ass kicked by Rockies fans, wearing that thing around town?"

He gives me a knowing look. A look that says, *I'd like to see them try.*

"We aren't as damn redneck as New Yorkers are, apparently." He smirks at me, and his rarely seen dimple peeks out.

"Riiiiight."

He seems to stop and contemplate the question for a moment, and then he confesses, "It was my dad's. He was born in New England. Landed in Poplar Springs after he met a raven-haired beauty from here at Arizona State University. He was there on a baseball scholarship, and she was visiting a cousin on campus for the weekend. Her name was Lily. He followed her home and never left."

"Not even to finish school?"

"Nope. He married her six weeks later, began working at a local farm, bought a little house out at Willow Gap, and started making babies."

"Six weeks. Wow, that was fast."

"He always said, 'When you meet her, you'll know. No use fighting it.' "

"That's a great love story."

He snorts. "Except for the part where a drunk driver runs a red light and T-bones the SUV his family is in, and those babies have to watch as their mother bleeds out at the bottom of the gap, unable to get free of the backseat and help her."

Dear Lord, I've never heard that part of their story before. *He had to actually watch his parents die?*

He gets a faraway look, and I know he is reliving the nightmare in his mind.

"Dad reached and took this hat from his head. He put it on mine right before he stopped breathing. So, no. No one in this town gives me shit about being a Red Sox fan."

A tear escapes as I bring my hand to my chest to touch the small rose-gold dandelion pendant my daddy gave me for my twelfth birthday. The necklace that I've held so dear to my heart because it contains a part of him. The pendant that lit a fire inside of me and inspired me to handcraft jewelry with heart. The one I never take off.

"I'm glad you have something of his. Something to make you feel close to him."

He shakes his head, uncomfortable with the sympathy from me. Then, he grabs a bucket and disappears into one of the stalls, ending the conversation.

I grab my own bucket and brush, and then I walk in to start brushing Huck down as I wonder to myself if Elle has anything special to remind her of her mom and dad.

Then, I decide that I will make her something.

Twenty

SOPHIE

I WALK INTO THE KITCHEN AFTER BRUSHING DOWN HUCK TO FIND Aunt Doreen and Aunt Ria rummaging through a huge stack of papers and receipts on the table.

"Here, you sort these into alphabetical order, and then we'll start by date, I guess," Aunt Doreen says as she pushes a pile in Aunt Ria's direction.

"Alphabetical order, you say?" Aunt Ria mumbles as she assesses the mess.

"What are you guys doing?" I ask as I pour myself a glass of lemonade and sit down.

"The books," Aunt Doreen answers.

I take in the table and the green ledger portfolio sitting in front of her. "You're joking, right?"

"I wish I were. Gram always handled all of this, and … well, the end of the year will be here soon, and we have to get our ducks in a row for the accountant."

"You mean to tell me, Gram was still keeping the ranch's records on a paper ledger?" I squeak in disbelief.

"Yes. She would keep it all recorded. She kept all the receipts and paperwork so nice and neat, and she wrote all the checks and kept the accounts balanced. Paid payroll to the employees and—oh my, we don't know what we're doing." Aunt Doreen places her head in her hands.

"Don't you guys have a computer?" I ask.

"Yes. There's one in Madeline's office. She uses it to run the stable's website for her camps for the children with disabilities."

"You guys need to get a QuickBooks account for the ranch and start moving all this over."

"What's a QuickBooks?"

"It's an online accounting and record-keeping program that you can use for the business. It will keep track of your accounts payable and accounts receivable and even do payroll for you. It's pretty user-friendly. A lot better than keeping all this straight."

"I don't really know my way around a computer." Aunt Doreen sighs.

"Surely, someone here does. Madeline? Elle?"

"Yes, Elle does, but she's not very interested in the ranch. She has big plans for being a news reporter or something."

"This week anyway," Ria adds.

"Think you could teach us?" Aunt Doreen turns her hopeful eyes to me.

"I guess it couldn't hurt to try. I'll grab my laptop."

"Oh, thank you, sweetheart." She exhales in relief.

We spend the rest of the evening with me giving a crash course tutorial for a basic QuickBooks home office program. None of which seems to sink in too well.

At some point, the men show up, looking for dinner, and Aunt Ria throws together some sloppy joes and serves it with potato salad she made earlier in the afternoon. We all eat and then get back to it.

"What's all this?" Daddy asks as he surveys us crowded around my laptop with both of his sisters frantically taking notes.

"Sophie is trying to teach us how to use the computer to keep better records of the ranch's business affairs," Aunt Doreen answers him as she narrows her eyes at the screen, trying to read the numbers in the columns. "I don't know how you can see that screen, Sophie. All I see is glare at this point. It's giving me the worst headache." She removes her reading glasses and pinches the bridge of her nose.

"Is that thing safe?" He looks at the computer like it might bite him.

"It has a firewall."

"A fire what?"

"A firewall. It's a security program that keeps your computer safe from malware and viruses."

"How does a machine catch a virus?"

All their eyes focus on me.

"Not an actual virus. You know what? That's enough for tonight. I don't want to overload you. We'll do some more tomorrow."

"Oh, thank goodness." Aunt Ria stands from the table and walks over to the freezer. "Anyone else need a drink?" She raises the mason jar in the air.

"I'll have a nip," Aunt Doreen accepts.

I stand and start to close my laptop.

"I appreciate your efforts, but I'm not sure we're going to be able to operate that thing," Daddy says as he sits opposite me.

"Somebody has to learn. You can't keep doing business this way. I can't believe Gram was still doing everything by hand. That's insane."

"Accountant's been complaining for years, but she'd put him in his place, and as long as all the numbers added up, I reckon he let her slide."

I shake my head. "How do you all measure profit and loss or forecast for the next season?"

"If there's money left in the accounts after we take the cattle to auction at the end of the year, it's profit. If there's not, it's loss."

"What?"

"Where'd I lose you?"

"You can't measure profit that way. You have to keep a record of material costs, man-hours, service fees like vet bills and heating and air contractors. How do you pay the ranch hands?"

"With cash."

"Cash? Are you serious? Are they considered self-employed

contract employees, or do you pay their social security and income taxes?"

"They are just guys who work, and I pay them with cash."

"You can't do that. What if one of them is hurt out there? Does workers' comp cover them? If you don't have a contract and they are working under the table, they could sue Rustic Peak."

"Those boys have been working for me for years. They aren't going to sue me."

"Really? You don't know that. If one of them ended up under the tractor and lost their leg and couldn't work again, what choice would they have? Or better yet, what if it killed them? Do you know every one of their next of kin well enough to know they wouldn't sue the ranch?"

"No," he reluctantly admits.

"Honestly, if the IRS found out the way you had been running this place, you would be in a heap of trouble. One thing you never want to do is piss off the IRS."

"Sophie, we're a small family business, and we've done just fine."

"You're an eight-thousand-acre cattle ranch. That's not small, and you, as a businessman, should want to protect that."

"I'm not a businessman. I'm a rancher."

"You need to be both."

He raises his weary eyes to mine. He's only fifty-five years old, but the lines around his eyes and the gray in his mustache make him seem older.

"We weren't prepared to lose Gram. She was healthy as a horse one minute, and the next, she was sick. It all happened so quickly. Too quick for her to teach us the ins and outs. But we'll figure it out. We have to. Too many people's families depend on us."

I sigh and calm down. "I'll help while I'm here. Maybe if I can get everything set up and all this"—I gesture to the mess covering the table—"sorted, then it will be easier to start from there and move forward. Although I'm not sure Aunt Doreen and Ria are the best choices to be taking over the operation. Madeline, Elle, or even Braxton would be easier to train."

"Braxton would love that." He snorts.

"I bet."

"Let me talk to Madeline tonight. I'm sure she'd be willing to learn, and I can try my hand at it, I guess."

"This is going to be a good thing. Once you get everything set up and see how much more efficient and how much more legal it is, you'll be glad you did."

"I trust you." He stands. "Thank you, Sophie."

"Don't thank me yet."

He smiles at me, and then he walks out the back door.

I take in the table. *Crap.* It's going to take more than a few weeks to straighten this out.

Twenty-One

SOPHIE

WE SPEND THE NEXT TWO DAYS SORTING RECEIPTS, scheduling a bank visit, and sitting down with the accountant, who is thrilled that we're moving to a system that will work with his program so that information can be easily imported to his office. Apparently, the ranch was paying for one of his employees to work overtime every quarter and manually enter everything that Gram had brought into his office. Who knows how much that cost the ranch over the years?

Dallas and I make a quick trip to Denver so that I can purchase a new desktop and printer and scanner. Daddy and Emmett clean out the storage room off of the kitchen, so we can convert it into an office. We're adding an old desk that Dallas's mom had stored at the bakery and the filing cabinet from Gram and Pop's room.

I print contract employee forms and have everyone working under the table fill out the proper paperwork. Then, Madeline and I start the slow process of inputting all the information into the computer. We split up the tasks; she enters all the utilities and office supply expenses as I sort all the labor and material goods expenses.

At one point, I have to call a very put-out Braxton in to explain some of the invoices to me.

"So, what's this one?"

He takes the paper from my hand and looks at the chicken scratch written across the carbon copy invoice from the local hardware store.

"Parts for the bush hog," he states as he throws the paper back down on the desk.

"What's a bush hog?"

"It's a type of mower."

"Why didn't you just say mower?"

"It's a big mower, and it has an attachment that's on hinges, so it can mow a field and go over rocks and stumps and things like that."

"Okay, so this files under equipment maintenance. What about this one?" I slide another paper in front of him.

"It's a receipt for fuel."

"I can see that, but fuel for what?"

"Tractors, mowers, generators, haulers—everything that runs on fuel."

I look up at him. He's sitting with his arms crossed over his chest, and he is annoyed.

I drop the pen in my hand and scoot back from the desk. "Look, I'm trying to help here. The least you could do is be nice."

"I don't have time to sit here all day and spoon-feed you this shit. I have a vet tech coming in a few hours to vaccinate, so we can start castrating calves. I need to get them corralled, and we have a fence down in the back pasture that we need to patch before nightfall."

"Fine. Go. I'll try to figure it out myself."

"You do that." He stands and heads for the door.

"You don't have to be such a jackass."

He stops, puts his hands in the doorframe, and looks back at me. "You can take your ass back to the city anytime you want. We've survived just fine around here without your help, and we'll be just fine once you're gone."

With that parting shot, he disappears out the door.

"Asshole," I murmur under my breath just as Aunt Doreen walks in.

"Where did Braxton run off to in such a huff?"

"Off to do something way more important than what I'm doing."

"Is he grumpy today? You have to overlook him when he gets like that."

"You mean, when he gets rude and condescending?"

She purses her lips. "I mean, when he gets distracted and over-whelmed. Running a ranch this size is not easy. It's pretty demanding, both mentally and physically. That boy takes a lot on his shoulders, and he takes considerable pride in the work and the quality of the cattle we produce. The Rustic Peak brand name means something to all of us, but it means a whole heck of a lot to Braxton."

"I get it, but he needs to understand that this—the balancing ac-counts and filing insurance and keeping good records—is a part of that brand too. If you can't pay the bills, that will do more to harm the ranch's good name than anything else will."

"Yes. Well, he is more of a hands-on type of man. We'll figure this office stuff out."

"You might need to hire someone once I leave. A part-time clerk or something."

She considers it for a second. "I can ask around the church and see if anyone is interested. For now, we will count our blessings that you are here. Now, are you at a stopping point?"

"I guess so. Until Emmett or Daddy can come in and help me sort some of these out anyway."

"Good. These boys are going to be starving after a day of castrat-ing. Let's prepare a good meal for them to come home to."

"All right. I'm going to check my e-mails quickly, and I'll be in to help in a few minutes."

"By the way, a package arrived for you this morning. Ria brought it in from the front porch when we got home from the market. I think she took it up to your room."

"Thank you."

After answering a few e-mails from Charlotte and scanning the designs I sketched for the women's watch for Maple and Park, I check the sales in our online store and schedule a conference call with Charlotte and Gail for tomorrow morning.

I place a quick call to Stanhope. I give him an update on our first-quarter sales and the new contract with the boutiques, and I forward it to him, so he can look over the fine print before I sign anything.

"We miss you, Sophia."

"I miss you guys too. I'll be home soon though."

"Not soon enough. Your mother is beside herself. She doesn't know what to do without her best girl."

"I know."

"Are you finding resolution there?"

"I don't know. Honestly, I think I'm more confused now than I was when I arrived. I was so full of anger, and now, I don't know how I feel."

"Just know that your mother and I love you very much, and no matter what, we have your back."

"Thank you, Stanhope. I love you both very much as well."

I end the call and head up to open the package Charlotte sent at my request.

I shut myself in my room and open the box.

Surrounded by bubble wrap is a small jewelry box from our shop. I open it, and nestled inside is the necklace I designed and sent to Justin with exact instructions.

I gently remove the delicate white-gold chain holding an elegant water lily pendant with a mother of pearl center. I wanted something to represent a mother's love, and when Braxton told me his mother's name was Lily, I knew exactly what I wanted to make.

The actual necklace turned out more beautiful than the sketch. I carefully place it back into the box.

I want to find the right time to give it to Elle without making too big a deal of it.

I hide it in the drawer of the nightstand, and I join my aunts to help them finish dinner.

Twenty-Two

BRAXTON

WE LOAD THE CALF INTO THE RESTRAINT STALL, AND Walker and I apply the elastrator band.

"Release," Jefferson shouts the command.

Emmett opens the door, and the calf staggers out of the stall.

"That's the last one for today, fellas. Anyone ready for lunch?" Emmett asks.

"Can't. Got to get out to the back pasture and get the breach in the fence patched before dark," I tell him as I snap off my gloves.

He removes his hat and scratches his head before looking up into the sky. "Looks like a storm might be blowing in. Think we have time to get it up before it hits?"

The wind started to kick up about half an hour ago. I glance off into the horizon and see the telltale signs of dark clouds over the mountains.

This is what I was afraid of—a storm catching us before we could finish. I shouldn't have been such an ass to Sophie this morning, but I didn't have the time to dick around, answering her questions, with the forecast calling for thunderstorms this evening.

"Hopefully. It looks like it's moving fast. I dropped a trailer with the lumber off at the site this morning," I reply.

"We'd best get going then. I'll let Doreen know we're headed straight out and get her to pack some sandwiches and water. I'll meet you guys there," Emmett says as he walks off in the direction of the house.

Jefferson, Walker, and I quickly put away all the banding supplies and load the back of the truck with a post-hole digger, a couple of bags of cement, and a mixer.

"You guys go on, and I'll fill the water tank and wait for Emmett. We'll be right behind you."

"You okay to load that tank, old man?" I rib Jefferson as I hop into the driver's seat.

"I can still work circles around you, son," he shouts back.

It's true. He might be getting up there in age, but the man is still solid and powerful.

Thirty minutes later, we are scarfing down ham and cheese sandwiches with one hand and unloading the trucks with the other. It's already been a long day, and we have hours of work ahead of us.

"Guess who's back in town?" Walker asks as he hands the digger off to me.

I raise an eyebrow in question.

"Morgan. I ran into her at the grocery store last night."

"I know. She's texted and called me a few times."

"Seems she's back for good. She said her dad's health is getting worse, and she moved back to be close to her mom and help out."

"I don't know about that. I heard from Jerry that the company she works for filed for bankruptcy last month. The deal they had to buy the old Stockman ranch fell through because of it. Apparently, the CEO was caught embezzling or some shit. My bet is, that has way more to do with her moving back to Poplar Falls than her dad's health does."

"I thought it sounded sketchy. Her dad has been on that oxygen tank for years. I saw him tying one on at Butch's last week, and he seemed just fine." He grabs a split rail log off the end of the tractor and wrenches it in the hole I just finished digging. "If she stays, you plan on starting that back up?"

"Nope," I answer instantly.

Morgan Cullman was my high school girlfriend. We dated for three years, and then she went off to college while I stayed and worked on the ranch. When she returned four years later with her degree in agricultural engineering, we resumed our relationship and were engaged within a year.

That was before she decided to take a job with a company that buys up local ranches and brands them under one corporate umbrella, and she made it her mission in life to convince struggling ranchers to sell for far less than their ranches were worth.

She tried to sell it to me as her doing them a huge favor and helping the local economy grow and expand, but all it did was cheat families out of the land they had owned for generations and line the pockets of a greedy company with no ties to Poplar Falls.

Once they set their sights on Rustic Peak and she started trying to feed their corporate bullshit to Jefferson and tried to manipulate me, I was done. The breakup was painful. I did love her, but ambition had changed her, and our dreams and ideals no longer lined up with one another.

After I broke off the engagement, which she didn't take well, she took off to work at the company's headquarters in Fort Worth, Texas. That was six years ago. The last thing I want is to get involved with her again.

Six weeks. Six weeks was all it took for Dad to know Mom was the one and get her to the altar. I figure, if Morgan and I couldn't get our act together after more than four years, she simply is not the one.

We work as fast as we can, but the downpour starts about an hour into our work. We jump into the trucks to take cover and let the worst of it pass. Then, we slip and slide through the mud and get a temporary patch in place until the land dries up in a couple of days, so we can come back and reinforce the fence.

Jefferson and Emmett head back to the house, and I drop Walker at home before I head back to wash up and eat.

"You sure you don't want to go back to the house for supper? Ria made a pot roast," I ask as I pull up to his door.

"Nah, man, I'm fucking beat. I'm just going to hose off this mud and pop a frozen pizza in the oven."

My back is aching from being bent over the fence for five straight hours and carrying split logs from the trailer to the line. I'm sweat-soaked and covered in dried mud, and my energy is zapped from barely eating lunch. Climbing the steps that lead to my room will take all I have left in me, so I grab my bag with a spare pair of jeans and thermal and opt for a quick hose off at the shower beside the last stall in the barn instead.

I start the spray and let it warm as I strip out of my boots and caked coveralls. Then, I step in and let the water wash the shitty day from my shoulders.

Twenty-Three

SOPHIE

"SOPHIE, CAN YOU GO CHECK AND SEE IF BRAX'S TRUCK IS IN the driveway? I don't want to take the roast out of the oven before he gets here," Aunt Ria calls into the office as I close everything down for the evening.

Dallas stopped in to help, and Aunt Doreen and Ria entertained Beau while we worked. A lot was accomplished. It turns out, Dallas is pretty efficient at deciphering chicken scratch and explaining what a lot of the invoices are for.

I walk over to the kitchen window that looks out toward the barn. "It's out there," I confirm.

"Can you go see what he's doing? I called up to his apartment, and he's not answering. If he's still piddling with unloading, tell him to get his hiney in here and eat, and he can finish that up later. Everyone is starving."

"Yes, ma'am."

Great. Just what I want to be doing, traipsing through the mud to find the asshole who's keeping dinner waiting.

He's not the only one who's had a long day. My stomach lets out an irritated growl.

The tractor is in the drive beside the truck, so he hasn't taken off on it. I walk toward the barn to have a look around.

I don't see him, but I can hear the sound of water running, so I walk to the back, and there he is—naked. The last stall was converted into a shower, and I've seen some of the workers use it to hose the mud and manure off before getting into their trucks to head home or entering the main house, but he's full-on showering out in the open.

I should turn around and go back, but I stand there and take in his broad back and sculpted ass. They don't build them like that in New York. Those muscled thighs and that rugged physique was not manufactured in a Gold's Gym on lunch hour. No, that body was built through hard work and good genes.

Very, very good genes.

I watch as he stands there with his hands planted on the wall of the stall above his bent head, so the water laps over him for a few more seconds, and then I start to slowly back out of the barn as quietly as I can manage.

Before I reach the doors, he calls out, "Tell 'em I'll be in shortly."

I freeze.

"I could smell you when you walked in, Sophie."

"Smell me?"

"Yeah, you always smell like jasmine."

Oh God, I can't believe I was caught watching him shower.

"I'm sorry. I didn't mean to invade your privacy. I just—"

"It's okay." He looks back at me over his shoulder. "I would've peeked, too, if I had found you showering out here."

His heated stare bores into me. I clear my throat.

"I'll let them know you're coming."

He raises his eyebrow, and I'm sure I'm blushing from head to toe.

"I mean ... you know what I mean," I stammer as I turn and flee to the house.

"Did you find him?" Aunt Ria asks as I enter the kitchen.

"Yep. He's in the barn."

"What's he into out there?" she asks as she starts to set the table.

I must look guilty because Dallas suspiciously looks at me and adds, "Yeah, what's he up to?"

I shrug. "I have no idea. I just yelled to him that supper was ready, and he said he'd be in here, in a minute."

"That boy. I swear, he'd work himself into the ground if we let him," Emmett says, shaking his head as he sits down at the table and starts loading up a plate.

"You talking about me again, old man?" Braxton booms as he walks through the back door.

His hair is wet and brushed back from his face like he ran his hands through it quickly. He's wearing a pair of faded jeans and a tight-fitting cream-colored thermal shirt. I realize he looks almost as good dressed as he does undressed.

I avoid his eyes as I walk to the sink to wash my hands before I sit.

He slides in beside me and speaks in a low tone, "I owe you an apology."

I turn on the water. "No, you don't. I'm the one who invaded your privacy and gawked at you while you were trying to shower. It's been a while since I've seen a naked man, especially a soaped-up, wet, naked man. I probably need to remedy that soon. Charlotte tells me that all the time. Anyway, I'm sorry. Hormones took over, I guess," I word-vomit all over him.

"Um, yeah, I was talking about this morning."

"Oh …" What I just spewed hits me. "Oh God." I turn to face him and grimace. "Can you forget everything I just said?"

He leans a hip against the sink and moves in a little closer. "That's going to be hard to do. Don't you think?"

I look up, and he's grinning at me.

"Now is not the time to tease me, Braxton."

"Who exactly is teasing who?" he asks.

It's a fair question.

"Hey, what are you two whispering about over there?" Dallas yells from behind us.

"Sophie here was just graciously accepting my apology for being short with her this morning," Braxton answers without looking away from me.

"Oh, that's wonderful. It's so nice to see you kids getting along. Now, both of you come and sit and eat. Supper is getting cold."

We do as Aunt Doreen requested and take our seats at the table with the others. Dallas eyeballs us curiously as she cuts up the roast beef on Beau's plate.

"Mind your own business and pass the potatoes, Dallas," Emmett says as he looks between the two of us with a mischievous grin.

I give him an appreciative smile in return.

After we've eaten dinner, I walk Dallas and Beau out to her truck. "Thank you for all the help today."

"You're welcome. Are you planning on working all day tomorrow?"

"No. I'm waiting on some information from the bank, and the rep that handles the ranch's account is out until Monday. I plan to get up and work on some designs for a few hours and then get Aunt Doe to take me into town. I want to get a manicure, and I'd love to find some-one to trim my hair."

"I'm off work tomorrow. Want me to pick you up? I was going to go see Janelle down at the salon next week anyway. I'll see if she can fit us both in."

"That would be great."

She shuts the door after buckling Beau in. "Maybe you'll tell me what's going on between you and Brax then too," she slips in as she rounds the front of the truck.

"Nothing is going on between Braxton and me. Trust me."

"Whatever. You have the worst poker face ever."

"I'm not lying."

"So then, what was with all the blushing and whispering in there?"

"He was just apologizing for being such a jerk this morning when I asked for his help. That's all."

"Really?"

"Yes, really."

"Hmm ... well, that's boring."

"What did you think was going on?"

"I don't know. Something juicier than that though. I'll see you tomorrow." With that, she hops in the truck and takes off.

I release a relieved breath and head back into the house. It's been a strange day, and I'm ready to call it a night. I look at my watch and see its eight thirty p.m. *Great.* I've acclimated to Poplar Falls' crazy schedule.

As I make it to the door, Braxton is coming out. He slides sideways to allow me to pass.

"Good night, Princess." He uses his annoying nickname for me, and for the first time, it doesn't feel like he's using it to insult me.

"Night," I return as I make a beeline for the stairs.

Yep, a strange day indeed.

Twenty-Four

SOPHIE

"I WANT A CHANGE. I WAS THINKING MAYBE AN OMBRE FROM dark to medium to platinum. What do you think?" I look up to see Janelle staring at me in the mirror with her fingers in my long blonde hair.

"An ombre, you say?"

"Yes. Why? You do know how to do an ombre, right?"

I should have asked before I came in. My hair is in desperate need of a trim, and Dallas brought me here with the promise that Janelle was a master of all things hair.

"Sure. I've seen it done before at a hair show one year. I've never had a client ask for it before though." She shrugs.

"Do you think you could pull it off?"

"Honey, I can pull off anything, but, um … are you sure you want to do that craziness to this beautiful mane you have?"

"You don't like it?"

"I think it's a little silly to tri-color your hair. Plus, you'd be stripping all the color out, and that is just damaging it for no good reason. Your natural hair color is gorgeous. Do you know how many women come in here, asking for this exact shade of blonde? If you want my opinion, I would just add a few highlights around your face to accent that. But, hey, it's your head, and you'll be the one who has to live with it. There are always hats."

I frown at her in the mirror. I'm not entirely sure if she's trying to talk me out of it because she has no confidence in her ability to pull it off or because she honestly thinks I'll look ridiculous.

I turn to Dallas, who is flipping through a magazine. "What do you think, Dal? Should I do the ombre or highlights?"

"Do the ombre if you want to look like a freaking unicorn walking down Main Street," she says without looking up from her page.

Great. The last thing I need is to stick out any more around here. I'll just have to shelve that idea until I return home to New York.

"Fine, Janelle. Please give me highlights and a trim."

"You got it, darlin'." She gets the color mixed and the foil ready, and then she begins the interrogation. "So, I hear you're helping your daddy get everything up-to-date out at the ranch."

Word sure travels fast in this town.

"Yes, trying to anyway."

"I'm sure his stubborn ass is having to be pulled, kicking and screaming, into the twentieth century."

"Twenty-first."

"Pardon?"

"It's the twenty-first century."

"Already?"

"Yes, Janelle, for about nineteen years now," Dallas chimes in.

"Wow, time flies," she muses.

Dallas rolls her eyes at me in the mirror, and I giggle.

"Honey, I'm real sorry about your grandma. She's sure going to be missed around here." She shakes out a cape that has seen better days and ties it around my neck.

"Thank you," I reply.

"I bet it's surreal, being back at the ranch. Everyone treating you nice?"

"Sure thing."

"How's that Braxton Young doing?"

"Still young enough to be your son," Dallas answers for me.

"But he's not," she whispers in my right ear.

120

"He's fine, I guess. Not much of a talker. Kind of ornery. I swear, he's a bigger pain in the ass when it comes to change than Daddy is."

"He might be an ass, but what a fine ass it is. Too fine to be out there on that ranch, all alone. People are starting to talk, if you know what I mean," she says as she starts dividing my hair into sections, adding color and wrapping it in foil.

"No, we don't know what you mean. Do tell." That finally gets Dallas's attention enough to put the magazine down and join the conversation for real.

"Oh, you know, every girl in this county has been trying to catch his eye for years, and he blows everyone off. Folks are starting to wonder if he bats for the other team."

"Are you implying you think Braxton is gay?" I ask.

"Well, the possibility has been considered," she admits.

"That's insane. He is not gay," I state matter-of-factly.

"And how do you know that for sure?" Janelle asks without looking up.

I can tell there is more to her question than the one she asked.

I shrug. "I just do. I mean, there is nothing wrong with being gay. I went out on a great date with a gay man before I left New York."

"Wait. What?" Dallas interrupts.

"It's a long story. I'll tell you later." I look back up at Janelle. "Braxton is not gay though."

"You said that. Now, how do you know that he's not?"

Because of the way he looks at me and the way he's touched me. Because a woman knows when a man is attracted to her; that's how, I think but do not say.

"Just call it intuition."

"Uh-huh. You heard her, Janelle. Intuition," Dallas repeats as she digs her elbow into Janelle's side, making her drop the color brush.

I give her a *shut the fuck up* look in the mirror, and she sticks her tongue out at me.

She and Janelle give each other a wicked smile that I do not miss.

Great, just what I need. Janelle's Big Hair Beauty Salon is the town gossip center. It's practically TMZ for Poplar Falls. The last thing I want is to be the topic of any conversations that take place within these walls.

We arrive back at the ranch to find Madeline in the porch swing, reading.

"Hi, girls. Don't you both look lovely?"

"Janelle gave us both a tune-up this morning," Dallas tells her as I take a seat on the steps.

"What are the two of you getting into this afternoon?"

"I have to pick Beau up from school in an hour, but we're going out to blow off some steam later," Dallas answers then turns to me, "by the way, you're driving tonight, Soph. I call dibs on drinking too much and showing your ass."

I laugh. "I can't be your DD, Dallas. I don't have a driver's license."

Her mouth drops open, and her eyes go wide. "What do you mean, you don't have a driver's license?"

I shrug. "I've never needed one."

"You're joking. How do you get around?"

"In the city, you take the subway or a taxi. Most apartments don't come with anywhere to park a car, and nobody wants to drive in Manhattan traffic anyway. We leave it to the insane cab drivers."

"You mean, you pay someone to take you everywhere? Work? The grocery store? Everywhere?"

"Sure. Or we walk. Depends on the distance and the weather."

"That's the craziest shit I've ever heard. Don't you think, Mrs. L.?"

"It's different that's for sure. Braxton and Elle couldn't wait to get their license. They were at the DMV the second the doors opened the day they turned sixteen," Madeline agrees.

"Really? I guess we don't pay it any attention. It's just the way it is."

"It's like you come from Mars or something."

"I've felt that way a time or two myself the last couple of weeks."

Twenty-Five

BRAXTON

"B̲RAX?"

"Over here, Elle."

I'm under the pickup, tightening the oil filter I just installed, when her face peers under the front of the truck.

"Hey."

"Hey yourself."

"Are you going to the pool hall tonight?"

Saturdays usually consist of Elle trying to convince me to go out with her, starting around noon and not letting up until I agree.

"I guess."

Might as well make it easy on both of us.

"Yay! Sonia can't come until later because she is babysitting Beau until Mrs. Henderson is home from her quilting class. Can I ride out with you?"

"Of course you can. We'll head out after supper."

"Awesome. I'm going to go and start preparing what I'm going to wear."

She stands and starts to walk off. Then, I watch as her feet turn, and she quickly paces back.

She looks back under the truck. "Thank you, Brax."

"You're welcome, sis."

Then, she runs off again.

Women. It's just clothes. Pants. Shirt. Shoes. That's all they need.

How it can take them six hours to decide which pants, shirt, and shoes is beyond me.

I finish up with the oil change and wash the truck. Then, I take Hawkeye out for a little exercise. I have only had the pup for six weeks, and he has tripled his weight. I think Doreen sneaks out and feeds him a couple of times a day even though I told her I feed him on a schedule. The vet is going to have a fit the next time he sees him.

When we return from our walk, I notice a horse trotting up the drive and a blonde ponytail swinging in the breeze. Madeline is standing on the front steps, watching the two of them.

We walk over, and Hawk drops onto the first step and falls fast asleep.

"Is that Sophie on Huck?"

"It sure is. I helped her saddle him a few minutes ago."

"And Huck didn't resist?"

"Not a bit."

"That damn horse never lets anyone ride him."

"I think he's become quite enamored with her."

I watch as she gets to the gate and turns the horse. Then, she brings him to a controlled canter.

"She's good with him," Madeline observes.

One more pass of the drive, and Sophie leads the animal toward the pasture and takes off in a gallop.

My heart skips a beat, and I start toward the field.

Madeline reaches out and halts me. "She's good. Let them run."

"I never run Huck like that. I don't know how he'll do."

It makes me nervous to watch as she picks up pace.

"She's a skilled rider. She can handle him. If she didn't think he was steady, she wouldn't have taken off."

The screen door opens, and Walker comes out with a beer.

"That Sophie on that horse?" he asks as he takes a seat on the step and starts to pet Hawkeye.

"Yep."

"Look at her go. City girl is just full of surprises, isn't she?"

I look back at her, laughing as she brings Huck back to a canter and heads toward the barn.

"Yep, all kinds of surprises."

After supper, Elle and I head out, as promised.

Dallas picked Sophie up earlier, and the two of them were eating at her house with her dad and Beau before coming to Fast Breaks.

"How do I look?" Elle asks as we pull out of the drive.

"Pretty, as always."

She beams at me. "Jeremy is going to be there tonight, so I have to look extra."

"Extra?"

"Yes. That's what Sophie called it. She helped me get ready tonight. She did my makeup." She turns and starts batting her eyelashes at me as if that helps me see her makeup better.

"Looks nice."

"And look, Brax!" She pulls a chain out from her blouse and shows me the necklace around her neck.

"That's nice as well."

"Isn't it? Sophie made it for me."

"She did?" I take a closer look at the delicate chain around her neck with the little silver flower.

"Yep. It's a lily, and the center is made of mother of pearl. She made it for me, so I could have something that reminded me of Momma." She sniffs as she reverently tucks the chain back close to her heart. "Wasn't that sweet of her?"

It was. Elle hates that she can't remember our mom. Not her face or her voice. She was so young when they died. I can remember everything about her in precise detail, but Elle just knows what Madeline or I tell her or what she sees in pictures.

"Very thoughtful," I agree as we pull into the parking lot, which is already filling up.

I pull into my usual spot and groan as I see the familiar Jeep parked in the spot beside it.

"Is that Morgan's car?" Elle asks.

"Looks like it."

I should have known she'd show up here when I didn't respond to any of her messages.

Elle's eyes go round, and she opens her door. "Don't look now, but she's headed this way. Good luck."

The little brat hops out of the truck and hurries inside, throwing her hand up in greeting as she goes.

I put the truck in park and roll the window down just as she makes it to my side.

"Brax."

"Hey, Morgan."

"You got a minute to talk?"

"About what?"

"About me moving back."

"What happened to Texas?"

"Oh, salary disputes, failed contract negotiations, and me just finally getting fed up and homesick enough to tell them to kiss my ass. Mom could use my help around here anyway."

"That's too bad."

I start to roll up the window, and she sticks her hand in and halts me.

"Come on, Braxton. We haven't seen each other in a couple of years. I just got home, and you aren't replying to any of my messages."

127

"I've been busy, Morgan, and you know I'm not much of a phone person."

She leans closer into the window. "I know. I just … I miss you."

She sticks her lip out in a fake pout, and it does nothing for me but make me want to laugh at her antics.

"I thought we were past this, Morgan."

"I don't think I'll ever be past it."

"You should be."

She lets out a frustrated huff. "You're never going to forgive me, are you?"

"There's nothing to forgive. We just had different dreams; that's all."

"What if my dreams have changed?"

"Then, I wish you luck at following your new ones, but I'm not a man who lives in the past."

She starts to tear up, and I consider putting my foot on the gas and plowing through the front of the bar.

"Are we at least still friends?" she finally asks.

"Friends I can do."

Her face falls, but she straightens up and takes a step back. "Well, come on then. Take me inside and buy your friend a shot."

I can already tell this is going to be a long night.

Twenty-Six

SOPHIE

W E PULL UP TO THE SITE OF THE OLD DYE HOUSE MILL A few miles outside of town. It still looks the same with its brick exterior, rusty tin roof, and huge, blacked-out, floor-to-ceiling windows.

I peer up at it through the windshield. "This is it? I thought this place closed down back when we were girls?"

"It did. Sat here empty for years and years until the town council finally decided to let Butch and his brother, Doug, buy it and turn it into a bar."

"Butch? As in Butch's Tavern?"

"Yep. He wanted to expand his redneck entertainment empire."

"Looks sketchy."

"It's not. They kept everything original on the outside, but the inside is cool as shit. Come on in and see."

We hop out and cross the parking lot where a large man in a black long-sleeved shirt that says *Security* across the chest is sitting in front of the enormous wooden beam doors.

"Hey, Fred."

"Hey, Dallas. Who's your friend?"

"This is Sophie. She's Jefferson Lancaster's daughter. She came in for Gram's funeral."

"Nice to meet you, Sophie. We sure were sad to hear about Gram. She was a great lady."

"Thank you."

"You two have fun and stay out of trouble." He winks as he opens the door for us to walk inside.

Dallas is right. It is cool as shit. The inside was gutted, and a sizeable raw wood bar was added to the far wall. The walls are exposed brick, and the high ceilings are accented with brushed silver, old ductwork, and iron pipes. High pub tables made of the same raw wood as the bar top are peppered in front, and off to the right are six large pool tables. The lights are low-hanging cascade chandeliers with antique amber bulbs that give off a subtle glow, granting the room lots of private, dark nooks and corners.

Music is coming from an ancient jukebox to the left of the bar, but it's not too loud that you can't carry on a conversation.

"Wow."

"Right! Pretty progressive for a beer joint in the woods of Poplar Falls, Colorado."

"I'm impressed."

"Wait till you order a drink."

We sidle up to the bar, and Dallas lets out a whistle to get the bartender's attention.

"I'll have a shot of tequila and a glass of whatever beer you have on tap," she shouts and then expectantly looks at me.

"Do they have a cocktail menu?"

She gives me a look that screams, *Are you kidding me?*

"Fine, I'll have a glass of whatever red wine they serve."

She shakes her head at me and shouts again, "Make that two shots of tequila and an iced tea."

I guess they don't serve wine here.

Dallas turns around and props both her elbows back on the bar as she surveys the room while we wait for our drinks.

"Uh-oh."

"What?"

I spin around to follow her gaze and see Elle and Braxton at one of the pool tables with a group of six. I recognize Myer and Walker but none of the others.

"Morgan's here."

"Who's Morgan?"

"Braxton's ex-fiancée."

I gasp. "He was engaged?"

"Sure was. But they broke up, and she moved to Texas. I heard she was back in town though. Looks like she came sniffing around, looking for him, right away."

There are two women standing at the table with them, one with a pool stick in her hand.

"Which one is she? The one playing or the one watching?"

"She's the one playing with the tight dress on. Who wears a damn dress to shoot pool?"

I assess the woman. She has long, dark hair that she has pinned back on one side. She is tall and slender, and she looks good in the cream-colored wrap dress and cowgirl boots.

I instantly hate her, and I have no idea why.

"I guess he has a type," I observe. Then, I turn back to the bar and wait for my shot.

"What do you mean?"

"I've seen a brunette sneaking out of his place early in the morning."

"Really? Was it her?"

"No, this girl was shorter, and her hair was a shade lighter."

"That dog. Keeping his hook-ups on the down-low."

The bartender places two salt-rimmed shots in front of us and two mason jars—one filled with draft beer and one with tea and lemon.

I pick up the shot glass and clink with hers before downing the shot. It burns all the way down, and I sputter and grab the jar with tea to wash it down. Which doesn't help. That burns too. I start coughing, and Dallas begins to beat me on the back.

"Are you all right? Did it have a bone in it?"

"Funny. What is that?" I rasp.

"It's iced tea vodka. What did you think it was?"

"I thought it was tea."

She wrinkles her nose. "Why would I order you tea at a bar?"

"Why would you order me a mason jar full of straight liquor?"

"Because it's a bar, duh. And you don't drink beer."

Jeez. I already know this night is going to take an interesting turn.

"Come on. Grab your glass. Let's go be nosy."

She picks up her beer and starts toward the pool tables. I follow a little less enthusiastically.

"Hey, guys," she bellows as we approach the crowd.

"Ladies." Walker scoots off a chair and makes room for us at the table covered with empty beer bottles and squares of cue chalk.

Elle comes over right away and hugs us both. "You guys finally made it." She drags a chair over from one of the other tables and sits with us.

Dallas gestures toward the pool table with her chin and asks, "Who's winning?"

"Braxton and Myer, of course—because they cheat!" Walker yells across the room.

"You're just mad because you shoot like a girl," Braxton retorts as he shoves the ball rack into Walker's gut.

"Hey," Dallas huffs, "that's offensive. Girls don't play as bad as Walker."

Myer spits beer across the floor, and Walker fakes an arrow to the heart.

"You wound me, Dal."

"Sorry, baby, but it's true. And we'll prove it. Sophie and I play the winners next."

I sputter, "Um, Dal, I'm not good at pool. You don't want me as a partner."

"You scared, Princess?"

I look up at Braxton, who is standing with his arms folded across his chest and a challenge in his eyes.

"I didn't say that."

"Then, rack 'em, and let's play."

"Fine." I grab my glass of horrible-tasting liquor, down it in one gulp, and stand. I'm swaying a little on the heel of my new boots.

"Whoa, you all right?" Walker asks as he catches my elbow.

"I'm good. Just stood up too fast."

I make my way over to the rack on the wall and grab a cue stick. Then, I nervously chalk the tip as Dallas starts to rack the balls.

"What's the wager?" Dallas asks the boys as she sets up the balls.

"No wager," I insist.

"There's always a wager," Walker leans in and says into my ear.

"What do you want it to be?" Braxton asks her.

"We win, and you have to teach Sophie here how to drive this weekend."

He raises an eyebrow and looks at me. "You can ride a horse that won't let anyone else ride it, but you can't drive a car?"

"I can drive. I think. I've never really tried before. I just don't drive."

He looks back at Dallas. "Done. What if we win?"

"What do you want?" she asks him with a seductive lilt to her voice that I don't like.

Wait, why do I care if she flirts with him? She always flirts with him.

He does a one-shoulder shrug. "Myer, you pick."

"If we win, you ladies cook us supper tomorrow night at Dallas's house."

"You're on."

She takes her cue and blasts into the triangle of balls, and they fly in all directions. She pockets three. Two solids and a stripe, and the game is on.

Walker buys everyone a shot and another round of drinks. This time, when I chase the shot with the iced tea, it's not so bad.

I'm a disaster of a partner. My third attempt to line up and shoot, I dig the cue tip right into the felt.

Ugh. I bang my head against the side of the table. *How did I let myself get roped into this?*

I'm still bent over the stick with my ass in the air when Braxton comes up beside me.

"Don't they have pool tables in New York?" he asks with a smirk.

I stand to answer him. "Of course they do. I just don't have the talent for this game."

He takes a sip from his beer bottle and sets it aside. "Yes, you do. Any girl who can ride a horse has the right hand and eye coordination to shoot pool."

He rolls his sleeves up to reveal his tanned forearms, and then he walks up behind me.

A shiver runs down my spine as he takes me by the waist, turns me back to the table, and continues, his warm breath at my neck, "You just have to stop focusing on where the ball is and keep your eye on where you want it to be." He wraps his arm around, and he slides his hands down the cue stick to mine. He takes my hands and adjusts my grip. "Hold it like this. All the weight on your back wrist, so the cue slides easy, and you have control. You ready?"

I nod, and he leans into me. We bend together over the edge of the table.

"Nice and steady. Strike firm. Too light, and you'll barely tap the other ball. Too hard, and you'll jump the table."

I pull back and strike the white ball, and it hits and sends the other into the side pocket.

"I did it!" I squeal as I turn in his arms.

We are so close that his breath licks across my lips. It smells like beer and cinnamon. One slight step, and our mouths would be touching.

"Very good, Princess. I bet there are a lot of things I could teach you."

In my inebriated state, I want to take him up on that, but better judgment grasps me before I say it out loud.

I quickly turn away from him, and five sets of eyes are all trained on us. Including Morgan's, and they are full of fire.

Wonderful.

Twenty-Seven

BRAXTON

"WE WON!" SOPHIE THROWS HER HANDS IN THE AIR and does a sexy little victory dance.

"Only because Dallas is a shark." Walker throws an arm around Sophie's neck, pulls her into his side, and musses her hair.

"Ew, get your sweaty pit away from my face." She makes a face and pushes him, and instead of him moving, she starts falling backward.

I start to reach out for her, but Dallas comes in behind her and catches her before she ends up on her ass.

Sophie starts laughing.

"I think maybe the iced tea vodka was a bad idea for you, lightweight," Dallas muses.

By my calculation, she has had four shots of tequila and three jars of whatever the hell she was drinking.

"Bathroom," she says to no one in particular and picks up her purse and heads toward the restrooms.

"Brax?" Morgan draws my attention from following Sophie's unsteady trek.

"Yeah?"

"Can you give me a ride home?"

"Your Jeep is outside."

"I've had too much to drink. Doug said I could leave it here tonight. One of the new guys working the bar offered to take me home, but I don't know him, and I don't think I want to get in a car alone with him."

I look back toward the hall Sophie disappeared down and then back at Dallas, who is shakily aiming a cue stick at the yellow solid instead of the cue ball.

"Dallas, who's driving you guys home?"

"Myer," she answers as she closes one eye and sticks her tongue out, trying to focus on her shot.

"I got them," Myer confirms.

I turn back to Morgan. "Sure, I can take you. Just let me know when you're ready."

"I'm going to pay my tab, and I'm ready if you are."

I look back at the hallway. "Okay. I'm going to the restroom. I'll meet you up front."

Just as I make it to the ladies' room and start to knock, it flies open, and Sophie stumbles out and right into my chest.

"Excuse me," she says as she rights herself.

Then, she looks up to see it's me.

"Oh, it's you." She moves to put her back against the wall of the hall.

I lean in, and I'm surrounded by the scent of jasmine. Her big blue eyes are glittering, and she is flushed from the alcohol.

"You okay?"

"I'm fabulous." She smiles huge, and my eyes are immediately drawn to her mouth.

A woman comes racing into the hallway with her hand over her mouth and two other women on her heels. I place my hands on either side of the wall above Sophie and move in close to shield her from being trampled.

I look down, and her eyes are squeezed shut. She opens one and looks up. I have her fenced in.

"Mrs. Janelle thinks you're gay," she blurts out.

I chuckle. "Does she now?"

"Well, she isn't sure, but she thinks it's a possibility. She just said no one ever sees you with a woman, so they wonder."

"They?"

"She wasn't very specific about who they are. Probably just a bunch of jealous girls you have shot down."

"What about you? Do you wonder?"

"Nope," she whispers as she barely shakes her head.

"Why not?"

"I just think you're busy and private. Plus, I'm pretty sure I saw a woman leaving your apartment at five a.m. last week."

"And what were you doing, watching my apartment at five a.m.?"

"I wasn't. I couldn't sleep. I was sitting on the porch swing, sketching and waiting for the sun to rise."

"Do you want proof?"

"Proof?"

I lean in closer and dip my head to hers. "Tell Mrs. Janelle that you are one hundred percent positive I'm not gay."

I press my lips to hers, intending to prove a point and back away, but she gasps in surprise, her lips parting, and I take the opportunity to deepen the kiss.

She grips the front of my henley and pulls me into her. Then, she stands up on her tiptoes to get closer. As our tongues wrestle, she releases her grip on my shirt and snakes her arms around my neck. She laces her fingers into my hair and tugs. A small moan escapes her, and it's not enough. I want more. I want her whimpering beneath me. I tug the hem of her tank loose from her jeans, and just as I'm about to skim my hand up her bare side, I hear a throat clear. I break away from her lips and look toward the hallway entrance.

"Sorry to interrupt, but I'm ready to go." Morgan's annoyed voice vibrates off the walls.

She is pissed.

"Be there in a minute."

"I want to leave now," she hisses.

I don't want her to cause a scene and embarrass Sophie.

"Okay. I'm coming."

I look back down at Sophie, who still has her arms around me as she stares at Morgan.

"You good?" I ask her.

She brings her stunned eyes to mine and nods. "I think so."

"Come on. I'm walking you back to Myer."

She disengages from me and starts down the hallway. Morgan gives her an angry scowl as we pass.

"Down, tiger. I'll be with you in a minute," I toss at Morgan as I follow Sophie back to the pool tables.

She makes it to Dallas and wraps her arms around her.

"You okay?"

"I'm drunk," she answers into her chest.

Dallas chuckles. "You think?"

I hand Myer the keys to my apartment. "Take them to the ranch and put them in my bed. I know she won't want to walk into the farmhouse in that condition."

He looks from me to Morgan and raises an eyebrow. "You got it."

"Thanks. Elle leave?"

"Yep. She and Sonia headed out a few minutes ago. She said to tell you good-bye."

I slap him on the back and head out to the truck with Morgan in tow.

I climb the steps to my apartment an hour and a half later.

Morgan lost her shit on me on the way to her house and refused to get out of the truck once we got to her place. She screamed and then tried tears and hurled every insult she could think of at Sophie.

Finally, after I refused her advances and threatened to wake her parents if she didn't get out of my truck, she gave up and went into her house.

I reach into the flowerpot off to the left of my door and grab the spare key. I enter as quietly as I can and flick on the small lamp on the table beside the door.

When my eyes adjust, I see Sophie fast asleep on my bed. It looks like she's wearing one of my old, worn-out John Deere T-shirts, and lying curled up in the crook of her side is Hawkeye with his feet in the air. No Dallas in sight.

Damn dog. He knows he's not allowed in my bed.

I walk on silent feet to the bathroom and brush my teeth. I change into a pair of lounge pants, and then I grab a blanket from the linen closet and head to the couch off to the left side of the bed.

"Hey," I hear her whisper into the dark.

"I didn't mean to wake you."

"It's okay. Myer and Dallas haven't been gone long."

"She could have stayed too."

"I know. She wanted to be home when Beau woke up, so she had Myer take her on home. You don't have to sleep on that sofa. We can share the bed."

I'm not so sure that's a good idea. I'm still wired, and I thought about that kiss the whole way home.

"Looks like you already have a bedmate."

She looks down at Hawkeye, who is still curled up to her, and she smiles and scratches his belly. "Little rascal snores too. But, seriously, you can sleep with us."

She scoots over to the far right to make room for me. I hesitate for a moment, and then I grab the remote off the coffee table. I lie down on top of the covers beside her and click on the TV.

She settles on her side, pulls the puppy close, and closes her eyes. Within minutes, she's fast asleep, and I don't sleep a wink all damn night.

Twenty-Eight

SOPHIE

I WAKE UP TO THE SOUND OF YAPPING. I'M PRESSED AGAINST something warm and hard. I peek one eye open and see a broad, muscular back.

Uh-oh.

I sit straight up. Too fast, and the room spins. I bring my head to my hand to steady it because it feels like my brain is about to pound its way out of my skull.

"Shut up, Hawk," I hear Braxton's sleepy voice command before he lightly chucks a pillow at the excited puppy at the end of the bed.

Hawk grabs the pillow with his jaw and yanks it back and forth before settling and chewing on it like it's a bone.

"This is why he's not allowed in the bed," he mumbles.

I look back down at the puppy. "But he's such a good snuggler. Aren't you, Hawkeye?" I coo at our furry bedmate.

He takes my soft tone as an invitation. He drops the pillow and hops his way up to my lap. Then, he plants his paws on my chest and starts licking my face.

I giggle, and that makes my head hurt worse. "Ouch. My head."

Braxton rolls over and looks at me. I'm sure I look frightful.

"You need some ibuprofen?"

"That would be great."

He reaches into the nightstand drawer and pops the top off a bottle of medication. He shakes two into my hand. Then, he twists the top off a bottle of water sitting beside him and takes a swig before passing it to me.

I take it from his hand and bring it to my lips. It's a big deal. Drinking after him. I don't do that. Not with anyone, but for some reason, I don't mind this morning.

"You're overthinking the water, Princess."

"Get out of my head," I snap.

"You have a horrible poker face."

"So I've been told." I hand him back the bottle and pull Hawkeye into my lap. "So, what's happening here exactly?"

"All we did was sleep last night," he reassures me.

"I know."

"What do you mean then?"

"We've kind of had this whole bitter, judgmental, standoffish relationship going on. It was comfortable. I don't know what to do with this. Are we calling a truce or something?"

He appraises me for a moment, and then he sits up and stretches. *Damn, he is pretty.* Then, he plants his arms on the bed and leans into me.

"You're in my T-shirt, in my bed, holding my dog. What do you think?"

"It's you, so I don't want to make any assumptions."

He grins.

Then, he jumps up and walks to the bathroom.

I look down at Hawkeye squirming in my arms. "Did that clear it up for you?"

He yaps.

"Yeah, me neither."

I hop up and grab my jeans from the armchair. I quickly pull them on while he is in the bathroom. I peer out the window beside the door that leads down to the side of the house. It looks quiet, but I know that my aunts and probably Emmett and Daddy are up. I wonder if they realize I'm missing yet.

"See anything good?"

I jump at his voice and quickly turn. "Just looking to see if anyone is stirring yet."

"It's late. They've been up for hours."

I look at the alarm clock by his bed. It's 7:06 a.m. These people have no concept of what is and isn't late.

"Madeline heads for the stables early on Sundays, and Ria and Doreen will leave for church soon. You can sneak in then."

Whew, that's a good plan. Emmett and Daddy will be much easier to slip by than the women.

"I bet Aunt Doe tried to wake me for breakfast and church. Think she'll believe that I stayed at Dallas's house last night?"

He shrugs. "Or you could tell her the truth."

"Tell them I slept up here?" I squeak out.

"It's not like I ravaged you, Sophie. You drank too much, and I let you crash up here, so you wouldn't wake the house up, stumbling in. They won't care."

My face heats at the thought of him ravaging me. He must notice because he moves closer to me. I instinctively back closer to the window.

"You kissed me," I whisper.

"Did I?"

He did. Didn't he? Did I kiss him? Oh God, it's all a little fuzzy, and I'm not sure.

"Let me know when you figure it out," he says as he leans in and slides his hand around my waist, running his little finger across my exposed skin. Then, he dips it low, and I gasp as it moves me into him, hip to hip. Then, he wraps his hand around something hanging at my back and pulls it from behind me. "Come on, Hawk," he says without looking away from my face.

The puppy hops up from his perch on the rug and trots over, and Braxton bends down to attach the leash to his collar. Then, he stands back up and reaches for the door handle.

143

"Be right back. Make yourself at home. There's a coffeemaker on the counter and supplies in the cabinet above it, but I'm fresh out of soy milk."

He leads Hawkeye out the door and closes it behind them.

I let out a breath. Get my hormones in check and make coffee.

When they return, I'm sitting on the sofa with my mug, checking e-mail on my phone.

"Coffee's ready."

He lets Hawkeye off the leash, and he runs to me. "I think you have a new best friend."

I reach down and scratch him behind the ear as I whisper conspiratorially, "That's why I let you in the bed last night. To buy your love and devotion."

"Just remember who feeds you, mutt."

I reach down and cover his ears. "Daddy didn't mean it," I utter softly.

I look up at Braxton as he pours a cup of coffee.

"This used to be my play space, you know."

He considers me as he stirs in the milk. "Is that right?"

"Yeah. It wasn't this." I gesture to the one-room apartment.

It's studio-style with a huge king-size bed that faces a fireplace with a large flat-screen TV mounted above it. The seating area with a small sofa and armchair are left of the bed, and a tiny kitchenette with a microwave, coffeepot, and refrigerator are to the right, with a small island and sink. The large walk-in closet and bathroom with a good-sized tiled shower but no tub are right behind the wall that rests against the bed. There isn't much in the way of décor but it's painted a soft cream and accented in rich dark browns and navy.

"It used to be an old loft over the barn where they stored hay bales until Daddy and Emmett closed it in for me one year. It wasn't anything fancy, just a big, open space where I kept all my art supplies. Dallas and I would play up here, and sometimes, when she slept over, Momma would let us set up a tent and camp in it. I would sit at an easel, facing those front windows, for hours and sketch the ranch, the horses, the house, everything. Gram would gush over and proudly display every creation."

"Yep. It was just drywall and windows and not much else. Walker and I spent the entire summer after graduation plumbing it, installing the bath and kitchen, and building the fireplace. Moved in it from the main house October of that year."

"It's nice. Cozy," I praise.

"It's not much, but it's all I need. It's home."

We hear Aunt Doreen's car start, and he looks out.

"You're all clear. They just pulled out of the gate."

I bend and give Hawk one last snuggle. Then, I stand and grab my things. "I'll return your T-shirt."

He looks me over. "No hurry."

He heads toward the bathroom again and then turns as I open the door.

"Don't forget; we have driving lessons this week. A bet's a bet."

Twenty-Nine

SOPHIE

I STEP OUT ON THE LANDING AND LOOK AROUND TO MAKE SURE THE coast is clear. Then, I start down the steps and beeline for the porch when I hear the crunch of gravel under tires. I panic, thinking my aunts have forgotten something and returned, so I freeze.

A black Jeep comes flying down the drive. I don't recognize it, so I start walking again, and just as I make it across the yard, a woman emerges from the driver's side and slams the door shut.

I put on my polite smile and greet our guest, "Hi. How can I help you?"

She removes her shades, and it dawns on me. I've seen her before. This is Morgan. Braxton's ex from the bar last night.

Great.

She looks me over, taking in his shirt that is several sizes too big and my bare feet. Then, her eyes follow the path I took from Braxton's front door to here, and they flare.

"You can't," she sneers.

I shrug and continue toward the steps to the porch, and she calls after me, "But I can help you."

At that, I take the first few steps up and turn to face her again, liking the advantage of looking down at her. "How's that?"

"Just some friendly advice."

I huff, "I don't need any advice, but thanks."

I turn and head up the steps toward the front door when she calls after me anyway, "You aren't his type, and he will never want you for more than that."

I look over my shoulder as she flits her hand out and gestures to my walk-of-shame appearance.

"He's stubborn and set in his ways. He doesn't like change, and he doesn't give a damn about anyone who has dreams bigger than living in this Podunk town for the rest of their lives. You obviously don't belong here, so he might play with you on his hook for a while, but he'll toss you back."

Before I can come up with a decent retort, she places her glasses on her head and struts off in the direction of Braxton's steps.

What a bitch.

After I shower and shoot a few e-mails off to Charlotte, I run down to the kitchen to scrounge for breakfast, trying to avoid looking outside to see if Morgan's Jeep is still here. It shouldn't matter to me. Should it?

Ugh. I walk over to the window above the sink and look up to Braxton's door. It's closed, and I can't see anything through his windows because of the sun's glare.

She's up there, and I don't like it. Not one bit. I decide it's not because I want him. It's because she's awful, and he deserves better.

I think he deserves better. *When did I start caring about what Braxton Young deserves?*

That kiss really messed with my head.

The front door opens and closes, and Elle walks into the kitchen and tosses her backpack onto the table.

"Is that Morgan's car out front?" she asks as she grabs a muffin from a basket on the counter.

"Yep," I say distractedly as I watch out the window, waiting for her to come down his stairs.

"Well, that didn't take long."

"What didn't?"

"She wants him back so bad. I just can't believe Braxton brought her home last night. I thought he was avoiding her. Guess she convinced him after all," she keeps talking as she opens the fridge and comes out with orange juice and a stick of butter. "You want a glass?"

I nod in answer, and she pours us both juice, grabs a knife, and sits at the table.

"He didn't."

She looks up at me as she slathers the muffin with butter.

"Bring her home last night, I mean. He did drive her home from the bar, but he came back alone. She showed up about half an hour ago."

"Hmm." That's her only reply.

"Do you think we should rescue him?" I ask, and she cuts her eyes to me.

"Rescue him?" she asks through a mouth full of muffin.

"Yeah, in case he wants to get rid of her and can't find a good reason."

She laughs around the muffin in her mouth, and it causes her to choke. She takes a sip of juice and answers me, "Braxton doesn't need us to rescue him. Trust me. If he wants her gone, he has zero problems telling her to get lost. He'd even pick her up, set her on her ass outside, and slam the door in her face."

"Oh."

She gives me a quizzical look. "You okay? You're acting funny."

Am I?

"Fine. Actually, I think I'm a little hungover, to tell you the truth."

"You know what helps with that? Junk food. Want to load up on snacks and veg out on the couch with me this afternoon?"

I shrug. "Sure. I was going to work a while, but maybe a day of rest is what I need. I can tackle all the things tomorrow."

"Awesome." She excitedly hops up. "I'll raid the pantry and fridge, and you choose the DVDs."

I take one last look out the window and head to the living room. If Morgan is what he wants, why should I care?

When Aunt Ria and Doreen return, they give us a passive-aggressive dressing-down for being out late and missing church.

I decide to go with the *I slept over at Dallas's house* story when Aunt Doreen asks where I was this morning.

"You guys should have heard the sermon today. Reverend Burr was so insightful. He was preaching on the importance of grace and how we should forgive others just as we were forgiven," Aunt Doreen shares.

Then, she gives me a pointed look.

"I'm forgiving when it's deserved."

"That's the point, sweetheart. Grace is forgiving someone even when they don't ask for it or deserve it. It releases you from the burden of carrying a chain of anger around your neck because carrying that heavy load does more damage to you than it does the person your angry with. It affects you physically and emotionally. It lives in every relationship you have."

"I don't think it's as easy as the good reverend made it sound."

"He didn't say it was easy; he said it was possible. And sometimes, to realize it's possible is all you need. Then, the power to hold on or let go lies in your hands and not in theirs any longer."

"This is getting heavy. We need more cookies," Elle says as she stands from the couch.

"Let's pop a fresh batch into the oven and *Bridget Jones's Diary* into the DVD player," she suggests as she starts toward the kitchen.

"Sounds good to me," Aunt Ria agrees, "I love that Colin Firth. His British accent gets me all kinds of tingly."

"Me too," we all say in unison.

Thirty

SOPHIE

"WHAT IS THIS RECEIPT FOR?"

I hold the sheet of paper up for Braxton to look at it. He carved out a small window for me this morning and is being way more amicable about the whole thing than he was last time.

"Semen."

I turn it around and look at it again. "That's what I thought it said. Why are we buying thirty thousand dollars' worth of semen?"

"To inseminate the cows and heifers. You know, so they will birth calves, and we have a herd to sell every year to keep the ranch running?"

He looks at me like I'm the crazy one.

"I thought bulls and cows did that … you know, the old-fashioned way."

"We have a few bulls to catch the ones that don't take to the artificial insemination, but it's more cost-effective to heat-synchronize the cows and inseminate them all at once. That way, we can concentrate the breeding and calving seasons and have a strong herd to take to auction."

"Can you not heat-sync the cows and still let the bulls do their thing and not pay all this money for semen?"

"We could, but we would have to purchase several more bulls. Those with good quality from a certified breeding line can be upward of five grand each. Then, you have the cost of feeding them and vet bills and hoping they don't catch any infections or die. With the frozen semen, we know the quality and the breeding stock. We inseminate all the cows at once and get about a sixty to seventy percent impregnation rate. The cleanup bulls take care of the other thirty percent, and we can keep our employment costs down by hiring extra hands only when the calves arrive in the spring."

"That makes sense."

He grins. "I know. That's why we do it."

"I guess this goes under material goods?" I ask.

"What qualifies as a material good?"

"A tangible commodity. Something you can hold, touch, or taste."

"I would say semen is definitely something you could touch or taste."

His stare bores into me, and it feels like the temperature in the room shoots up about ten degrees.

"Are you flirting with me, Brax?"

"Depends. Does bull semen turn you on?"

"Ew, no."

He laughs.

"Material goods. Got it," I mumble.

He sits with me for another hour before his patience runs thin, so I let him off the hook, and we join everyone for lunch.

"I appreciate the help today," I tell him as I pass the pasta salad.

"You're welcome, Princess."

I smile at him and reach for the plate of burgers as Daddy hands it in my direction. I catch the look he's giving the two of us—a look that is skeptical and curious. Not that I can blame him. I'm thrown by our behavior too.

After we finish eating, Aunt Doreen drives me into town for the meeting with Mr. Stroupe, the branch manager at the local bank. She has to sign off for him to be able to share the ranch's financial information with me. After which, she heads to Janelle's salon for her appointment while we sit in the conference room and go over account statements and set up all the banking online.

"And these debits, what are they for?"

"About ten years ago, your Gram and Pop decided to give family members shares in the company instead of paying them as employees. Making everyone a shareholder or a part-owner of Rustic Peak. So, they are no longer paid a salary, and instead, they get a profit share percentage at the end of each season. If the ranch has a good year, the split is a sizable sum." He gestures to the spreadsheet on his computer. "These are the debits for those payments from Rustic Peak's main account, and these are the accounts they deposit into."

He loads the accounts on the screen. Pop and Gram have a joint account, as do Daddy and Madeline. Doreen, Ria, Braxton, and Elowyn have individual accounts, and then there is another account under Gram's name.

"Gram has two accounts?" I ask for clarification as I make notes.

"No, she had her name put on that one as a joint account, so she could make the deposits and move the money around if she ever needed to."

"Who does the account belong to?" I ask as I begin to load the information into the system.

He looks at me in confusion. "Why, you, Sophia."

"Excuse me, what?"

"You have been getting an equal share of the ranch's profit since you turned eighteen. That's the age that each grandchild was added. Being as you've never made a withdrawal, it's a fairly sizable account at this point."

"I don't understand."

"Didn't you know that you were named a shareholder?"

"No, I had no idea."

"This is your social security number, correct?"

He pulls up the account on his screen, and I verify all the information as mine. Then, I get a good look at the balance. *Holy shit.* There is enough to pay Stanhope back every single penny he's invested in Sophia Doreen Designs and then some.

We finish up the meeting, and by the end, we have all the ranch's banking set up online and linked to the QuickBooks program. We have the utilities set up to auto-pay and all the payroll on automatic draft.

Aunt Doreen arrives to pick me up, and I thank Mr. Stroupe for all his help.

"It was my pleasure. I tried for years to talk Gram into letting me get this all done for her to make her life easier, and she wouldn't hear of it. She didn't place much trust in technology."

On the ride back to Rustic Peak, I get lost in my thoughts.

"You all right, Sophie?" Aunt Doreen asks as we turn onto the old country road leading to home.

"Did you know that Gram has been putting money in an account in my name all these years?"

"She has?"

"Yes. A profit-sharing account."

"I didn't, but that makes perfect sense. You are a Lancaster."

"But I'm not part of the ranch."

"You're a part of the family, Sophia. Her granddaughter. Do you think she ever forgot that?"

"I just ... I didn't expect it."

"No one here ever stopped loving you or stopped waiting for you to come home, Sophie. Least of all Gram."

Guilt and grief wash over me like a tidal wave. I could've come

AMBER KELLY

sooner. I could have picked up the phone and called or visited. I just assumed that everyone in Colorado had forgotten all about me and moved on to love the new family members, just like Daddy had. That wasn't fair. So much wasted time all because I was scared to face him.

"I always intended to come see you guys one day. I thought about it a lot, especially when I was younger. Then, time slipped by, and I was in college. Life got busy, and the longer I waited, the harder it was to imagine just showing up here. The scarier it seemed. I would push it to the back of my Someday list. I ran out of somedays while I wasn't looking."

For the first time, I cry. Really cry. I let the sobs take over, and I cry for the girl who lost her grandmother—not just a few weeks ago, but a lifetime ago. I cry for wasted time.

Time is the most valuable thing any of us owns. We can't hoard it or save it, can't borrow it from another person, can't buy it or even pray for more of it. You are allotted only so many days on this Earth, so many birthdays and Christmases. Some get ninety, and some get far less. Gram got seventy-four birthdays. Braxton and Elle's momma got only thirty. Some get less than that. Yet time is the one thing we waste more of than anything else, and we never even notice. We always think we have more until we don't. We are even so careless as to wish it away. Wishing for the weekend to hurry up and come or the workday to be over with or the winter months to pass. Never appreciating the moment we have right now and never stopping to truly live it.

Aunt Doreen takes a long, out-of-the-way route home, so I can get it all out.

When we pull up in front of the house, I open the door, and she calls to me, "Sophie Doe."

"Yes?"

"Now that the dam's starting to break, don't build it back up, sweetheart. Feel it. Let it flow, all of it, and let it go."

"I'm trying, Aunt Doe. I'm truly trying."

Thirty-One

BRAXTON

I THROW THE COOLER INTO THE BACK OF THE PICKUP AND SHUT THE tailgate. The next two days, Jefferson, Emmett, and I will be attending the National Western Stock Show and Rodeo in Denver. We attend every year as a part of our membership in the National Cattlemen's Beef Association. They sponsor the event, and it's always top-notch. Each year, the trade show offers training and education in better breeding and feeding techniques to area stockmen, and the stock show features all the latest and greatest equipment to hit the agricultural market in the last year. Several of the local ranches send a couple of representatives. It's important to stay on top of the market and to get continuing education in the ever-changing industry.

Jefferson steps out of the house onto the porch, followed by Aunt Madeline. Dallas's pickup pulls up just as he kisses her good-bye, and she and Sophie hop out.

"See you gals in a few days," he greets as he heads my way.

"Where are you going?" Sophie asks as he passes.

"Denver. We have the Stock Show and Rodeo to attend."

"A rodeo? Really?"

He stops and takes in her expectant face. "I forgot how much you loved rodeos when you were little."

"I love them! I haven't been to one since I was eleven years old, but I still watch them on television from time to time."

He ponders her statement for a moment. "You want to come with us?"

"Can I?" Her face is alight.

"I don't see why not. We have two rooms booked, and Brax can bunk in with Emmett and me."

She brings her hopeful eyes to me. "I don't want to put you out of your room," she says, a little deflated.

"Go, pack a bag quickly. We need to get on the road," I say in response.

She squeals in delight and runs into the house.

I can't believe the same girl who showed up here in designer duds gets that excited at the prospect of spending two nights in a crappy hotel and attending a rodeo. She is full of all kinds of surprises.

"Man, I wish I could go. I'd love to watch some real cowboys competing," Dallas says as she starts to follow.

"Why don't you?" Jefferson asks. "Sophie isn't going to want to spend all day talking shop during the actual show. You girls can hang out in the city, and I'll scrounge you up some badges for the rodeo competitions in the evening."

"I can't. I'm on the schedule at the diner tomorrow, and I have Beau. Momma and Daddy watch him while I work all week. I don't want to ask them to keep him at night too."

"He can stay here with us," Ria offers as she rounds the house with a watering can in hand. "Doreen and I would love his company. It's been a while since the pitter-patter of little feet graced this old house."

"He has school."

"I think we can manage to get him to and from the schoolhouse for a couple of days. It would be our pleasure."

Dallas looks like she is considering it.

"Let me call Faye right quick and see if she can cover my shift." She runs off into the house.

"You sure you're okay with giving up your room, son?" Jefferson asks me once they are inside.

I shrug. "I don't mind. As long as I don't have to babysit her and Dallas."

"They're big girls. They can take care of themselves."

Dallas was unable to get coverage for work, so she is driving up tomorrow night. That means Sophie had to come up with us. Jefferson is driving, and Emmett is riding shotgun. We waited until the workday was done and headed out after dinner. That way, we can be up and at the expo early in the morning. Sophie and I are sitting in the backseat of the king cab while the two of them bicker over the radio in the front.

I look over, and she is yawning.

"Look who's ready to crash at seven p.m.," I tease her.

"I can't help it. You crazy people have me up at the crack of dawn every day. My internal clock is all off." She grins.

She puts some earbuds into her ears and turns her music on, and about ten minutes later, she is fast asleep. In her slumber, she lulls to the side, and her head rests at a strange angle. She looks uncomfortable, so I gently pull her forward and tuck her into my side, so her head is lying on me. She looks so beautiful and peaceful. I absentmindedly run my fingers through her long, silky hair.

"Brax." Jefferson gets my attention.

I meet his eyes in the rearview mirror. "Yeah?"

"How's my girl doing back there?"

"Good. She's sleeping."

He nods. "She comfortable?"

I know he sees her curled up in my lap.

"I got her."

"That's good, son."

We pull up to the hotel a little over an hour later. It's a budget establishment because us men couldn't care less how fancy the place is as long as it's clean and it has hot water. I look down at Sophie and feel a bit guilty that she'll be sleeping in the old, smelly, run-down place.

"You think there are any other hotels with vacancies?" I ask as Jefferson parks the truck.

"Why? We always stay here," he asks.

"Because the beds are lumpy, the rooms smell like stale cigarettes, and the coffee tastes like turpentine."

"Yeah, and?"

"And that's fine for us three, but I hate for Sophie to be stuck here because we don't mind it."

He looks into the backseat at his sleeping daughter and sighs. "I doubt there's anything available around here. Everything has probably been sold out for months because of the show. She'll be fine." He opens his door and steps out. "You guys wait here, and I'll go check us in and see if they can put an extra cot in our room."

Emmett turns in his seat. "I have to take a leak."

Then, he gets out and darts after Jefferson toward the hotel's office. At the sound of his door slamming shut, Sophie starts, and then she rolls over and snuggles in deeper.

I like the feel of her, and I love the smell of her. My mind flashes back to her wrapped around me the other night. She stayed on her side of the bed until five minutes after she fell asleep. I lay there, watching television, and she rolled into me and wrapped herself around me. Her bare legs hooking my thigh and her arm going around my middle. It took every ounce of self-control I had not to move on top of her and continue that kiss from the bar, but I knew she'd had too much to drink. So, I just held her. All night long, I held her, and I haven't been able to think about much else since.

Morgan showed up the next morning and caught Sophie sneaking back to the farmhouse. I had just stepped into the shower when I heard the pounding on the door. I thought maybe Sophie had forgotten something or was spooked back to the door by her dad, so I jumped out, wrapped a towel around my hips, and opened it. I tried to block Morgan's entrance, but she forced her way into my space. I spent the next two excruciating hours convincing her that there was nothing left between us to save and that what had or hadn't happened between Sophie and me, or any girl for that matter, was none of her damn business. She told me how much she still loved me and made a lot of hollow apologies and hollow promises if I would reconsider.

When I finally got her to the door, she threw her parting shot.

"If you think any girl is going to be satisfied with living her life above an old barn and only having your attention ten percent of the time without getting restless, you're crazy. Especially that girl. It might be fine for Madeline, but even Elle wants more than this. I love you enough that I'm willing to try. Maybe we could find a compromise because having everything I ever wanted wasn't as wonderful as I'd thought it would be without you."

That all sounded great, and it might have worked if she had come to me before she went after Rustic Peaks at her company's whim. I could never trust her after that. Money and ambition trumped love and loyalty, and that is a character flaw I can't overlook. I'd rather wake up alone every day for the rest of my life than wake up with a snake in my bed.

I look back down at Sophie. I don't know how, but somehow, in the past three weeks, she's managed to get under my skin. I can't let her though. Morgan is right. Sophie doesn't belong here, and because of that fact and out of respect for Jefferson, I should keep my distance and my damn hands to myself.

Thirty-Two

SOPHIE

I WAKE TO A BOOMING KNOCK AT MY DOOR.

I open an eye, and the light peeking in beneath the dingy brown-and-orange curtains that barely cover the dirty windows of the motel blinds me.

"Coming," I croak out as I roll over and set my feet on the floor.

My neck and back are stiff as a board from sleeping on the threadbare mattress. I was poked by springs all night long.

I stand and stretch, and my back cracks all the way down. That helps.

I undo the sliding lock and open the door.

"Why did you open the door?" Braxton asks as he walks into the room, carrying a tray.

"Because you knocked on it."

"You didn't know it was me on the other side. You need to ask before you unlock the door to strangers."

He sets the tray with two coffee cups on the small, round Formica table in the corner. Then, he spins and pins me with his stern look of disapproval.

"It's too early, and I'm too tired to fight with you, Braxton," I groan.

I ignore his annoyance and walk to the table where I open the bag perched on the cardboard tray. It is filled with warm doughnuts. I pluck a powder-covered one from the bag and grab a cup of coffee. Then, I sit on the edge of the bed.

"Jefferson and Emmett are getting their showers, and we'll be ready to go in about thirty minutes," he informs me.

"Okay," I say as I swallow. I dust the sugar from my hands and stand. "I'll hop in the shower quickly and be ready to go."

"Are you going with us?"

"Of course I am."

He looks confused. "I assumed you would want to call whatever that car company is of yours and get a driver to tote you around Denver today."

"No way. I want to go to the show."

"It's a lot of boring industry crap today. Nothing exciting. You could go shopping or to the spa or something like that. Cherry Creek Mall is just a few miles away."

I stop and turn on him. "You know, back in New York, I don't sit around, sipping champagne, eating bonbons, and getting massages all day. I run a company, and I'm pretty good at it. I want to see what you guys learn. I'm interested in how things run on the ranch. Especially after going through the records this past week. You never know; I might be able to help find ways to cut cost and promote efficiency that you guys miss when you're distracted by the big, shiny, new toys."

He gives me a half grin. "Well, all right then, get in the shower. I'm going to wait here." He snatches the remote and stacks pillows up against the headboard.

I dig my jeans and long-sleeved tee from my duffel bag and head into the bathroom. It's crusty, and the sink is covered with dark spots where cigarettes have been set. Ew, I might not drink champagne all day, but I am just prissy enough to wish I had a pair of flip-flops to wear in this shower. I turn the water on as hot as I can and let it run for several minutes, hoping it kills anything that could be living on the shower floor.

When I emerge from my scalding hot shower, Daddy and Emmett have joined Braxton in my room. They're all eating doughnuts and watching television.

"Hey, Sophie. How'd you sleep last night?" Emmett asks as I take my wet hair and gather it into a knot on top of my head.

I decide to skip makeup and just add a little bit of moisturizer to my face and swipe on a thin layer of lip balm.

"Great," I lie.

The last thing I want is to make them feel bad for my restless night's sleep. I was the one who invited myself along on their trip, so I have no right to complain about the accommodations.

"See, Braxton? She's fine."

I look in the mirror at Braxton, who has his eyes on the TV.

"She's lying," he calls out.

"He was worried about you all night. That's why he got up so early and drove into town to get coffee and doughnuts. He didn't want you drinking what they have here," Daddy informs me, and a warm feeling overcomes me as I realize his concern for my comfort.

"It's not that bad," Emmett says, looking into the cup in his hand. "Of course, it's not that good either."

"Thank you, Brax," I say as I shove the lip gloss in the front pocket of my jeans.

His eyes move from the television to meet mine in the mirror. "You're welcome, Princess."

Then, he focuses back on the news.

I place my stack of belongings back on top of my bag and sit to pull on my socks and boots.

Daddy moves closer, and I catch him looking over my pile. Braxton's T-shirt, the one I stole and now sleep in at night, is sitting on top.

Crap.

He looks at the shirt and then to Braxton, who is still watching the television.

I hold my breath, waiting to see if he recognizes the shirt. I have no idea how we would explain it. My mind starts reeling for an explanation when he looks back to me.

"We'd best get moving. We don't want all the best bulls spoken for before we arrive."

I relax as I finish putting on my boots and coat.

Fifteen minutes later, we are in the truck and heading for National Western Center.

I'm excited as we enter the complex. It's a massive two-hundred-fifty-acre facility, and it is filled to the max with attendees, vendors, animals, and equipment. There is so much to see and so much to learn.

Daddy and Emmett head to the livestock building to check out the quality of the bulls that are for sale while Braxton and I sit in on a demonstration of a new cattle feedlot. Then, we move on to a presentation on more straightforward insemination techniques.

I learn a lot. There is so much more to running a beef cattle ranch than I ever realized. The scheduling and new advancements in technology are fascinating. We leave the demo with me convinced we need the new feedlot immediately.

"We don't need it." Braxton sets me straight.

"But it would save so much time, and time is money," I regurgitate the spiel.

"True, but we don't overpopulate our land. We have enough acreage per head that eighty percent of our cattle's diet is grass off the land. We don't have to supplement with grain enough to justify the cost of a new lot. We're in most need of a new tractor and a new hauling trailer at the moment. We've been patching and repairing the ones we have for the last couple of years, and it's not cost-effective to keep throwing money at them every time they break down. Plus, it takes man-hours to do the repairs."

He guides us to the equipment sales area, and we start pricing new tractors.

"I never realized how expensive tractors are," I muse as we stroll down the line of mid-size tractors with price tags in the mid- to high-five figures.

"Now, you see why we've patched Ole Big Bird as long as we have. They are definitely an investment but a necessary one."

"Do you have a preference?" I ask as I run my hand over one of the massive machines.

"I'm a John Deere fan; you should know that," he answers.

I laugh. "Of course you are."

"They're a tad too pricey though, so we'll probably go for one of the middle-tier brands."

"Doesn't it make more sense to get the best brand for your money?"

"Sometimes, you have to make the best with what you can afford. We'd rather get second best and pay cash for it than have to mortgage anything. Pop and Jefferson aren't fans of debt. Debt is why some of the other ranches in the county had to sell. We stay afloat because we are smart about what we spend."

"True, but a calculated risk is not always bad. If the better brand does a more efficient job, you can place the money to cover the debt aside in an account and take out a loan for the tractor. Interest rates are so good right now that you could probably get locked in at a one and a half to one-point-seven-five percent rate, which is peanuts. Pay it off in installments and never touch the original amount."

"I don't know much about the banking side. Gram always handled that stuff. I'm better at calculating birthing cycles and feeding schedules."

"I've gotten pretty good at it in the past year. Stanhope took me under his wing and mentored me through the legal and financial aspects of starting my design company."

"Stanhope?"

"My stepfather. He's built several successful companies from the ground up. He's probably the smartest man I know when it comes to finance."

He considers me for a moment.

"Maybe you could sit down with Jefferson and discuss what you think our best options are."

"I can do that."

Thirty-Three

SOPHIE

AFTER A LONG DAY AT THE SHOW, THE FOUR OF US HEAD BACK to the hotel to get ready for the rodeo tonight.

When we make it into the parking lot, Dallas's truck is idling outside the door to my room.

She jumps out as we pull into the space beside her.

"Do you know that the manager of this here fine establishment let me have a key to your room? He didn't ask my name or anything. He just handed it to me when I told him I was here to stay with you. Isn't that some shady shit?"

"I told him you would be coming before we left this morning. Described you well. I'm sure he felt confident you were you," I say as I take the bag off her shoulder, so she can carry the cooler bag she has on the other.

"He still should have asked to see some ID before handing out keys to your room. I'm going to go have a chat with him." Braxton stomps off toward the office.

"That boy has gotten awfully protective of Sophie as of late," Emmett says to no one in particular.

"I've noticed that too. Weird, right?" Dallas asks him.

"I think he'd be pissed even if it were your room they handed someone a key to," I point out.

"Maybe so, but he didn't bring me any coffee this morning," Daddy says as he watches Braxton enter the office.

"He probably just used me as an excuse to go get it for himself. He just didn't want to admit he wanted a latte."

Both of them cut their eyes to me and shake their heads.

"The Ritz it's not," Dallas says as she looks around our home for the next two nights.

"Not exactly."

"Good thing I brought plenty of provisions."

She unzips the Yeti cooler on the floor and starts to pull out mason jars of moonshine, a bottle of tequila, a bottle of bourbon, and a pitcher of lemonade. Then, she unpacks grocery bags of microwave popcorn, chips, and cookies.

"We can't drink all that in two nights."

"I got a text from Russ Eastman. He and his brother, Trey, are here for the show too, and they'll be at the rodeo tonight. I thought maybe they could swing by afterward with some of their friends and have a few drinks with us."

"Dallas, my daddy, Emmett, and Braxton are right next door. We can't have a room full of boys over here," I explain unnecessarily.

"We're not teenagers, for goodness' sake. If we want to have company, it's none of their business."

"You're crazy."

"You say that, but you haven't seen Russ and Trey yet." She wags her eyebrows at me. "Come on, let's get all gussied up for this. That arena is going to be full of dirty, rugged cowboys. We have to look our best."

"Dirty cowboys?" I ask.

"Oh, yes, that's just the way I like them. Extra dirty."

Daddy and Emmett turn in early, and Braxton escorts us to the arena.

"I'm going down to help with the bucking chutes. You two okay?" he asks as we enter the event.

Dallas waves him off. "We're fine. I have friends coming."

"All right, I'll find you after the bull-riding events. Keep your phones on vibrate. It'll be too loud in here to hear it ring."

He takes off down the stadium stairs to the arena floor.

"Let's get in line. You grab hot dogs and fries, and I'll get the beers."

I wrinkle my nose.

"I know, I know, but they don't serve rosé here, so you'll have to make do."

I pay for our food and take it to the condiment table to add mustard, ketchup, and relish, and Dallas joins me, followed by two tall, handsome men.

"Sophie, this is Russ and Trey. Fellas, this is my bestie, Sophie."

They each shake my hand. Russ, the oldest, has a short beard, piercing green eyes, and a well-worn cowboy hat covering his hair. Trey is a little more clean-cut than his brother with the same dark hair and green eyes, but his face is clean-shaven, and he isn't wearing a hat. They graciously help us carry our food and drinks to our seats on the bleachers.

"Which event are you most interested in?" Trey asks as I look over the event program.

"Me? I like the barrel racing and the calf roping. You?"

"Bull riding."

"I should have guessed."

"One of our buddies is a competing bull rider. He's won several Professional Bull Rider events in the last few years. He's a rising star on the circuit."

"I get nervous, watching the bull riders. My daddy took me to a Professional Rodeo Cowboys Association rodeo in Montana once, and one of the riders was bucked off. Before he could get away, the bull trampled him. Shattered his arm and broke several ribs. It was awful. He was lucky it wasn't worse."

"Yeah, it's a dangerous sport, but most sports are. Even football players are one bad hit away from being paralyzed the rest of their life. That's why they train so hard. And everyone doesn't have the talent for it. Still, accidents happen."

"I know you're right. Those bucking bulls still make me nervous. My … my, um … my daddy's nephew-in-law, Braxton, is helping with the chutes tonight."

I point down to where Brax is straddling the side of one of the chutes while the rider gets positioned on the bull.

"Braxton Young. Yeah, I know him. We went to school together. You're related?"

"Not really. His aunt married my dad, but we just met recently. I live in New York."

"New York? Wow. That's pretty cool. How long are you in Colorado?"

"I'm not sure. A couple more weeks at most."

"We should get together back in Poplar Falls. Maybe Russ and I can take you and Dallas out to dinner one night."

I look over to Dallas, who is a hundred percent enthralled by whatever Russ is talking about.

"We could probably arrange that."

He smiles, and I realize how attractive he truly is.

"So, what do you think?" Dallas asks as she loops her arm in mine as we make our way to the ladies' room.

"They are friendly and easy on the eyes."

"Right? Russ has been coming into the diner every day that I work. He's asked me out a few times, but I always say no because of Beau. Dating is hard when you have a little person at home."

169

"You shouldn't feel guilty for wanting a life, Dallas. Being a mom doesn't mean you can't do anything for yourself."

"I know. I don't want to introduce anyone into his life that doesn't plan to stay awhile. Plus, I want to go home to him the nights I don't work the Tavern. I spend enough time away from him."

"Tell you what. When we get back, we'll go out on a double date. That way, you can feel him out without all the pressure."

"That would be amazing. I think Trey is into you."

"Yeah, well, I'm only here a little while longer, so it can't be more than a one-time thing."

"Maybe not, but if you play your cards right, it could be one hell of a memorable one time."

Thirty-Four

SOPHIE

WHEN WE RETURNED FROM DENVER, I SAT DOWN WITH Daddy and Braxton and discussed the merits of buying a new middle-of-the-line tractor outright or getting a loan for a top-of-the-line model. I laid the entire thing out on spreadsheets to show how, at a low-interest rate, the second option made more sense in the long run.

After my presentation and going over the figures a few times, Daddy agreed to talk to Mr. Stroupe at the bank to discuss the loan. So, he and Aunt Doreen and I are on our way to town. I want her along for all the business discussions and decision-making because she will more than likely be the one to take over for Gram running the administrative side of the ranch.

"Do you agree with Sophie that this is a good idea?" Daddy asks the bank manager.

"I do. You'll have use of the better tractor, which will be more efficient on the ranch, and the better brand will probably save you in maintenance fees down the road. We have your monthly payment extremely reasonable, and the interest rate is the lowest we've seen in years," Mr. Stroupe explains.

"And you can write the interest off on your taxes at the end of the year," I add.

"Honestly, this is the best way to purchase all the equipment you need on the ranch, including vehicles. You paid cash for your last truck by pulling the money out of a CD. Gram could have left the money in the CD and financed the truck—not only saving you money, but also making you money."

"How's that?" Daddy asks.

"The money was making two percent more per month in the CD than the interest rate would have been to finance the truck. For example, if you have ten dollars in an account that is making three percent interest and you decide to buy a toy truck that cost five dollars, you can finance at a one and a half percent rate or take the whole five dollars out of your account and pay in cash. It makes more sense to leave the whole ten dollars in the account and finance the toy truck because it's gaining double what the loan would cost. Does that make sense?" I try to illustrate the concept as simple as possible without talking down or disrespecting him.

"Perfect sense," he agrees.

We leave the bank after signing all the paperwork and getting the loan process started.

Aunt Doreen nervously prattles on about keeping up with it all, so I decide to broach the subject of hiring some help on the way home.

"Have you thought any more about hiring an administrative assistant?" I ask her.

She eyes Daddy and then cautiously answers, "Not everyone is comfortable with hiring someone outside of the family."

"That's silly. Companies do it all the time."

"We're a family company," Daddy insists.

"I realize that, but someone has to take care of the administrative side of the business with Gram gone, and I think it's a little bigger than Aunt Doreen can manage."

Even if I sat and trained her nonstop for the next week, she's never going to catch on. She has zero experience using e-mail, much less a computer and accounting program. The mountain is insurmountable in the time we have.

"I trust that you know what you're doing," he replies in answer.

"I do, but I'm only here for another week or so, and you'll need someone once I leave."

"We'll make do."

That's his infuriating answer.

"It's not that simple," I start to argue.

"We'll figure it out, Sophie. We aren't hiring anyone. If Doreen can't manage it, then Elle will help."

Elle has dreams that don't include being Aunt Doreen's assistant. She wants to go to school next year.

I drop the subject for now because the stubborn man is not going to budge. It's not really my problem anyway, so I don't know why I care so much.

I'm skipping dinner with the family tonight because Dallas and I are going on a double date. Russ and Trey are taking us to a farm-to-table restaurant the next county over, and then we're going to the drive-in theater to watch the latest Marvel movie. I'm truly just going along for moral support. I like Trey well enough, but it's not like we have any kind of possible future, whereas Dallas would very much like to see where things go with Russ.

I decide that comfortable is the way to go, so I dress in my low-slung jeans, a soft-pink cashmere sweater with a broad neckline so it falls off one shoulder, and brown cowgirl boots. I load a bag with thick wool blankets and homemade snacks provided by Aunt Ria for the drive-in. The nights are so cold, so we'll be wrapped up to stay warm in the back of Dallas's truck. I haven't been to a drive-in before, so I'm excited to experience it for the first, and probably last, time tonight.

Aunt Ria tucks some hand-warmers into my bag along with the brownies and deer jerky. "You have fun tonight and keep your eye on Dallas."

"I will. I think she's a little nervous, which is odd. I don't think I've ever seen her nervous before."

"It's good that you're here. That ex-husband of hers did a number on her. She works so hard, and she is a good momma, but she deserves more than just Beau in her life."

"Says the woman who never remarried after her husband was killed in the war. You've never batted an eyelash at another gentleman in all this time, have you? Aunt Doreen and Emmett have been sneaking kisses for years since Uncle Lee took off but not you."

Uncle Arthur was killed in Vietnam in 1975. They had only been married for two short years, and Aunt Ria has never so much as looked sideways at another man. At least, according to Dallas.

"Sometimes, a love so big comes along, and even if you only get to hold on to it for a little while, it can fill you up for a lifetime. That was my Arthur. I've never felt the need to fill his place in my heart. I have my family and friends and have never suffered a single moment of loneliness. One day, I'll be back with him, and until then, I'm quite content."

"That's beautiful. I hope I find that kind of love someday. I'm not the best at maintaining relationships," I admit.

"Why not? You're so easy to love, Sophie."

"I think I'm always waiting for them to decide they want to leave. I expect it. So, I never really let them in, and eventually, they do." I shrug.

She opens her mouth to say something and is cut off by Elle, yelling down the hallway, "Sophie, a hot guy in a sweet Range Rover is here to pick you up."

Thirty-Five

BRAXTON

I TOSS ANOTHER BAG OF GRAIN DOWN TO EMMETT FROM THE STORAGE loft off the side of the barn. He grabs it and throws it up on the truck bed.

"That's the last of it, old man. Time to wash up and eat," I say as I make my way down the ladder.

It's been a long day. We finally got the fence patch reinforced in the back pasture, and I'm exhausted and starving.

We bring the ladder down and toss it on the truck bed with the feed. Just as I shut the tailgate, a shiny new Range Rover comes rolling to a stop in front of the house. A man I slightly recognize but can't place steps out and speaks to Elle, who is on the front porch. She walks inside, and he waits by his truck.

"Emmett, who's that?" I gesture toward the visitor with my chin.

He looks up and scans the driveway. "It must be that Eastman boy come to pick Sophie up for dinner. I heard her telling Ria about it this afternoon," he answers.

Eastman—that's it. We went to high school together. The guy was a real tool, always flaunting his family's wealth.

"Dinner?" I question.

"Yep. He and his brother were out at the show in Denver, and they met the girls. I reckon he's taken a fancy to Sophie."

I don't like the thought of her being alone with that guy—not one bit.

"He's an idiot. Why would she have anything to do with him?" I ask the rhetorical question.

He answers me anyway, "I guess because none of the idiots around here have offered to take her to dinner."

He slaps me on the back and walks toward the backyard.

I stand there and wait until she comes out the door. She looks beautiful in jeans and a fuzzy pink top that is feminine and still looks substantial enough to keep her warm. She greets him with a big smile and a hug, and then he opens the passenger door for her. She shrugs an overnight bag off her shoulder and hands it to him. He shuts her in, and then he opens the back door and tosses in her bag.

Surely, she doesn't plan on staying the night with him. They just met.

I stomp my way across the yard and enter the back door. Everyone is seated for dinner with two open chairs—mine and Sophie's. I roll up my sleeves and wash up. Then, I take my seat. I load my plate and start eating, still thinking about Sophie's overnight bag sitting in that asshole's backseat.

"Something wrong, Brax?" Jefferson gets my attention.

"No. Why?" I ask with my mouth full.

"Well, son, you poured gravy all over your baked apples and started shoveling it in like we were going to steal your plate. And your aunt Madeline has asked you the same question four times."

I stop and look down at my plate. I did indeed pour gravy on my apples instead of the sliced turkey breast.

I look back up, and everyone's amused faces are staring back at me.

"What?" I bite out.

"No need to shout," Doreen gently scolds me, "and no need to worry about Sophie. She's a big girl who can take care of herself."

"Who said I was worried about Sophie?"

She keeps talking as she salts and peppers her plate, "Aren't you?"

"Why aren't you? Do you know that guy? Does she? She took an overnight bag with her, for fuck's sake."

"Language," she reprimands.

"I'm sorry. I just don't like it."

"She took a bag with supplies for the drive-in tonight. It's loaded up with blankets and snacks, not pajamas and toiletries. She'll be home tonight," Ria reassures me.

Relief washes over me for a second, and then I notice they're all still staring at me.

"Okay. I overreacted. I still don't like it. Just because she met him once doesn't mean she knows the guy."

"Just how do you expect her to get to know him if she doesn't go out with him?" Jefferson asks.

I shrug. I don't exactly have an answer for that.

"Can we all just eat now?" I ask, hoping to end the conversation.

"Sure," he answers, and we all finish our meal in silence.

Afterward, I head up to my room and let Hawkeye out. I check the showtimes at the drive-in and see that the show starts at eight thirty-five p.m., and it's a double feature. Damn it, they won't even be done until after midnight.

I build a fire in the fireplace and settle in with a beer. It's going to be a long night. Hawkeye jumps up on the bed beside me. He has been sleeping with me since last week when Sophie let him. Now, he thinks he's always allowed to sleep with us.

Us? Did I just think of Sophie and me as an us?

What the hell is wrong with me? The girl has gotten under my skin.

Hawk starts barking, and I look down at him.

"Yeah, I wish she were here too."

Thirty-Six

SOPHIE

"GET UP. IT'S TIME FOR YOUR DRIVING LESSON."
I wake to the sound of Braxton's voice at my bedroom door.

We got in late last night. After a fabulous dinner at The Heirloom Restaurant, we went to the drive-in. It was so much fun. Seriously, we got in for twenty dollars a carload. That was four adults watching two full-length new releases for twenty dollars. That would cost no less than a hundred twenty dollars in New York, and the drive-in lets you bring your own food. Charlotte and I usually hide food in our purses and sneak it in, but they allow you to bring it right on in and eat it out in the open. It was the craziest thing I'd ever seen. The night was beautiful, and the sky was clear, so once we got all cozy in the blankets, we were very comfortable.

Trey and I tried our best to pretend we didn't notice when Russ and Dallas started making out halfway through the second feature. I was nervous that Trey would expect the same, but he was a gentleman and didn't attempt so much as a kiss until he brought me back to my door. He walked me up onto the porch. Just as our lips touched, Braxton's front door flew open, and Hawkeye shot across the yard, heading straight for us. He wedged himself between the two of us and started jumping up for me to pick him up. Braxton rounded the front with the leash in his hand, yelling after him. He apologized. We had pulled up just as he was leashing the puppy, but when Hawkeye heard our car doors shut, he darted right past a sleepy Brax and came looking for me.

The interruption had ruined the moment, so Trey wished me a good night and promised to call me today as Braxton and I wrangled an excited Hawkeye.

A sharp knock comes at the door.

"Go away, Braxton. I need a couple more hours of sleep," I answer and roll over as I pull the covers over my head.

The door creaks open, and he snatches the comforter from the bottom of the bed, yanking hard.

It slides right off of me, exposing my bare legs. I'm not wearing anything but panties and his John Deere T-shirt.

"Lazy …" he starts. Then, his eyes glide down my body, and whatever he was about to say dies on his lips.

"Hey!" I protest as I sit up and grab the sheet. I pull it up to my chin, a little embarrassed that he caught me still sleeping in his shirt.

"Sorry. Just trying to get you moving. Daylight's a-wasting."

I roll my eyes. "We were up late last night. The world won't end if we spend one morning sleeping past eight a.m.," I gripe.

He grins and leans in close. "Keep pouting, and I'm going to bite that bottom lip. Now, get up and get dressed. Everyone is waiting for us downstairs."

I gasp at his threat and suck my bottom lip in between my teeth.

That makes him flat-out smile.

"Who's everyone?" I ask.

"Payne, Dallas and Beau, Silas and Chloe, Elle, Walker, and Myer. It's been raining all morning. We're going mudding down at Henry's Knob."

"Mudding? What are we, unruly teenagers?"

"Today we are. Now, get up."

"Ugh, fine. Go away, and I'll be down in a minute."

I throw on jeans and a sweatshirt and run downstairs. The kitchen is filled with everyone chatting loudly as they load plates with bacon and eggs. Aunt Doreen is bent over the oven, pulling out a pan of biscuits, and Aunt Ria is cutting up a bowl of fruit.

I slide into one of the chairs at the table.

"You want coffee or juice, Sophie?" Aunt Ria asks.

"Coffee," I groan.

"Here, eat this. You'll need your energy," Dallas says as she places a plate in front of me.

"How are you so bright-eyed and bushy-tailed this morning? You were out as late as I was last night," I complain as I take a slice of bacon and pop it in my mouth.

"I'm a momma. We're used to functioning on little to no sleep." She shrugs.

"Well, I'm not. I need sleep," I whine.

"We're going mud-slinging, Miss Sophie," Beau's animated voice calls across the table.

He is sitting in his uncle Payne's lap, and his mouth and hands are covered in grape jelly.

"I heard," I say as I grin at him.

"Yaaaaay," he squeals.

"It is a lot of fun," Dallas says as she nudges me in the side.

"I'm sure it is," I grumble.

One hour later, we are in three trucks out in the knob. Payne, Dallas, and Myer have Beau in one truck. Silas, Chloe, Elle and Walker are in another, and Braxton has me in his truck.

"I don't know if a muddy field in a huge truck is the best place for me to learn how to drive," I say nervously as I grip the stirring wheel so tightly that my knuckles turn white.

"Relax. It's the perfect place. There's no traffic out here. No one but you and me and the field."

"And everyone else I know in Poplar Falls," I snap.

"They're playing in the mud. They aren't paying us a bit of attention."

"I don't know about this, Braxton. I don't even need to know how to drive."

"Everyone should know how to drive. I taught Elle how when she was fourteen years old. You can do this."

I take a deep breath and decide to try. "What do I do first?"

"First, adjust the seat. You want to be able to comfortably reach the pedals without being right up on the steering wheel. Then, adjust your mirrors. The button is in the door above the handle."

I do as he instructed and nervously wait for what comes next.

"Now, the truck is in neutral, so push the clutch in. It's on the left. Start the car and put it in first gear."

He places his hand over mine on the gear shift and helps me move the truck into first.

"Here comes the tricky part. You want to let up off the clutch as you press the gas until you are completely off the clutch and moving forward."

I do as he said, and the truck starts jumping under us.

"Easy. Try to do it at the same time."

I try again, and the truck stalls.

I put my head against the steering wheel and groan, "Ugh."

"It's all right; no one gets it without stalling out the first time. Try again."

He spends the next two hours patiently talking me through stall after stall. He never loses his cool. Even as I grind his clutch over and over. Finally, I get a feel for it and am able to take off and switch gears easily. Then, he spends time having me back up and stop and start on a hill.

It is fun once I get the hang of it.

"I did it!" I say excitedly as I put the truck in park. Then, I leap at him in the passenger seat and throw my arms around his neck.

"You did," he says proudly into my hair.

"Thank you for teaching me how." I beam at him.

"You're welcome, Princess."

He reaches his arms around my waist and pulls me closer to him. My arms are still around his neck, and as my excitement settles, I realize how close we are. I raise my head from his neck, and we are nose-to-nose.

"What's next?"

"What do you want to be next, Princess?"

I stare into his eyes. Then, I nervously lick my lip. We are so close that my tongue touches his lip, and he groans.

His hand at my back presses me in closer, and my breath catches.

I thread my fingers into his hair and let him have my weight. He shifts slightly, and just as I'm about to climb across the cab of the truck and into his lap, a bang comes at the window beside his head.

Our hot breath has the window fogged up, and I hit my head on the roof as I jump back toward the driver's side.

He rights himself and rolls the window down. A little blond head and a pair of round glasses peers up over the window at us.

"Miss Sophie, can I ride with you next?"

"I don't feel comfortable driving with you as a passenger, but I bet, between the two of us, we could talk Braxton into slinging us around for a while."

"Please, Mr. Braxton," he pleads with his snaggle-toothed lisp.

"Pretty please, Mr. Braxton," I add in my best little-girl voice while batting my lashes at him.

He slings open the door, grabs Beau, and hoists him up into the truck with me.

"Hop in, little man. It's time to get this truck good and dirty."

"Yay!" Beau squeals as I slide over and let Braxton in the driver's seat.

After he shuts the door, he revs the engine and starts spinning the tires.

He slams the truck in gear, and we take off like a shot as mud rains over us like a wave.

Beau cheers with delight the entire time.

Thirty-Seven

SOPHIE

AFTER OUR MORNING ON THE KNOB, WE RETURN TO THE RANCH and have lunch out in the backyard. I look around at this motley crew, and I see true friendship and sincere joy. I watch my aunts flit around, bringing out food and beverages and loving their people in the way they know best, and I realize that Dallas is right; this is perfect. Riding around in the mud with people you genuinely like and eating a good meal prepared by people who love you, getting rest and sunshine and fresh air and just being—it's all joy. Poplar Falls doesn't need more commerce or big buildings to be a great place to live and raise a family. It already has all it needs.

We disperse for a few hours while the boys head out to get some work done on the ranch, and Dallas and Payne take Beau home for a nap. Tonight, we're building a bonfire and grilling out in the meadow behind the barn.

I take the opportunity to place a call to Charlotte.

"Hi, Char. How are things going at the office?"

"Strumming right along. I got the contracts you and Stanhope signed off on over to Gail. Manufacturing started on the new order. By the way, you knocked the watch design out of the park. Justin showed me the first sample yesterday, and it's gorgeous. Lightweight and elegant. I told him I was keeping it and that he had to make a new one for Gail."

"I'm glad you love it. I was nervous that New Yorkers weren't going to dig the vine design."

"It's perfection. It's different and delicate. Oh, and the quill brace-lets went nuts in the precious metals. We've had over five thousand or-ders. That's over seven hundred grand in profit on those sales alone."

"Amazing."

"Your little dream has exploded." She squeals.

"I have new sketches to send you this afternoon, and I uploaded a few new pieces on the website. I have a call with Justin and his team in an hour to discuss what quantities they can fulfill before we go into automatic backorder. I don't want to overload them with Maple and Park's orders going in."

"Those guys are like machines. I talked to him about the possi-bility of them hiring a second and maybe a third shift for the month of November to make sure we can get everything shipped in plenty of time for Christmas. He was on board for that. After this season, we might want to look into expanding their workshop. A birdie told me the space next door might be available to lease after the first of the year. It would be great if we could knock out a wall," she continues.

"I'll have Stanhope talk to Lamar and get the 411," I offer.

The building we lease for manufacturing is owned by Lamar Chessler, one of Stanhope's golf buddies. I wanted both spaces from the beginning, but only the smaller space was open at the time.

"Enough business. What are you up to?" I ask as I settle on the porch with a glass of iced tea and my pad.

"I'm on my way to spin class. Just waiting on the Uber now."

"You are taking a car to your exercise class around the corner? Isn't that counterproductive?" I say through a laugh.

"I don't want to wear myself out before I get there. Plus, I'm crushing on the instructor, and I don't want to walk in all sweaty. He needs to see what this looks like pulled together before he reduces me to a puddle."

"You're ridiculous."

"I know, right?"

"I miss you."

"I miss you too."

"Have fun at spin, and I'll e-mail or call you after I talk to Stanhope."

"Sounds good."

We disconnect, and I take a moment to enjoy the feeling of pride that overcomes me at the success our little business is experiencing. It's more than enough to keep our small workforce employed another year, and we are creating beauty in the world.

I pick up my pad and start to sketch a sparrow as it sings me a sweet tune.

"Oh my goodness, that is huge!" I exclaim as I take in the bonfire.

"That's what she said," Walker retorts and curls his tongue out to his chin as he walks past me with a cooler in his arms.

I punch him in the side.

"That's what he *wished* she'd said," Dallas calls after him loudly.

He laughs. "Give me a couple of hours and a few beers, and I'll be happy to whip it out and show you, Dal."

She makes a disgusted face as we sit in the lawn chairs set up a safe distance from the rising flames.

"I invited Russ tonight. He said he and Trey might swing by later," she says as she opens a bottle.

"That's cool. You like him, huh?"

She shrugs. "I guess. We had a good time the other night, and when he took me home, we made out in the truck for a while before he left. He rounded a couple of bases. It was nice. What about you? How did things go with Trey when he brought you home?"

"Fine. He walked me to the door, and we started to kiss good night until we were interrupted. He called me this morning while we were out at the knob and left me a sweet voice mail."

"Interrupted?"

"Yeah, Braxton was letting Hawkeye out, and he got away from him and came for me. Braxton chased him onto the porch, and it kind of killed the moment."

"He just happened to be letting his dog out at the same time Trey was walking you to your door?"

I nod.

She scoffs.

"What?"

"He was waiting up for you."

"No, he wasn't. He was asleep, and that's why Hawk got away. He wasn't quite awake."

She gives me a look that says, *You cannot be that dense.*

"He was."

"Whatever. He's gotten territorial over you lately. He doesn't act like that. Not even over Elle."

Has he gotten territorial? Yes, he's a little protective at times, but that's just the man in him. I don't think it's jealousy.

I look off to where he and Myer are chatting as they man the grill. He seems so much younger at this moment. Carefree and laughing. His brow is usually creased in concentration or from exertion while he works. Either that, or he's scowling at me. However, right now, he's casual and relaxed. I think it's because the work is done, and both Elle and I are close. There is nothing for him to worry over.

His eyes find me in the firelight, and he smiles. His smiles are rare, but man, it's nice when he grants one to you. A shiver runs down my spine.

"See what I mean? He doesn't look at anyone else like that," Dallas voices her observation of our eye contact.

"Like what? He just smiled at me."

"Like he wishes the rest of us would go the hell home."

That takes my attention from Braxton, and I snap my eyes to her.

"He does not!"

"Uh-huh. You're blind."

"No, I'm not. You're just picking up something that's not there."

"We'll see."

She gives a conspiratorial raise of her eyebrow as she turns her bottle up. I have a sneaky suspicion this is going to be an interesting night.

"Food is ready!" Myer calls out.

"Myer, can you bring Sophie and me a burger and chips?"

"Sure, Dal. Mustard, ketchup, and cheese, right?" he answers.

"And pickles. Thank you!"

As I watch Myer jump to do her bidding, I wonder exactly who the blind one is.

Thirty-Eight

BRAXTON

I'M HAVING A NICE TIME. IT'S A BEAUTIFUL, CLEAR NIGHT. THE FOOD is good. The beer is good. Everything is good. That is, until the Range Rover pulls up.

I grab another beer from the cooler and dry it off with my shirttail.

"Toss me another one, will you?" Walker bellows from his perch on the guitar case.

I snatch another bottle from the cooler and walk it over to him.

"Who are the dudes with Dallas and Sophie?" He throws his chin in the direction of the girls and their guests.

"Russ Eastman and his brother, Trey."

"Russ Eastman? That douche. He was a whiny little pissant in high school. Why are they hanging out with that pair?"

"They ran into them at the rodeo last week, and they took them to dinner and the drive-in last night."

"We just going to allow this?"

I cut my eyes from Sophie to him. "What exactly do you want to do? They're grown women; they can talk to whoever they want."

"No, sir, those are our women, and I will not let assholes objectify them."

I laugh. "I dare you to walk over there and say that to Dallas."

"I will. Right after I finish this here beer," he says as he raises his fresh bottle in the air.

To make the night even better, Lori's red Mercedes pulls in next. I have been avoiding her the last couple of weeks, and I guess her patience has run out.

"All we need now to make the night a complete disaster is for Morgan's Jeep to come down the road," Myer notes.

I look over, and he is shooting daggers at Russ. I guess I'm not the only one sloshing through shit tonight.

I slap him on the back as I make my way over to Lori. "Don't speak that on me, man."

Lori gets out of the car and walks to meet me.

"Hey, stranger," she says as she takes in the scene. "I didn't realize you were having a party."

"It wasn't planned. Just threw it together a few hours ago."

"It's Saturday night, and you aren't answering my texts, so I thought I'd ride out and see if you just weren't getting them or you had other plans. Now, I know."

I feel a little guilty for blowing her off. I'm not even sure why I have been. We've always enjoyed each other and our no-strings-attached arrangement, but something doesn't feel right about it anymore.

"I'm sorry I didn't answer your messages. I'm not sure why I didn't."

"It's okay, Braxton. You and I are just having fun. If you're otherwise engaged at the moment, all you have to do is tell me." She lets me off the hook.

"Come on," I say as I wrap my arm around her neck and lead her back toward the crowd. "Since you're here, you might as well grab a cold one and some food."

I introduce her around and set her up next to Walker with a plate piled high.

I catch Sophie's eye as she watches me hand Lori a beer.

Doesn't look like she's any happier to see my friend arrive than I was to see hers.

Eastman has had his hands all over Sophie. Anytime he can think of a reason to touch her, he does. The night has gotten chillier, and the wind has kicked up, so he takes that as an opportunity to pull her close to him and wrap his coat around her shoulders. He uses his hands to warm hers and then tucks them under his arm.

I want to break that arm off his body and throw it in the fire.

I've tried to keep my attention diverted from that side of the fire, but I can't focus on anything, except for how close he is to her and how she blushes every time he leans in and whispers in her ear.

Last night was the longest night of my life. I sat, watching television, until I saw the headlights from his truck pull into the driveway. I watched from the window as he got out of the truck and opened her door. Then, he walked her, hand in hand, to the front porch. I knew he was going to kiss her, and I just reacted. Before I could think better of it, I woke a sleeping Hawkeye up and opened the door. It took him a second to catch on, but as soon as he caught sight of the lights, he darted straight for her. I followed, and I could see the embrace Trey had Sophie in as I made my chase. That was the first time I wanted to break his arm.

"Braxton, man, you in outer space tonight or what?" Walker snaps me out of memory lane.

"What?"

"Lori here needs another beer."

"I'll get it." I get to my feet and head to the cooler. I look over my shoulder and ask if anyone else needs anything while I'm up. When I turn back around, I collide with something soft.

"Oops, sorry," Sophie says as she grabs my sleeve to balance herself.

"Where are you headed?" I ask her as she hurries past me.

"The barn. I have to pee," she calls over her shoulder as she makes haste toward the barn.

191

I walk the beer over to Lori, who is enthralled by whatever bullshit Walker is spewing.

Then, I look around as everyone chats, and against my better judgment, I decide to follow after Sophie.

As I enter the barn, she is coming out of the door where the toilet is and walks over to the old sink where she washes her hands. She dries them on the leg of her jeans and turns to leave when she sees me and jumps, letting out a little yelp of surprise.

"Oh my God, Braxton, you scared the bejesus out of me."

"Sorry, Princess."

"What are you doing up here?" she asks as she looks behind me.

Looking for you. I don't say it aloud, but it's the truth.

"I'm going to let Hawk out."

"Oh, okay." She starts to walk past me, and then she stops. "Don't let him in the bed with you two tonight," she says.

Then, she starts walking again, and I grab her arm to halt her.

"What's that?"

"Hawkeye. Don't let him sleep with you and her tonight."

I pull her close and whisper in her ear, "You feeling some kind of way about my dog, Princess?"

"Yes. He's my snuggly sleep partner. Not hers."

"Is that right?"

"Yes."

"In that case, maybe you should stay the night with us and not her."

She opens her mouth to say something and then stops as she processes what I just said. She blinks up at me and replies softly, "What?"

"You heard me."

I snake my arm around her back and pull her flush to me. Then, I do the one thing I have been dying to do since this morning in the truck before Beau's interruption. I crash my lips to hers.

It takes her off guard for a second, and she stiffens, but then she melts in my arms and opens to kiss me back.

192

I back us up toward the door.

She whimpers as I press her into the door and disengage our mouths, so I can look down at her.

"This is a bad idea," she says.

"The worst," I agree.

Then, I pick her up at the waist, and she wraps her legs around me. She gasps as our bodies make full contact, and I take the opportunity to enter her mouth again.

I hold her in place with my hips and run my hands up her sides, taking her sweatshirt with them. I pull back from our kiss, and she raises her arms, so I can slide it from her body. Then, I'm kissing my way down her neck to the tops of her breasts. I push the straps of her bra down until it falls free from her. I take one pretty pink nipple into my mouth, and she arches her back, breathing my name into the air.

I move to her other breast, suck it between my teeth, and gently bite down. She moans and starts circling her hips against me. I grow so hard, it's painful. I want so damn bad to slide into her right here against the splintered wall of a dirty barn.

I reach down and cup between her legs, and she softly purrs, "Yeeeesss."

I want to make her feel good. Right now. So, I force my hand into the front of her jeans. She's bare. *Fuck.*

She's slick and ready, so I circle her clit and then give it a little pinch. She bucks her hips into me.

"You like that, Princess?"

She nods.

I coat my finger in her wetness, find her opening, and slide inside her.

"Oh God," she murmurs as she starts moving with me.

That's when we hear the voices. Her eyes fly open.

"Shh." I try to calm her as I slide my hand away from her.

A whimper of protest leaves her mouth as I lower her to the floor. I move a few steps to the side, so I can look out of the door, and I see Eastman and Dallas approaching as he calls out Sophie's name.

She pulls her sweatshirt back over her head and tries to right herself.

I tug her to me and give her one last deep kiss before I tell her, "You're in my bed tonight, Princess. Get rid of him."

Then, I dart off into the barn.

Thirty-Nine

SOPHIE

I HAVE EXACTLY TWO SECONDS TO PROCESS WHAT JUST HAPPENED before Trey and Dallas walk into the barn. I scurry over to the sink, turn it on, and place my hands under the flow.

"There you are. We were starting to get worried," Trey says as they walk fully in.

I take a moment to calm myself down, and then I plant a smile on my face and turn to face them.

"Here I am," I squeak out just a little too loudly.

Dallas raises an eyebrow, and her eyes start flitting around the barn.

"Sorry I took so long. I'm not feeling very well. I think maybe the burger disagreed with me." The lie falls easily from my lips.

Trey gets a look of concern, and I feel a tad bit guilty.

"I ate the exact same thing, and I feel fine," Dallas unhelpfully replies.

"Maybe yours was done better than mine," I say slowly and punch out each word.

She grins. "Maybe."

"I'm sorry, Trey. I think I might have to call it an early night tonight," I offer the apology as I lead them back out of the door. I'm not sure where Braxton ran off to, and I want to get them out of there, so he can make his escape.

"You do look a little flushed," he says as he lays the back of his hand against my forehead. "You're a bit clammy too."

I smile weakly at him. "Nothing a good night's sleep won't cure."

The three of us walk back down to everyone else, and I say my good nights as Braxton comes from the other side of the barn and takes his seat next to his female visitor. I don't like him sitting beside her at all. Walker seems to be holding her attention though, and Braxton's eyes meet mine.

Heat. I feel it all the way to my toes.

I wave one last time to Russ and Trey and to the crowd at large.

Dallas stands to hug me and speaks low into my ear, "Don't think I didn't notice that both you and Braxton were missing for a long-ass time. I wasn't the only one who noticed either. You're lucky I was the one to come looking for you."

I hug her tightly. "Thank you," I whisper back because there is no way to hide it.

She pulls back and gives me a wicked grin. "You have a good night, Sophie." She winks at me and lets me go.

I jog up back toward the barn and straight to Braxton's steps, trying to stay tucked into the shadows.

I grab the key from the flowerpot I have seen him use before to let myself in. Hawkeye yaps and comes galloping at me from his spot on the floor.

I bend and scoop him up. "Shh, calm down. Your daddy will be home soon, and he'll take you out."

He licks my face, and I sit him down. I remove my boots and jeans and make myself comfortable. I curl up in nothing but my sweatshirt to wait for Braxton, and I fall fast asleep.

I awaken by a hand sliding up my leg. For a second, I forget where I am and start to kick it away.

Then, I hear Braxton's low voice. "Easy, Princess. It's just me."

I relax and curl back into the pillow I'm hugging and close my eyes.

"Oh no, you don't. I was going out of my mind out there, waiting for everyone to leave, knowing you were up here."

"Mmm," I respond as I start to drift back into la-la land.

Then, I feel a tongue in the dip of my low back, and it starts to slowly trail its way up my spine. His hand glides over my bare hip, and he gently turns me till my back is against the bed. I blink the sleep from my eyes and look up into his handsome face.

"Hi," I whisper.

"Hi."

"You took long enough."

"My apologies. I had to make sure the fire was put out properly and get all the riffraff sent home."

He's already changed into his lounge pants, and his hair is damp.

"You showered."

"I smelled like smoke. Didn't want you to have to sleep next to that all night."

"That was thoughtful."

"I have my moments."

I snake my arms around his neck and lace my fingers through his hair.

He hesitates for a moment, and then he bends down and presses his lips to mine. I immediately open to him, and he deepens the kiss. He nips at my bottom lip and then gently soothes it with his tongue. His weight shifts fully on top of me, and I wrap my legs around his hips as he settles between them. I'm completely exposed to him. There is nothing between us but the thin material of his sleep pants and my panties, and I can feel every hard inch of him. He laces his hands into the hair at the side of my face and kisses me hard as he thrusts his erection against me.

I reach between us and undo the tie to his pants. "I want to touch you."

He bears up slightly to give me room, so I can dip my hand in.

"Fuuuuuck," he groans.

AMBER KELLY

I tug his cock loose, and his pants slide down his hips. I wrap my hand around him and slide down his length and back up again. He grows harder in my hand.

He lets me play for just a moment, and then he stands and drops his pants to the floor. I sit up to watch as he steps out of them. Then, he puts a knee on the bed, grips the hem of my sweatshirt, pulls it over me, and tosses it on the floor. I lift my hips, and he slides my panties down my legs and flings them.

He prowls back up my body and puts his mouth on my shoulder where he gently bites down. I drag my nails down his bare back in response, and he kisses a trail down my collarbone to my breasts. He kneads one as he laps at the other. Then, he moves down to my belly button where he dips his tongue as I thread my fingers into his hair and tug. He continues his descent until his mouth is right there.

I watch as he lifts my right leg and wraps it around his shoulder, spreading me wide. Open completely for his viewing pleasure. I'm too turned on to be the least bit embarrassed. His hot breath feathers over me, and I shudder with anticipation.

He brings his thumb to my clit and starts to run lazy circles around it. Each one shooting an aching sensation up my spine.

"Braxton," I beg because I need more.

He dips his head to where I need him. He runs his tongue from my opening to my bud, and then he sucks it into his mouth. My hips come off the bed to meet his mouth, and he starts lapping at me. It's amazing. I start moving my hips with his mouth, and it feels so damn good. He slides a finger inside me as he continues to lick at me and then another. He pumps his fingers in and out as he curves them to hit the exact spot I need.

I grab on to his head and hold on as he brings me to the edge, and I tumble off. His name is on my lips as I fall.

When I recover, he moves back up my body. His lips coated in my taste, he takes my mouth again in a hungry kiss.

"You're beautiful, Princess," he says as he sits up and looks down over me. Then, he reaches in the drawer of the nightstand, pulls out a foil packet, and tears it open with his teeth.

He comes up onto his knees, and I watch as he stretches the latex over himself. He's at my entrance a moment later, and he pauses, waiting for permission. I grab his ass and bear up to bring him inside me. His tip enters, and I moan as he slowly rocks forward until he fills me completely. *There it is.*

He moves inside me, and it feels exquisite. I lock my left leg around his waist, and I thrust my hips up to meet him as he pushes inside me deeper and deeper until I'm screaming his name into the dark room as I climax again.

"Oh, yes, Braxton!"

He quickens his pace until he lets out a cry of his own. I wrap my arms up under and around to grip his shoulders and hold on until he finishes and collapses on top of me.

We lie there in a sweaty, entangled mess while we catch our breath until we hear loud scraping at the bathroom door, followed by rapid-fire barking.

I burst into laughter, my face buried in his neck as Hawkeye tries to claw his way to us.

"Calm down. I'm not hurting her, Hawk," he yells down the hall.

"I'm good, Hawkeye. I'm very, very good," I call reassuringly.

Braxton looks into my eyes and gives me one last, long kiss. Then, he hops up and heads for the bathroom. As soon as he opens the door, Hawkeye shoots past him and straight for the bed. He puts his front paws up and peeks over the edge at me, waiting for permission to get up with me.

"Just a minute, Hawk," Braxton says as he returns to the living room, sans the condom. He slides on his pants and picks the puppy up and walks to the door. "We'll be right back. Don't fall asleep."

He grabs the leash, and they walk out the door.

I roll over on my side, and a feeling of euphoria rushes over me, quickly followed by a sense of panic.

I just slept with Braxton. Shit. I just slept with Braxton.

I snatch the cover at the end of the bed and pull it up over me.

What now? Should I get dressed and go back to the house? I look around for the rest of my clothing and freeze when the door opens again.

He takes me in with the cover pulled up to my chin, my distress obvious.

"I leave you alone for five minutes, and you're already overthinking," he says as he reaches down to release the puppy from the leash. Amusement in his voice.

He picks Hawkeye up and drops him on the bed next to me. Then, he plants his arms on the bed on either side of my body, caging me in. "Relax."

He takes his hand and tugs at the blanket as I tightly grip it up under my chin.

He smiles and plants a loud kiss on my lips. "Relax, Sophie," he gently demands again.

I let out a breath and let go of the blanket. He pulls it aside and slides under it with me. I watch as he stacks pillows behind his back and turns the television on. He side-eyes me until I settle in next to him. Hawk tottles up between us and turns in a circle a few times before he lies down. Braxton wraps his arm around the two of us and scoots us closer to him. I give in and lay my head on his chest.

"You done freaking out?" he asks once I settle.

"Probably not," I admit.

I can feel his silent laughter through his chest.

Asshole.

Forty

SOPHIE

I WAKE UP, CURLED INTO BRAXTON'S BACK. MY LEG IS SLUNG OVER HIS thigh, and my arm is around his middle. I'm wrapped around him like a burrito. I scooch closer to him and let his warmth seep into me. I slide my hand down his abs and find his morning erection tucked against his stomach. I take a moment to peek over his shoulder and have a look. Last night, it was dark, and I was in a blissful haze. It's an impressive sight. I stroke the length of him with one fingertip, lightly grazing him with my nail. His cock twitches, and he stirs. I halt my finger and wait. I think he's still asleep, and I continue my exploring when he suddenly clasps my wrist and yanks me over him as he turns.

I'm now flat on top of him. I fold my arms and rest my head on them. He opens one eye and looks at me. My nose is resting on his chin.

"Morning," he greets as he slowly runs his hand up and down my back.

"Good morning," I whisper.

I caress the inside of his calf with my big toe as I gaze at his face.

"Now what?" I ask into the silence.

"You ask that a lot."

"I just like to know where I stand."

"It's too early for hard questions, Princess."

"Is it a hard question?"

"It's not an easy one."

"Yeah," I say as I look away.

"Tell you what. Let's enjoy at least another hour in this bed and then get some food in us before we have a serious conversation. Can we do that?"

I consider it and decide. "We can do that."

"Good."

I slide off to his side and snuggle into him. He kisses the top of my head and runs his fingers into my tangled hair.

I drift right back to sleep.

I wake back up to Braxton's hands on me, and he finally lets me explore in the daylight. I decide that whatever this is, I'm just going to enjoy it. I'm only here for another week. There is no reason to try to define something that is going to be over so quickly.

We shower together. Then, I dress and wait once again for my aunts to leave for church before I sneak down to the main house.

Emmett is sitting in a rocking chair on the front porch, whittling a piece of wood, when I tiptoe up the steps.

He grins without looking up from the knife. "Good morning, Sophie. I take it, you enjoyed yourself a nice long walk this morning." He spoon-feeds me my alibi.

"I did."

"That's nice."

I take a seat on the chair beside him and rock. "I wasn't really taking a walk."

"You don't say."

"I'm an idiot, Emmett."

"Oh, I don't know about that. Seems to me you're just done fighting a losing battle."

"I am?"

"You and Braxton have been circling each other for weeks now. I'm just surprised it took this long for me to find you sneaking across the lawn."

I blush from embarrassment. "You don't think badly of me?"

He looks up and meets my eyes. "Think highly of you, Sophie. Think highly of him as well. Always have. Why would that change just because you finally started thinking highly of each other?"

I lean over and kiss him on the cheek. "Thank you, Uncle Em." I use my old nickname for him for the first time since I arrived back in Poplar Falls.

It earns me a teary smile just as Daddy walks out the front door.

"Ah, Sophie, I was looking for you."

"You found me."

"The attorney called this morning, and he'll be home Wednesday. He scheduled the will reading for Friday morning."

"Okay."

"I know you have a life to get back to. We appreciate all your help around here the last few weeks."

At that, I stand. "I guess I'll go make some airline reservations."

I make my escape before I burst into tears. Never in a million years would I have guessed it would be hard to leave this place, but now, I wish time would slow down. I'm not ready for Friday.

I stop by the kitchen and find a plate of food on the stove with a handwritten note from my aunts, saying they didn't want to wake me. I make myself a cup of coffee and carry it up to my—*Aunt Doreen's* room. I check my phone, and I have a ton of missed calls and messages from Dallas.

Call me.

You'd better call me as soon as you wake up.

You'd better call me the second you finish what you're doing once you wake up.

CALL ME, DAMN IT.

I hit her number and call before she storms the farmhouse.

"It's about time," she says in way of a greeting.

"I called as soon as I got to my room."

"Well?"

"Well, what?"

"Don't pull that with me. How was it?"

I sigh. "It was nice."

"Nice? Nice? I'm on my way over."

"What? Why?"

"Because I can't read your face over the phone, and I know good and damn well it was better than freaking nice."

"All right. It was better than nice."

"Too late. I have my keys. I'll be there in twenty. Be ready."

The line goes dead.

Grr.

I make a call to Mom as I wait for Dallas. She's so relieved that I'll be home by the weekend. She's been growing more and more distraught, the longer I stay in Colorado.

Elle is downstairs when I hang up with Mom.

"Good morning," she greets as she types away on her laptop.

"You working on something new?"

"Yes. I'm working on a research piece about climate change and the truth behind carbon footprints."

I consider her before determining. "You have a heart for environmental causes."

She thinks about that for a moment. "I do. Which is strange. I have always wanted to move off to the big city and live this glamorous life, but I think we can do that and still protect the planet for future generations. Something so simple as using a washcloth instead of a paper towel or using white vinegar to clean our homes instead of a harmful chemical spray, which creates a cloud of poison that floats up into the atmosphere, can make a huge difference. It might take a little more elbow grease to get the job done, but isn't it worth it? We are all so concerned with convenience when we should be more concerned about the state of the world we are passing on to our babies."

"I couldn't agree more. Tell you what. Once you finish this paper, send it to me. I'd like to read it, and I'll have my stepdad read it. He is on the board of several environmental charities in New York, and I bet he can answer a lot of questions or put you in contact with someone who can help you."

"Really?"

"Yes. It's essential to start making the right connections now. Then, you work hard and finish school. After you graduate, he might even be able to help you get on at a paper or magazine or an independent organization in New York, Chicago, or Denver. He works with people all over the world."

"You'd do that for me?"

"Of course."

She leaps from her spot on the couch and throws her arms around me. "Thank you, Sophie."

"Don't thank me yet. You still have to do the work, but I believe in you."

I hear a throat clear behind us.

"Braxton!" She disengages from me and runs to her brother.

"Did you hear? Sophie believes in me, and she's going to help me."

"I heard. That's awesome."

He gives me an appreciative look over her shoulder. He loves his little sister so much. It's written all over him.

Forty-One

SOPHIE

DALLAS MAKES IT TO THE RANCH JUST AS THE AUNTS PULL IN from church. Madeline, Elle, and I decided to make lunch. We're just pulling the chicken casserole out of the oven when the front door swings open, and their excited chatter fills the house. That's one thing I'm going to miss when I return home. All the noise of a house full of people. When I first got here, I hated it. I was so used to the solitude of my one-bedroom apartment that I never realized how lonely and quiet it actually was.

"Something smells divine," Aunt Doreen says as they make their way into the kitchen.

"We thought we'd make lunch today. Madeline taught me how to make a chicken casserole," I state proudly.

I can't wait to show Charlotte all of my newly acquired culinary skills. I bet she's never eaten a casserole in her life.

Dallas sidles up to my side and speaks under her breath, "After lunch, you spill."

Then, she grabs a plate and starts to load it up.

A few minutes later, and we are joined at the table by Daddy, Emmett, and Braxton.

"How was your night last night, kids?" Aunt Doreen asks as she passes the green beans to Braxton.

Dallas props her elbows on the table and focuses on Braxton. "Yes, Brax, how was your night?"

"Fine, I guess," he answers without looking at either of them.

"I bet it was," Dallas comments as she shoves a forkful into her mouth.

I kick her under the table.

"Ow, did you just kick me?"

"Sorry," I bite out as I shoot arrows with my eyes that are pleading for her to shut up.

"You guys must have been out there late. I could still see the flames rising over the barn when we turned in, and you look a little haggard, dear," Aunt Doreen continues as she assesses Braxton.

Dallas nods as she chews. Then, she points her fork at him. "She's right; you look like you had a long, sleepless night there, Brax. Something keep you up all night?" She feigns concern.

She's like a dog with a bone.

He gives her a pointed look. "Nope. I slept great. Better than I have in a long time."

She raises an impressed eyebrow. "Really?"

"Really."

"Well then." She gives me an impressed smile.

My aunts look at each other in confusion over their odd exchange, and Emmett just grins at Braxton like a proud father. I want to crawl under the table and hide.

I quickly try to change the subject. "Daddy told me the attorney set the reading for Friday morning. That means I'll be heading home soon. We need to spend some more time this week going over the computer program."

The room as a whole goes silent.

Aunt Ria places her hand over mine on the table. "We're not ready to think about you leaving us yet. These last few weeks sure have flown by."

"They have," I admit sadly.

"You'll come back for Thanksgiving and Christmas, won't you?" Elle asks.

"Um, I haven't thought about it. I suppose I could. I've always spent Christmas in the city while Mom and Stanhope are in the Bahamas."

"The Bahamas?" Daddy asks.

I look up, a little stunned he's even paying attention to our conversation.

"Yes. They rent a house on the beach. They fly down the week before and stay through the New Year."

"Why?"

I don't actually know why.

"It's just what they've always done. I guess New York gets so crowded with tourists during the holidays, it's usually bitterly cold, and business slows down that time of year, so they choose to spend it in the islands where it's warm and quiet."

He throws his napkin on his plate and roars, "You mean to tell me that you've been spending every single Christmas by yourself all these years?"

I wince. "Not every single one. Just since she and Stanhope have been married."

"How long's that been?"

"They were married the summer before I graduated high school."

The table goes quiet as my words echo around the kitchen.

"Fourteen years," he mutters as he shakes his head.

"It's not as bad as it sounds. I have some friends in the city."

"Stop it. Don't defend her. All these years, I thought ..." He stops and looks me in the eye before he continues. Then, he changes his mind, gets up from the table, and storms out of the kitchen.

Madeline gets up and follows him.

"That's not Christmas, Sophie. Christmas is a time for family. We're all so busy year-round, and it's a time to slow down and spend quality time with each other, celebrating the birth of our Savior and another year of bounty that the good Lord has blessed us with," Aunt Ria says softly.

"I'm sorry. I didn't mean to upset anyone," I start.

"He needs to process these feelings." I look to Emmett as he speaks, "He's been guilty of turning a blind eye to things for long enough."

Embarrassed, I tell the table, "My mother loves me. I've always been welcome to go along, but with school and then work, I just couldn't."

"Oh, honey, no one is questioning Vivian's love for you," Aunt Doreen consoles.

Dallas grabs my hand under the table and holds on while we finish our meal in silence.

Daddy and Madeline never returned to finish lunch, so we wrapped their plates and cleaned the kitchen.

Dallas and I decide to spend the afternoon taking Beau to a pumpkin patch about an hour outside of town.

On our way to her house to pick him up, she starts the interrogation.

"Are you going to tell me about last night or not?" she blurts out as soon as the truck hits the road outside of the ranch's gate.

"What exactly do you want to know?"

"Every single detail."

I spend the next fifteen giving her a blow-by-blow account of the night, starting from when Braxton followed me into the barn and ending with him kissing me senseless this morning before I snuck back over to the house.

"Wow," she breathes.

"I know."

"I can't believe you've been in town a little over three weeks and already trapped *the* Braxton Young in your snare. That's some impressive shit."

"I haven't trapped anyone. We are just enjoying each other's company; that's all."

She gives me a pointed look.

"Okay. Really enjoying each other's company," I admit.

"From hate to love. It's a tale as old as time," she muses.

I spit coffee across her dashboard. "We are not in love," I sputter as I try to dry the mess.

"That's right; it's hate to 'enjoy' each other." She air-quotes the word *enjoy*.

I roll my eyes at her. "I'm pretty sure the only reason he pursued me at all is because he knows I'm leaving soon, and there is zero chance of me expecting more than a fling."

"Do you though, only expect a couple of nights of sex, and that's it?"

"Well, yeah. I don't know how I could expect more."

"So, you'd be completely okay if you came back for Christmas and Braxton and Morgan were happily married and her belly was swollen with his baby?"

"Christmas is only a couple months away, Dallas. Unless she's already carrying his seed, that's impossible."

"You know what I mean."

I consider her question, and the truth is, I would be devastated. *How did I let myself catch feelings for him?* I need to get out of Poplar Falls and back to my real life as soon as possible.

Forty-Two

BRAXTON

I FIND JEFFERSON LOADING THE TRAILER WITH CHAIN SAWS AND straps. Everyone gave him a wide berth after he stormed off during lunch, but the boys just showed up for our foray into the woods to cut firewood for the winter.

"You all right?" I ask as I pick up one of the saws and lay it in the truck bed.

"Fine," he grunts as he lifts another one on.

"Talk to me, old man," I push.

He removes his hat and wipes his brow. "I just thought she was living a good life. That her momma married a rich man, who gave them both everything they ever wanted. Everything I couldn't give them. And to hear that my baby girl has been up there, spending Christmas all alone all these years, while I'm here, surrounded by a huge, loving family … fuck. No wonder she hates me."

"I don't think she hates you, Jefferson."

He places his hat back on his head. "Well, she should. I hate myself enough for both of us."

He slams the tailgate shut and walks off.

I don't know the story of what went down with Jefferson and his first wife. I don't even think Aunt Madeline knows the whole story; however, I think Sophie deserves to know, but I don't get a chance to voice my opinion before the rest of the boys show up.

We return hours later with a trailer full of logs. It takes a lot of wood to run the fireplaces in the farmhouse and my loft as well as the wood we go through while building bonfires. Every fall, we stockpile as much as we can, so we don't have to go back out during the cold, wet winter months.

We get the logs unloaded, and Jefferson and Emmett head up to start cooking the ribs for supper while Walker, Silas, and I start splitting logs and chopping up the wood to stack in the woodshed.

"Jefferson was grumpier than usual today," Silas points out as he swings his ax at the stump in front of him.

"Damn near took Emmett's arm off with a chain saw too," I agree.

"Did he find Sophie in your bed this morning?" Walker asks.

I slide my eyes to him. "I don't know what you're talking about."

"Don't play that shit with us. I saw the way you were staring a damn hole through Trey last night. I'm surprised the boy didn't spontaneously burst into flames."

"Yeah, and then you disappeared into the barn after Sophie. We tried our damnedest to keep him from going looking for her. Even Dallas tried. When he said he was going to check on her and make sure she was okay, Dallas jumped up and offered to look herself, but he trailed after her," Silas adds.

I keep loading logs on the stump and hurling my ax.

"And, when Chloe and I went to leave, there was a light on in your apartment. We could see someone moving around up there. Seeing as Lori had left right before us—"

"Enough," I cut Silas off.

"What are you doing, Brax?" Walker asks, a look of concern on his face.

"I have no idea," I admit.

He nods. "Not that I blame you. She's smoking hot and fun as hell, but I'm smart enough not to touch Jefferson's daughter."

"Like you had a chance." Silas smacks him in the ribs.

"Nobody does against this handsome devil." Walker grabs my chin and starts making kissy noises at me.

I push him off, and he starts laughing.

"I have an ax in my hand, dumbass," I warn him.

"Seriously, does Jefferson know you have sleepovers with his girl?" Silas asks.

"I don't know. If he does, he hasn't said a word to me. I think Emmett knows though."

"If Emmett knows, Jefferson knows, and so do Ria and Doreen," Walker notes.

"We're adults," is all the explanation I offer.

"Are you a couple now?" Silas asks.

"No," I answer honestly.

"Fuck buddies?" Walker interjects.

"No."

"What then?" he asks the million-dollar question.

"She goes back to New York in a few days. Until then, we are what we are."

"You just going to let her go back without a fight?" Walker asks incredulously.

"Of course I am. She lives there. Her business is there."

"But you wish she'd stay," Silas guesses.

"Wouldn't matter if I did."

"Have you considered telling her?" Walker asks.

"No."

"Maybe that's something she'd like to hear," he suggests.

"Why? To make it harder for her to leave? I'm sure Doreen and Ria are going to make her feel bad enough."

Walker opens a bottle of water and shrugs. "There's always Morgan."

"Or Lori," Silas adds.

"Nah, I took care of Lori for him last night," Walk says with a wink before downing his water.

Dallas's truck pulls up around three p.m., and Sophie emerges with a sleepy Beau in her arms. She has her hair pulled through a green-and-pink camouflage ball cap and her face full of green and pink paint that looks like a butterfly mask. She's so damn beautiful. They disappear into the house.

"Hey, Brax. Can you guys come unload these for us?" Dallas bellows from the driveway.

Walker and I make our way to the truck and look inside the bed.

"Damn, did you guys leave any pumpkins for the other patrons?" he asks as we take in the massive haul.

"We went a little overboard. It turns out, Sophie is as good at telling Beau no as I am."

"Looks like you guys had fun," I say as I start grabbing pumpkins and setting them on the porch.

"Sophie sure did. Do you know she hasn't been to a pumpkin patch since she left Colorado? She said that some churches in the city truck in a bunch of pumpkins from upstate, sell them on their lawn, and call it a pumpkin patch. Isn't that pathetic? It hurt Beau's little heart to hear it, and he made it his mission to do every single thing Smithfield Farms had to offer, so Miss Sophie could do it. Wore himself out." She shuts the truck. "Those are all of Sophie's."

Walker looks at the massive collection of pumpkins in every size and shape that litter the porch. "What's she planning to do, pack them in a bag and take them on a plane with her?"

Dallas shrugs. "Beats me. I reckon she just wants to enjoy them as much as she can the next few days. Thanks for the help."

Forty-Three

SOPHIE

WE HAD A BIG DAY. THE PUMPKIN PATCH WAS SO MUCH fun.

"Look at this one, Miss Sophie! It's as big as my head," Beau exclaimed as he picked up a tiny pumpkin from among the others and raised it for me to see.

"It is, and look at your muscles. You're so strong," I praised.

"Momma, can I have this one?" he asked.

"Yes. Add it to our wagon," Dallas said as she walked through the patch. Between the three of us, we filled two wagons with pumpkins.

We got ourselves lost in a corn maze, picked three baskets of apples, had our faces painted, rode a tiny train around the orchard, and ate our weight in both apple cider and pumpkin-flavored doughnuts before I paid for our treasures as Dallas loaded a sleepy Beau into his car seat. Two burly teenagers packed our wares onto the truck with the crate of pie pumpkins we had picked out for Aunt Doreen earlier.

We drove around for a while, enjoying the fall foliage, while Beau napped. The Colorado mountains sure were beautiful this time of year.

"I'm exhausted," I say as I lay the sleeping child on the couch. I collapse beside him and close my eyes.

"Beau is a handful. He can wear you out," Dallas says as she walks in the front door.

AMBER KELLY

"You look all wide-awake and alert over there. I don't know how you do it."

"I'm used to it. He's been running me ragged since he learned to walk. Besides, some of us got plenty of sleep last night, and some of us didn't."

"Touché."

"Are we going to carve pumpkins tonight?" Beau asks as he eats his grilled cheese sandwich at the table.

Aunt Doreen and Aunt Ria are teaching Dallas and me how to make pumpkin pies from scratch. I'm covered with flour and rolling out dough as she checks the pumpkins that are roasting in the oven. Aunt Doreen is scooping the roasted flesh from the ones that have cooled, and Ria is mixing the eggs, milk, and spices.

"We can do it when we get home tonight," Dallas answers as she pulls the pan from the oven.

"You can do it here," I say as I lay the dough across the pie pan and trim.

"It'll be messy."

"I can get the boys to put a tarp down in the front yard," Aunt Ria offers.

"I've haven't carved a pumpkin in twenty years. I don't think I even remember how."

"See, Momma? Miss Sophie needs me to teach her how to do it," he pleads.

"Are you sure? That means, you guys will have two more mouths to feed at dinner again." Dallas looks at Aunt Doreen.

"Jefferson is smoking ribs out on the grill. I'm making my broccoli casserole and mac 'n' cheese."

"Yay! Mac 'n' cheese!" Beau approves of the menu.

Dallas looks over at him. "What do we say to Miss Doreen?"

"Thank you, Miss Doreen," he says through a mouthful of grilled cheese.

"After you swallow, baby," she scolds.

"Sorry, Momma." He grins at her.

Daddy and Emmett cooked a mess of ribs and slathered them with Emmett's homemade barbeque sauce.

"These are amazing," I say as I lick the sauce from my fingers.

"Can I have another one, Miss Sophie?"

I look over at Beau, who is covered in sauce. It's on his nose, his chin, both hands, and even in his hair. I grab another rib from the center of the table and plop it on his plate.

"The secret ingredient is cherry soda," Emmett whispers to me through the side of his mouth.

"Can I know the other ingredients?" I ask.

"I'd tell you, but I'd have to kill you," he says with a wink.

"I've been trying to get him to tell me for years," Aunt Doreen says as she nudges me with her elbow.

"All done." Beau raises his sticky hands in the air. "Can we carve pumpkins now?" he asks Dallas.

"As soon as everyone else is finished. We haven't had pie yet."

"But I'm full of pie," he whines.

Aunt Doreen kept sneaking him bites of pie filling all afternoon.

"We have to wait for everyone else to have theirs," she tells him.

He deflates, but he doesn't argue with his mother.

"I can eat pie later," I say, and he smiles. "If you think you can talk Braxton and Walker into getting us that tarp before they have dessert, you and I can get started."

"Please, Mr. Braxton," he begs with his little sauce-covered hands folded in a prayer under his chin.

"You got it, little man. Go let Sophie wash you up, and we'll meet you around front."

"Yay!" He leaps from his spot at the table and runs toward the house.

I get up to follow him, and I get him washed up. Daddy gives me an old, raggedy sweatshirt to wear.

By the time we make it out front, Braxton and Walker are spreading the tarp in the drive and helping to bring our larger pumpkins down to the yard.

"Ew, look, Miss Sophie!" Beau pulls his hand from inside his pumpkin, and with it comes a bunch of clumpy goo covered in seeds.

"Yucky." I fake disgust, and he giggles.

I draw a firefly on the front of a giant, oblong pumpkin and carve it so that its tail flickers with a candle lit inside.

"Damn, that's gorgeous," Dallas praises when I'm done.

"Whoa, Miss Sophie, that's a big bug with wings. Cool!"

"It's a firefly," I tell him.

"What's that?"

"You've never seen a firefly before?"

"No."

"Colorado doesn't have fireflies," Dallas informs me.

"Well, they are these tiny beetles that come out at night, and as they fly, their butts glow, so other beetles can find them. When there are a bunch of them together at once, the entire park looks like stars are twinkling close to the ground. It's pretty amazing."

"Wow," he says. "Momma, can we visit Miss Sophie and see their glowing butts?"

"Maybe we will one day, but for now, we have to help her get all this mess cleaned up and get you to bed. Someone has had a big day, and he has school tomorrow."

"Me?" He points his thumb into his little chest.

"Yes, you," she says as she starts to tickle him, and he curls up on the tarp in a fit of laughter.

"You guys go ahead. I'll get Elle or the boys to help me clean all this up. You need to get him home and in a bath."

"Are you sure? I hate to carve and run."

"I'm sure. Just load him and your jack-o'-lanterns and get on the road."

"I'm leaving mine here," Beau says.

"You are?"

"Yes. I made it for you." He picks up his hacked-up pumpkin and hands it to me.

"I love it so much. Thank you."

"You can take it home with you, so you'll remember me."

I tap him on the nose. "As if I could ever forget you, Beau Stovall."

Forty-Four

SOPHIE

AFTER ELLE AND I CLEAN UP MOST OF THE MESS WE MADE OUT front, Braxton takes a hose to the tarp, and he and Emmett put it away. I place the pumpkins on the steps leading up the porch and add candles, so they glow.

Braxton comes, sits on the first step, and watches as I light the last one.

"Thank you for helping," I say as I close the top.

"Well, I was promised pie."

"Is that right?"

I stand and start up the steps. He wraps his hand around my calf to stop my progress.

"Where are you going?"

"I'll be right back. Stay here."

I run inside, and Aunt Doreen and Madeline are in the kitchen.

"Where are the pies?" I ask as I grab a fork from the drawer.

"In the refrigerator on the back porch," Aunt Doreen answers.

"Thanks."

I grab a pie and a can of whipped cream from the refrigerator and walk back through the kitchen. They watch me the entire time, but neither asks what I'm doing.

I make it back out to the front porch, and Braxton is right where I left him.

I take a seat beside him and remove the foil from the top of the pie.

Then, I shake the whipped cream can and spray small circles on top of it. I set the can down and turn to Braxton. "Your dessert, sir."

He takes the pie from my hand and holds it as I stick the fork right in the center and dig in. I take the big bite and moan as I chew.

His eyes never leave my mouth.

I dig in again, and this time, I turn the fork for him to take the bite. He does, and I smile as he swallows.

"You like it?"

"Uh-huh," he replies.

I take another bite, and he brings his hand to the side of my face and swipes a tiny bit of the cream from the corner of my mouth. Then, he licks his finger.

I imagine him licking whipped cream off other body parts, and a shiver runs through me. He notices.

He sets the pie aside. Then, he twists to pick me up from my seat and plants me in his lap. I'm straddling him, and his hand cups my ass and moves me against him.

I gasp.

He brings one hand up, fists it in my hair, and pulls me to his mouth. Then, he runs his tongue across my bottom lip, and I plant my lips on his.

I don't know how long we kiss, but at some point, I feel him grow hard beneath me, and I start moving my hips against him, bearing down harder and harder to feel the friction I need.

He finally can take no more and halts my movements by gripping my hips.

I let out a little cry of protest, and he stands with me in his lap and picks me up.

"What are you doing?"

"Taking you to bed." He starts walking to his front door.

"Braxton, they're going to see us." I look back at the light coming from the kitchen window where I can still see Madeline and Aunt Doreen moving around.

"Don't care," he says as he takes the steps two at a time.

He grabs the handle, opens the door, and kicks it closed behind us. In a few long strides, he has me tossed on the bed and is over top of me.

He undoes his jeans, and then he sits on the bed and pulls me on top of him. We are nose-to-nose, and he reaches between us to my jeans and pops the button. He seals his mouth to mine. We are in the exact same position as we were on the steps. Me straddling him, except this time, his cock is free, and he's unzipping my pants.

His hand finds me, and I lean back to give him full access.

"Wet for me," he groans as he slides his finger in my entrance and then another.

"Right there," I breathe as he starts pumping in and out.

I move against him until he hits the exact spot I need, and I ride his hand.

"That's it. Look at me, Princess. I want to see your face as you come."

I give him my eyes, and I try to focus on him as the first wave hits me, but I close my eyes and lean back further, so I can get him deeper. He brings his thumb to my clit and strokes, and I tumble over the edge as pleasure overtakes me.

"Beautiful," he murmurs as I come down from my high.

Then, he bucks his hips and twists until I land on my back on the bed. He tugs my jeans down my legs, and a moment later, he is inside me.

He takes his time. Building me up and then bringing me back down. He leisurely makes love to me. He kisses my forehead, my eyes, and my nose. He nips at my earlobe, and it drives me wild. I want him to go faster and harder, but he controls the pace.

When I can finally take no more, I demand, "Harder, Braxton. I'm so close. I need it harder, baby."

He dips his head and bites at my nipple, and I buck off the bed. Then, he grins.

"Yes, ma'am."

And he finally starts drilling into me until my toes curl as the sensation shoots from my core, and I scream his name into the room. He arches his back as he releases with me.

We lie there, naked, me against his chest, and he plays with my hair in the darkness.

"We probably shouldn't have come up here while everyone was still awake," I say as I try to figure out how I'm going to explain where we ran off to.

"You started it on the porch," he accuses.

I raise my head. "I did not. You pulled me into your lap, remember?"

"Yeah, but you're the one who pulled that whipped cream stunt."

I did do that.

"I was trying to feed you your dessert," I say innocently.

"You were trying to tease me, Princess."

"Are you going to miss me when I leave?" I blurt out of nowhere.

He considers me for a second.

"Never mind. I shouldn't have asked that."

I try to hide my face from him as mortification washes over me for putting him on the spot.

He lifts my chin with two fingers and looks at me. "I'll sure miss your pie." He grins.

I grab the pillow at my back and smack him with it as he laughs while I struggle to pull back and strike him again.

He snatches the pillow from my grasp and asks, "What about you? Are you going to miss anything around here?"

"I'll miss lots of things. I'm going to miss the hell out of Huckleberry and Hawkeye," I tease.

He flips me to my back. "That damn dog trumps me every time."

He kisses me again, and I proceed to show rather than tell him how much I'm going to miss him. Then, we finally let a very put-out Hawkeye out of the bathroom, and he settles in with us.

I wake up with his arms around me, and I feel his morning erection on my backside.

"What time is it?" I ask as he slides his hand around to caress my breast.

"Early. I have to get out to the cattle."

"Oh," I say as I back up and push myself closer to him.

His hand travels down between my legs, and I spread for him and open myself in invitation.

He finds my opening and gently slides into me, making love to me from behind.

"I like having you in my bed in the morning," he says as he buries his face in my neck.

"Me too," I manage to get out before I spasm around him.

He lies with me a little longer before he gets up, and I hear the shower start. I drift back off to sleep.

When I wake up again, Hawkeye and I are tightly tucked in, and there is a fire dancing in the fireplace. I'm warm and comfortable and satiated. I pull Hawk closer and snuggle his little body.

I finally get up after sleeping in the longest I have since I arrived in Colorado. I take a quick shower and dress, and then I look to make sure the coast is clear and head toward the house.

I get about five feet from Braxton's steps when Daddy and Emmett emerge from the barn.

"Sophie?" Daddy calls, and it sounds like a question.

I squeeze my eyes tightly closed and pray that I will just disappear. No such luck.

I slowly turn to face them.

"Good morning," I mumble.

"Ain't it though?" Emmett replies as he places a calming hand on Daddy's arm.

Daddy looks from me to Braxton's steps and back again.

"Well, got to go. Lots of work to do today. I'm teaching Aunt Doreen how to run payroll later. You guys have a good day out, doing whatever it is ranchers do all day," I spew and then awkwardly salute them before I turn and jog toward the house.

My heart is racing as I make it to the porch where Aunt Ria is rocking as she reads.

I calmly walk up the steps, and as I pass, she says, "I cleaned the pie and whipped cream from the porch this morning before anyone else was up."

I stop and turn to her. "I'm sorry I left a mess."

"That's all right. We just don't want to attract ants. Next time, you take it on up to Braxton's and put it in his fridge, and then you'll have breakfast for the morning," she says casually without looking up from her pages.

"Yes, ma'am."

I text Braxton to let him know about my run-in with Daddy and Emmett as I left his apartment. He didn't respond for a couple of hours, and then all I got was a thumbs-up emoji. *I've been freaking out all day, and that's all he has to say?*

I spend the majority of the afternoon in the office with Aunt Doreen, going over the computer one more time. She gets flustered, and we finally have to call it a day.

"I think I can do it well enough," she says as I close everything down.

I don't have much confidence in her "well enough," but there is nothing I can do about it.

"I'll just have to call you if I get stuck."

I imagine her calling me a couple of times a day, every single day.

I ride into town with Elle, who is meeting her friends for lunch at the diner. Dallas is working, so I wait till her shift is over, and she and I pick Beau up and go shopping for Halloween supplies.

"Sophie, I'm telling you, they all already knew," she says when I finish telling her about my morning.

"No, they didn't. Aunt Ria figured it out when she found our mess on the porch, and you should have seen Daddy's face."

"Okay, so maybe Jefferson didn't know, but the rest of them knew. Nothing happens in that house without the aunts knowing."

"I'm so embarrassed," I groan.

"Why? If it were me having all the hot, sweaty sex with Braxton Young, I wouldn't be embarrassed."

"Because … I don't know why. I just am."

"Whatever. At least the cat's out of the bag, and you can spend your final nights with him."

That is a plus.

Beau picks out his Halloween costume from a selection at the general store. It's the cutest little Batman suit and mask.

"Momma is going to be Robin. Miss Sophie, will you be Batgirl and go trick-or-treating with us?" Beau asks as we make our way to the register.

"I'm sorry, Beau, but I don't think I'm going to be here for Halloween."

"But you have to stay. You want to see me dressed up, don't you?" he asks as his face falls.

"You can try it on for me tonight," I offer as I kneel, so I'm face-to-face with him.

"I can't put it on before trick-or-treating."

"Why not?"

"'Cause then it won't be special."

"Trunk-or-Treat is Saturday night at the church. They do it the weekend before Halloween. That's the trick-or-treating he's talking about," Dallas informs me as she joins us with their purchase in hand.

"In that case," I turn back to Beau and whisper excitedly, "I'll still be here. Let's go pick out my Batgirl costume!"

His face lights up. "Yay!"

He grabs me by the hand and leads me back to the racks. They don't have a Batgirl costume, so I purchase the exact same mask and cape as he did. I'll wear it with the black dress I brought from home.

I'm getting all kinds of firsts in before I leave.

Forty-Five

SOPHIE

FRIDAY CAME FAST. WHEN I FIRST ARRIVED IN POPLAR FALLS, I couldn't wait to leave, and now, I'm sad because it's almost time to go.

"The will reading is what time today?" Mom asks over the line.

"Soon. We're leaving for the attorney's office now."

"Who all is we?" she asks.

"All of us. Pop, Daddy, Madeline, Aunt Doreen, Aunt Ria, Braxton, and Elle."

"Us. You're part of an us now?"

"Mom, please don't."

"I was just pointing out how, a few weeks ago, it was them, and now, it's us."

"They're just words, Mom."

"When is your flight home? Stan and I will pick you up at the airport."

"Sunday evening. I think I land at nine p.m., but I'll double-check with Charlotte. She made my reservation."

"Sunday? Why aren't you flying home tonight?" she whines.

"Because, Mom, tomorrow is the Halloween Trunk-or-Treat at the church, and I promised Beau I would be Batgirl."

"Excuse me, what?"

"Trunk-or-Treat. They do it the Saturday before Halloween. Everyone parks in the church parking lot, and they dress up and decorate their trunks. The kids dress up and go from car to car, trick-or-treating. It's a safe alternative."

"Who's Beau?"

"Dallas's son. I told you about him, remember? He's going to be Batman, and I promised to be Batgirl and trick-or-treat with him."

"I see."

Aunt Ria calls to me from downstairs.

"Mom, we're leaving. I have to go."

"All right. Call me when it's done. I love you, my onliest only."

We disconnect, and I clasp my necklace around my neck and race down the steps.

Everyone is waiting in the driveway, and I climb into the truck with Pop and Daddy and Madeline.

We all assemble in the office of Dennis Phillips and wait for him to join us. Once he does, he flies through the niceties and gets straight to business.

"Okay, folks, we are here for the formal reading of the last will and testament of one Mrs. Betty Sue Lancaster. I have requested the presence of all of you here today because each of you is mentioned in Mrs. Lancaster's will. I have a letter that she wished for me to read to you all."

He waves a sealed envelope in the air. Then, he takes a letter opener from his desk and slides it open. He clears his throat and begins to read aloud.

Dear family,

I guess if Dennis is reading this to you, I'm in heaven and my Lord has taken me by the hand. Now, I don't want you all to be sad for me. I'm seeing glorious sights right now as I stroll down the streets of gold, arm in arm with my Savior. I'm sure I'll only get a quick look around before you all join me. Remember, with the Lord, a day is like a thousand years.

Now, on to the good stuff. You girls divide up my jewelry. Be fair and don't fight. The thing that mattered most to me was my wedding band, and I'm assuming it's in the ground with my remains. As far as everything else, Pop gets everything in our accounts, and my share of the ranch will be divided equally among the other seven of you.

Donald, my sweetheart, you were the greatest love of my life. Greatest pain in my ass too, but I wouldn't have traded a single minute of our life together. I'll keep your side of the bed warm in our mansion in glory. Don't be in a hurry to join me, sweetheart. I'll be here when you get here.

Maria and Doreen, your momma loved you with her whole heart, but you know that. I am so proud of my girls.

Madeline, Braxton, and Elle, you're as much a part of this family and my heart as anyone else seated here today.

Jefferson, my stubborn boy, you've been walking around with half a heart for so long. It's time, son. You've protected Vivian long enough. Tell Sophia the truth. Don't spend one more minute of your life with that chain of regret holding you hostage.

Sophia, oh my precious girl, I'm sorry it took my passing to bring you home, but you're here now. Listen to him, baby girl. It's time for forgiveness.

Now enough of this, I want you all to go live your lives and love each other well until we meet again.
Gram

He finishes, and then he folds the letter. He returns it to the envelope and gives it to Pop.

We all sit there in silence and let her last words sink in.

I don't understand any of it.

"What did she mean, it's time to stop protecting Mom?" I ask to the room in general.

"Sophie, darlin', we should talk about this when we get home," Daddy whispers without looking at me.

I take him in, and the room at large. My aunts' grim demeanor and looks of concern scare me. What could they possibly be hiding?

Panic starts to overtake me. My chest is tight and I can't catch my breath.

I decide I don't want to know. I want to leave. I want to get on a plane and go home where things make sense.

I stand and start toward the door.

"Miss Lancaster, I need your signature," Mr. Phillips calls after me.

"No, you don't. I don't want it. I don't want any part of her shares. I don't want the shares I have. I just want to leave."

I open the door, and I run from the building. I pull my purse up on my shoulder, and I sprint across the road. I have no idea where I am or where I'm headed. I just know I have to go.

I get to the next corner before I hear footfalls behind me. I try to keep running, but I can't. I'm lost and out of breath. I turn and throw my hands up in front of me just as Braxton makes it to my side.

"Don't," I yell as he reaches for me.

"It's okay, Sophie," he says carefully.

"No, it's not okay. I don't want to hear it. Whatever it is they think I need to know about my mother, I don't want to know."

He steps closer and takes my bag from my hand. "Why?"

"Because I'm scared."

"Of what?"

"Being angry with her too. She's all I have," I admit before I crumple.

He wraps me in his arms. "That's not true. Not anymore."

I bury my face in his shirt, and I sob.

He holds me while I let it all out. "Come on, let's go home."

When we walk into the house, Madeline is in the living room. She stands as I enter and starts to speak.

"Don't," I say as I raise my hand to halt her words. "I don't want to hear anything you have to say. My mother is not the villain here. You are," I spit my vile at her.

She lowers her head and says nothing as I move to pass her.

"Sophia Doreen, you apologize to her," I hear Daddy's command as he enters from the kitchen.

"No. Why should I? You replaced us. You threw Momma and me away, and you replaced us with her."

"You be angry with me, darlin'. I deserve it. I will take it. But this is her house, and you will show her respect."

I turn quickly and mutter the words, "I'm sorry."

The truth is, I have grown to like Madeline these past few weeks. It's confusing to both love and hate someone at once.

I turn, and with my back to her, I continue addressing Daddy, "I *am* sorry. I'm going to get my things. I should have never come back here. It was a mistake. I don't know what I expected. An apology, maybe an explanation. Something. Perhaps I just wanted to see what was so good about them that you would want them instead of me. And I get it now. They're great. Your family is great."

I run up the stairs to my room and start packing. Braxton follows, stands in the door, and watches as I toss everything into my suitcase.

My phone keeps ringing, and I'm sure it's Mom or Charlotte wanting an update, but I just don't have it in me to talk to them.

"You want to sleep at my place tonight?" he asks.

"I'm going to go to the airport and try to book an earlier flight to New York," I say in answer.

"Running away?"

I turn on him and hurl my anger in his direction. "What's it matter to you if I am? You and your sister and your aunt can have this place. You can have him. I'm done."

He walks in and picks my bag up off the bed. "Okay. Have it your way. Take your ass back to New York and hide. I'll drive you to the airport myself, but first, you're going to sit your ass down and hear what Jefferson has to say."

Forty-Six

BRAXTON

WE WALK DOWNSTAIRS, AND I LEAVE SOPHIE IN THE LIVING room and go in search of Jefferson after she reluctantly agrees to sit down with him before leaving. I have no idea what secrets he's keeping, but they need to clear the air before she walks out that door.

I hear yelling from the backyard, so I follow the voices.

"You need to tell her the truth, Jefferson. It's time," Doreen demands.

"I don't see the point. It's only going to hurt her. Let her be mad at me."

"For goodness' sake, stop playing the martyr. That girl has been hurting her entire life because of the lies. She deserves to know. Maybe if she does, she can finally move past it."

He throws his mug against the side of the house, and it shatters into a million shards.

"You mad?" she yells.

"You're damn right, I'm mad."

"Well, so am I. You didn't just cut her out of your life. You cut her out of all our lives, and we're not having it any longer. She is our flesh and blood, and you're going to darn well start treating her that way, or so help me, you are going to be fending for yourself all alone out here on this ranch."

"What good would it do now? You saw her face in that office. She doesn't want to know."

Jefferson, Aunt Madeline, Doreen, and Ria are in a standstill on the back deck.

"She needs to know the truth, Jeff," Doreen iterates.

"I can't change what happened back then, and I don't want to cause her any more pain."

"She's spent her whole life in pain, and you have the power to do something about it."

"She's leaving," I announce, and they all turn to face me.

"She's been up there, packing. I told her I would take her to the airport, but she had to face you first. It's now or never, old man. I don't think she'll ever come back here if she leaves without answers."

"Maybe that's for the best," he says.

"Best for who? You?"

"Son, you don't know …"

"You're right; I don't know. But the man she thinks you are is not the man I know you to be. Doreen is right; she is hurting. She's shut herself off so much that she thinks that sitting home alone on the holidays is perfectly normal. She's content in isolation because no one can hurt her there." I point an accusing finger at him. "That's your fault."

His face falls, and he stands there, facing us all.

"It will hurt; you're right. But she's been so confused all these years. She thinks you abandoned her, Jefferson. That you didn't love her. It's time to tell her. She deserves the chance to start forgiving, and maybe she'll finally be able to heal," Aunt Ria gently pleads.

"I know you thought the only person suffering was you, being painted the bad guy, but can't you see how we all have suffered? Sophie most of all," Doreen adds.

"It has to be you, sweetheart," Aunt Madeline encourages. "She needs to hear it from you."

He lifts his eyes to meet mine, and he focuses behind me. I see the moment he surrenders as his eyes fall on Sophie.

"I'll be on the front porch," she murmurs.

He nods, and I follow her.

Forty-Seven

SOPHIE

I TIGHTLY HOLD BRAXTON'S HAND AND LET HIM LEAD ME TO THE porch, Daddy follows a few minutes later and sits in a rocking chair.

Braxton turns me to face him and lets go. He cups my face with his hands. "Hear him out. It can't be worse than what you already imagine in that gorgeous head of yours."

I nod, and he kisses my forehead. I take a seat on the porch swing, and he grasps Daddy's shoulder for a moment before he walks back inside.

We sit in silence with nothing but the crickets and tree frogs groaning around us.

Finally, he leans his elbows on his knees and starts to speak, "That year was a hard one for us. There was a severe drought throughout the county, and as a result, wildfires ravaged the mountainside. One took out over half our grazing pastures and most of our cattle. Pop and I saved what we could, but it spread too fast, and we had to fight it with all we had just to save the house and the barn. Some of the ranches west of us lost everything, including some lives, so at the end of the day, we counted ourselves lucky. Lucky but in dire straits. We had no steers to take to auction that year. We lost our best heifers. We knew it was going to take years to recover, if we recovered at all.

"So, when a Hollywood scout showed up at the door one after-noon, looking for a location to film for a big motion picture that was in production, we had no choice but to accept. They paid us a decent sum of money for the use of one of the grain silos and a few acres of land off the backside of our property line. They were going to be here for eight weeks. Eight weeks, and he promised we wouldn't even know they were here."

I vaguely remember the fires but not the severity he's describing.

"I hated the thought of them on our land. I hated them trampling the fields, cutting back trees, and littering our space with trailers and campers and equipment. It was a nuisance, but Vivian, she loved it all. She was always enamored with Hollywood. She liked to sing and dance, and she was fairly good at it—as far as her little bit of experience at the local town theater. She was always on the piano, practicing for some production they were putting on."

He gets a far-off look in his eyes.

"She had the sweetest voice. I loved to come home and hear her singing in the kitchen."

He looks back at me. "She was vulnerable. I should have paid better attention, but Pop and I were so preoccupied, working sunup to sundown, trying to repair the damages as much as we could ourselves. Once you were off to school, she would spend her entire day down there, watching the goings-on with the filming. Then, it got to where she wasn't picking you up at school on time or doing anything at the house. One day, I happened to be coming to the barn for some tools—I can't remember what exactly—and Mrs. Martin was pulling up with you in her car. You had been sitting at the school for over two hours, waiting for your mother to pick you up, and finally, she brought you home when they couldn't get anyone to answer the phone at the house."

I recall that day. I was so embarrassed that my teacher had to bring me home.

"You were upset. You had sat there for hours. I got you inside, and your mother was nowhere to be found, but I knew where to look for her. I got you settled, and I headed for the filming location. When I got there, it looked like they had finished up for the day. A few people were milling around, and I asked for the director. They pointed me to a trailer that I assumed was his office. I stormed in to ask if he had seen your mother."

He stops for a moment as pain crosses his face. He focuses his eyes on the porch floor.

"He knew where she was all right, and it wasn't an office. It was his personal trailer. They were in his bed together. In the act. I lost it and flew into a rage. I pulled him off of her, and I beat the man. Beat him bad. She kept screaming and trying to get me off of him, but all I could see was him defiling my wife. My love."

He takes a deep breath.

"I dragged her from the site. Told them to pack up their gear and get the hell off my land. Your mother wasn't even remorseful. She was angry. She told me that they were in love and that he was going to take her to New York and make her a star. He was full of shit. He saw a pretty, naive girl, and he took advantage.

"The film crew packed up the next day and headed out. I sat and watched until the last truck pulled out. Then, I went to the fishing cabin for a couple of nights. I needed to clear my head, and I didn't want to lash out in anger, not in front of you. I needed a little time to calm down. I could forgive her. I loved her that much. She broke my heart, and I was furious. But I could forgive her, and that was what I came to tell her when I found the note you'd left for me. She had packed the two of you up in the middle of the night and taken off."

He stops his trip down memory lane there and waits. I let his story rattle around in my brain.

Fragments come to my memory. The film crew leaving abruptly. Mom's frantic state that night. Daddy's odd fishing trip in the middle of the week. All of it.

"Sophie, sweetheart, say something."

"She lied to me," I whisper.

Forty-Eight

SOPHIE

I STAND FROM MY SEAT ON THE SWING AND WALK OVER TO HIM.

"Daddy, why didn't you come for me?" I ask as I sit in the rocking chair next to him.

He stares off into the night sky for a few moments, carefully choosing his words. "I tried. Once she got you to the city, it was hard to track you down. That director fella—Patrick Stone was his name—he had moved you two into an apartment. He, uh, was worried about the scandal of it all. See, he had a wife and two kids back in California. He tucked you and your mother safely away in New York and paid me a visit a few days later. He threatened to press charges for the assault, and he threatened to sue Pop and Rustic Peak for breach of contract because I'd forced them to leave before the eight weeks was up. We had already used some of the funds they had paid for sod and to do one of the major fence repairs, and we needed the rest to pay the lean we had against the ranch and purchase new heifers and just survive for the rest of the year. I couldn't pay him back, and I didn't even have the money to fly to New York to get you and fly us both back. My back was against the wall. He knew it.

"My plan was to come and get you after the next season. By then, I was sure he was going to shake Vivian loose. He was only keeping her up to try to hush everything until after his movie released."

"You never came."

"I did. Once. Your mother met me in the city, and she came without you. The director had cut her off, just as I'd predicted, but she had moved on and was seeing some wealthy businessman. She was so happy and full of light that I hadn't seen in years. She begged me not to take you from her."

"And you just walked away?"

"I did. I knew that man could give you two a life I couldn't. I was a broken man back then. I wanted to get myself together, and I did. I met Madeline and fell in love again. She's a good woman. By the time I planned to come visit you and try to mend fences, the accident happened, and we took the kids in. Things were hectic, and then time passed. Too much time. So much time that I thought it was better for you if I just stayed out of your life because if I came back around, I was going to have to tell you some hard truths, and I thought it was better you hate me than your mother," he says.

"Why?"

"Vivian is codependent. I knew she had married a couple of times, and I didn't know if the current one would last. She needed you. She needed you to believe in her."

"But I needed you."

Pain passes his eyes as he explains, "I failed you. I was still trying to take care of and protect Viv. I guess I have been all these years. Even now." He shakes his head in disbelief.

"Your mother was the most beautiful woman I'd ever seen. I still remember the first day I met her. She came to the door, selling fresh eggs from her parents' chickens. She was wearing this simple yellow cotton dress, and her hair was in a braid. She took my breath away. I think I fell in love right then and there. Pop wouldn't buy her eggs because we had chickens of our own, so I kept sneaking out and meeting her at the gate to buy a couple with my own money each morning just so I could see her. Gram made me eat eggs for breakfast, lunch, and supper, but I didn't care. The days were better when they started with her smile. You have the same one."

He looks over to me with a soft expression.

"I'd have done anything back then to make her smile, and when the time came, I even let her go to see it."

"I don't understand."

"She didn't belong here. She had to escape this life. Our life. She was suffocating here. Did I like the way she did it? No, ma'am. Hurt like a son of a bitch. Coming home and finding my girls gone. I knew that man was no good and was just going to use her up and spit her out. But she had stars in her eyes and wouldn't listen to reason, and I had to stop trying to hold on to her. She was like a caged bird. Every day, she grew a little bit sadder, and it broke my heart to see her light fading. I loved her so much, and I wanted to keep her forever, but I couldn't."

I look around the porch as a light wind kicks up, and the tinkle of the wind chime dances in the air. "I can see that. Mom is too much personality for this place."

He nods in agreement. "I think you and her have that in common."

"I don't know. I was happy here with Pop and Gram and Emmett and you. I hated leaving. I missed Dallas and my horse. I was so homesick. Don't get me wrong; I love the city now. I love my life there, but this feels like home too."

"You are the best parts of both your mother and me. You have her curiosity and thirst for adventure and my stubborn attitude and appreciation for your roots." He looks over at me with tears in his eyes. "I think that makes you pretty special, sweetheart."

He takes a deep breath.

"She loved you too, you know. Anytime I brought you up, she would fall apart. Like even thinking about you was too painful. I thought you'd broken her heart, and that was why. After a while, I stopped mentioning you."

"She did love me but not enough to stay. Love is defined by choice. If there were only one option, then you are just that—the only option. Choosing to love another person in spite of all the other options available … that's the part that makes it special. That's the part that makes it all worth it. I chose her, but she didn't choose me. That's our love story in a nutshell."

Forty-Nine

SOPHIE

DADDY AND I SIT AND ROCK FOR A LONG TIME WITHOUT SAYING anything.

"I forgive you, Daddy," I finally say into the darkness.

He reaches over, takes my hand, and squeezes it tightly, and I see a tear roll down his cheek. I don't think I've ever seen him cry before.

"You're going to have to forgive her too, darlin'." He motions toward the headlights that are coming down the driveway.

A black SUV pulls in front of the porch. The back door opens, and my mother steps out.

"How?" I ask.

"I called her this morning when you bolted from the attorney's office. She got on the first flight she could."

Mom speaks to the driver, and he pulls an overnight bag from the hatch and sets it on the step. Then, he returns to the truck and pulls away.

Mom stands in the drive, watching the taillights fade off, and then she turns and brings her eyes to mine. She is a mess. Her eyes are puffy, and her nose is bright red. Vivian Marshall is always put together. I don't think I've ever seen her so distraught.

"Hi, Mom," I say.

She looks up and smiles. "Hi, baby," she replies carefully. "Jefferson."

He stands and walks down the steps toward her. "Hello, Viv."

She bursts into sobs as soon as her name leaves his lips.

He wraps her in his arms and whispers soothing things into her hair. Words I can't make out, words that are private, just between them.

Once she has better control of herself, he lets her go. He picks up her bag and carries it up the steps. He stops and looks down at me, waiting for permission. I nod that I'm okay, and he walks into the house.

She stands in the drive, wringing her hands for a couple more minutes. Then, she musters the courage to come up and take a seat beside me.

As she sits, Braxton comes barreling from the front door. He looks down at me.

"You all right?" he asks as Daddy comes up behind him and clasps his shoulder.

I smile up at him. "I'm fine."

He looks at my mother and back to me. "Are you sure?"

"Yes, Brax, I'm sure. We'll be inside in a minute."

Daddy tugs at his shoulder, and Braxton reluctantly backs into the house.

"Brax?" Mom asks.

"Braxton Young. He is Daddy and Madeline's nephew."

"He seems … intense."

"That's one way to describe him."

"Is he the reason you have stayed all this time?"

"One of them," I admit to her and myself.

"Sophie, I love you—" she starts.

I interrupt, "I've never doubted that, Mom. But that's not the point. You lied to me. You have been lying to me my entire life. You let me feel unwanted. You let me hate him."

"I know."

"Why?"

"I didn't want you to hate me because I was the one who had done the terrible thing to your father. Because I was selfish and scared of losing you."

"None of that makes it okay."

"I know."

"I'm angry, so angry, with you right now."

"I deserve that, but I hope you can forgive me, Sophia. You're my onliest only, and I can't lose you. Please."

"You'll never lose me, Mom. But you can't make me be who and what you want me to be. You can't manipulate me any longer."

"I won't. I promise. Just come home, and I'll make it up to you," she begs.

"You can't. You can't make up for the twenty years I lost with Daddy. You can't bring Gram back and give me back those missing memories."

I take a deep breath and make a decision.

"I'm not going back to New York."

"What? Sophia, please. What about your apartment and your business? You can't give all that up because you're angry with me."

"I'm not going to give anything up. I'll figure it out. Charlotte and I have been handling things just fine the past month, and they need me here now that Gram is gone. They need help running the ranch."

"You're punishing me," she whispers.

"No, I'm not. I'm just righting a wrong. You stole time from me, Mom. New York is wonderful, and there's so much to appreciate about it, but it can feel cold and unfriendly sometimes. I stand on a street teeming with thousands of people, and I feel lonesome. I've had this sadness living inside me all these years that I didn't understand. Now, I do. New York is not home. Not for me."

Her head falls in her hands.

I get up, and I kneel in front of her chair. I take her hands in mine, and she looks down at me.

"You're not losing me. I'll be flying up to the city all the time. I'll still have to be in the office for meetings, and I'll visit. Besides, if I give up my apartment, I'll have to stay with you and Stanhope or Charlotte when I do."

"You'll stay with us," she insists, and I know I have her.

"Okay. I'll stay with you."

"Promise that you won't stay out here and fill your life with all these people and forget me." She sniffles.

"My heart is big and roomie, Mom. It doesn't have to be you or them. Not anymore. I have enough to go around. It's a well that won't go dry if other people drink from it."

She wraps her arms around my neck, and we hold each other for a long while.

"You know, I think you'll find you needed to be released from the weight of these secrets too," I say over her shoulder, and she nods.

Braxton and I drive Mom to the hotel in town. On the way, she grills him about his age, his responsibilities on the ranch, if he wants to get married one day, and if he wants children. He's polite, but I know his patience is running thin by the time we drop her at her room.

On the ride back to the ranch, I get lost in my thoughts as I stare at the countryside passing by the window.

"Penny for your thoughts," he says into the silence.

"Just trying to figure out how I'm going to break the news to Charlotte that I'm staying in Poplar Falls."

"So, you've decided for sure?"

"Yes, at least for now. Aunt Doreen can use my help, and I think Daddy and I need more time. What do you think about me staying?" I bring my knees up onto the seat and turn to face him.

"Are we having a real conversation?" he asks as he slides his eyes to me.

"It doesn't have to be if you don't want it to be. I just need to know how to proceed from here. I know that what started between us happened when we both assumed I'd be gone in a few weeks. I don't want you to think I expect anything from you."

"What do you want, Princess?"

"I really don't expect …"

"I didn't ask what you expected. I asked what you wanted."

"I know I want to wake up, curled up with Hawkeye every morning," I tease.

"That damn dog, always stealing my girl." He pulls over on the side of the highway, and he pulls me into his lap. "I guess I'll just have to learn to share."

Then, he brings his lips to mine and kisses me breathless.

"If you're planning on waking up there every morning anyway, you should probably go ahead and move your stuff in. It'd be easier than trying to sneak back to the house every day." He chuckles.

"I think they know," I whisper.

"They might have a clue," he confirms.

"You think there's room enough for us both?"

"If there's not, I'll build you another room. I'll build you a studio. Whatever you need, we'll figure it out."

I grin. "Would you be willing to install a bathtub?"

"I bet you could persuade me."

Epilogue

BRAXTON

"You and Sophie coming to the house for supper tonight?" Jefferson asks as we finish herding the cattle back into the newly fenced pasture.

She's been moved in for a little over a month now. She flew back to New York over Thanksgiving to see her mother and to pack up the rest of her belongings. She took part of the money in the account Gram had set up for her all those years ago and repaid Stanhope the money he had invested. Then, she made Charlotte an official partner in Sophia Doreen Designs. The two of them run the business together with Sophie taking on a more creative role and Charlotte running the office in New York. Their little business venture is booming, and since Sophie took the financial reins of Rustic Peak, the ranch is thriving too. We were able to purchase more heifers for the year, and we should have an amazing calving season. We even hired a few extra hands, and Sophie hired Dallas to help her in the office. Not that they get much done together, but it allowed Dallas to quit her part-time job at Butch's Tavern and Beau to have his momma tuck him in every night.

"Nope. I have plans for us tonight."

"Did you tell Doreen? You know how upset she gets when you two are missing, and she was expecting you." Emmett winks at me over Jefferson's shoulder. "I'm going to wait in the truck while you two figure this out."

We watch as he hops in the passenger side of Jefferson's truck.

"I did. I called her this morning."

"Good. Well, you two have a good night."

He starts to walk to the truck, and I call after him, "Jefferson?"

I don't know why I'm so nervous.

"Yeah?"

"I need to ask you something," I say as I reach in my pocket and pull out the box that has been tucked there all day.

I made the mistake of showing it to Silas and Walker yesterday, and the two have been giving me shit ever since.

"I have this for Sophie, and I'm going to give it to her tonight."

I open the box to show him the ring inside. It was my mother's. Nothing fancy—just a simple diamond in a simple setting.

He looks at the box and then to me. "You ready for that? It's only been a couple of months since she showed up here in Poplar Falls. You sure it's not too fast?"

"Six weeks," I say as I look down at the ring.

"What's that?"

"Six weeks. That's how long it took Dad to know that he wanted to marry Mom and to put this ring on her finger. It only took me four."

He nods his head, and a smile graces his face.

"I'm ready if she'll have me and if I have your blessing."

"My blessing? I couldn't have asked for a better man for my Sophia. You've been my son since the day God brought you and your sister to our doorstep. I'd be awfully proud for you to make that official."

"Are you ready yet, woman?" I ask as I round the hall and see her sitting in the closet floor rifling through a pile of clothes.

I look around at the mess. It's been a tight fit since Sophie moved all her things into the loft. Women sure come with a lot of extra stuff.

"I'm trying to find my brown scarf. I swear I packed all of my scarves in one box and I can't find them now," she huffs in frustration.

I reach down and pick up a brown wool scarf and hold it out on one finger for her to see. She looks up and blows a piece of stray hair from her face and mumbles, "Thanks," as she grabs it.

"You're welcome. Now, can we go?"

She stands and wraps the scarf around her neck.

"I promise I'll get this all sorted eventually. I need to throw out almost everything and only keep the essentials."

She looks over at the shelf of shoes and sighs. I follow her eyes.

"You aren't getting rid of those," I state matter of fact.

Her eyes snap to me.

"You made fun of me for wearing this very pair when I first got here," she reminds me as she lifts a pair of nude stilettos.

"I did. They're impractical as hell, but I didn't say they weren't sexy," I say as I pull her to me.

She places the shoes back on the shelf and turns in my arms.

"Well, I have to give up something because all of my stuff and I don't exactly fit."

"We'll make it work," I say as I kiss her lips, "now, let's go. I'm getting hungry."

"Where are we going anyway?"

"It's a surprise."

We walk out into a clear but cold December night. She starts toward the truck, but I wrap my arm around her waist to steer her in the direction leading behind the barn.

"We're walking?" she asks in disbelief.

"It's just a short distance. I promise."

I tuck her into my side and we walk down the back of the ranch through the forest of trees and toward the river. About twenty minutes later we make it to the spot. It's a clearing on a hill that overlooks the water. A fire is crackling, and picnic basket rests on a quilt along with an ice bucket and two champagne flutes. She untangles from my arm and walks toward the site. Then she turns around and beams at me.

"What's all this?"

"Your Christmas present."

She looks confused for a moment before her eyes go soft.

"It's perfect."

She doesn't understand, so I walk over and take her hand and lead her to the blanket. I spin her to face out toward the valley and the water below, wrap her in my arms, and rest my chin on her shoulder.

"I wanted our first supper in our new kitchen to be special," I whisper into her hair.

"What?" she breathes.

"Pop and Jefferson gave this parcel to us. We are standing in what will be our kitchen with huge bay windows so we can look at this view every morning. I'm going to build you a wraparound porch, so you sit out here all you want and sketch, and your new closet will be able to hold all the sexy shoes you can buy."

"You're going to build us a house?"

"Yes, ma'am."

"With a bathtub?"

"Oh yes, can't forget the Princess's bathtub," I tease.

"It *is* perfect," she chokes out on a sob.

"Not quite yet," I say as I hear the rumble approach.

She hears it too and turns to look back toward the trees. We hear laughter and then Beau's impatient voice loudly whisper, "Now, Mommy?"

"Now, baby," Dallas answers as she plucks him down from the four-wheeler.

He releases the excited puppy in his arms, and Hawkeye shoots off like a rocket in our direction.

I reach down and scoop him up as Dallas gets back on the machine and pulls Beau up into her lap. She winks at us, and they drive back off into the trees.

I turn to Sophie, and she watches me closely. Her eyes are full of amusement and question.

Hawk is squirming in my arms, and she reaches for him as he leaps. He starts licking at her jaw as she giggles. Once he finally settles, she notices the red bow and box around his neck.

"What's this?" she asks as she starts to untie it. She sets Hawk down and opens the lid. She gasps and turns back to me with shock written all over her face.

"I know it's not much, and we can get you another one if you want, but it was my mother's, and I think she'd like for you to have it," I say as I take the ring from the box and lower to one knee.

She gasps.

"Sophia Doreen Lancaster, I know it seems fast, but I'm a man who knows who he is and I don't need a lot of time to ponder when I know something is right. I love you, and I want to spend the rest of my life loving you. If you'll have me."

I slide the ring on her finger, and it's a perfect fit.

Tears immediately fill her eyes, and before I can get another word out, she launches herself at me. I catch her as we both tumble onto the blanket.

"Yes, yes, yes …" she starts repeating over and over as she peppers my face with kisses and Hawkeye jumps up and down around our heads yapping, trying to get in on the action.

She finally stills as I settle on my back with her on top of me.

"You chose me," she whispers.

I nod, and she continues.

"I choose you too, forever."

She presses her lips to mine as a symphony of hoots and whistles from beyond the trees fills the air around us.

The End

BOTH
of Me

Prologue

Gabby
Four Years Old

I AM GETTING ALL DRESSED UP LIKE A PRINCESS.

Papa and Mamma are expecting company for dinner tonight, so Nonna has dressed me in my prettiest dress. It is purple, and it has yellow butterflies on the front. Purple is my favorite color.

I twirl and twirl until I am dizzy.

"Hold still, so I can finish your hair, Gabriella," Nonna scolds.

She helps me get my shoes on as she explains that the Scutari family just moved two estates down from us. Mr. Scutari is in the same business as Papa. He and his three boys—Emilio, Atelo, and Christoff— as well as their grandparents are coming to meet us all tonight, and Papa wants me and my brothers to be on our very best behavior. She holds my hand and leads me downstairs.

"There is my *bambina*." Papa reaches out for me, and he picks me up and spins me around as I laugh with glee. He turns, and I see a group of people huddled in the foyer.

"Say hello to our new friends, Gabriella. This is Papa's friend Mr. Scutari and his boys and their grandparents."

"Hi." I wave shyly and lay my head on Papa's shoulder.

They all say hello in return, and Papa shows us into the dining room where Mamma and Nonna are placing food in the center of the table. My tummy growls loudly, and everyone laughs.

"My baby girl is always hungry." Papa smiles down at me as he places me in my seat between Nicco and one of his friend's sons.

I sneak a peek up at the stranger. He has long, dark hair that falls into his face. His eyes are dark green, and when he smiles down at me, he has a dimple in his cheek, just like Nicco.

"Hey, I am Christoff."

"Where is your mamma, Crisscross?" I ask.

"No, Chris-toff," he repeats.

I wrinkle my nose. That's what I said.

I mimic him, "Criss-cross."

He laughs, and so does Nicco.

"Gabriella, he said Christoff, not Crisscross. Crisscross would be a silly name."

"I didn't say Crisscross. I said, Criss-Cross," I state in aggravation.

"You just said it again."

"I did not."

Nicco is always mean to me, and he always tries to embarrass me.

"It's okay," Christoff whispers to me. "You can call me Crisscross if you want to."

"I don't want to call you that. People will laugh at me. I want to call you Crisscross."

Nicco laughs out loud again, and I don't understand what is so funny.

"It can be a thing just between you and me, okay?" he says. "I'll call you"—he scratches his head—"Gabby. You call me"—he stops, and his forehead crinkles like he is thinking—"Cross. What do you think?"

I look up into his green eyes, and I smile.

"Nicknames just for us?"

"Yes, ma'am."

I smile big at him. He is so nice. I think we will be the bestest friends ever.

Cross's papa tells us that his mamma was in an accident, and she is with Jesus and the angels now. His mamma's parents came to live with them afterward to help. I look up at Cross, and when his papa talks about the angels, his lips quiver. He is sad. I would be sad, too, if my mamma went to live with the angels and did not come visit me. I will have to love him extra hard for her, so he is not sad anymore.

After dinner, the adults have yucky coffee while we all enjoy dessert that Cross's grandmother, Una, made. Then, they excuse themselves. Nicco looks to Cross and asks if he wants to ride bikes, and I ask if I can come, too.

"No, you can't even ride your bike without training wheels." He rolls his eyes.

I start to get upset because I want to go with them. I don't want to stay while the older boys play video games and the grown-ups talk in the study.

Why can't I go?

"Tell you what, Miss Gabby." Cross bends down and looks me in the eye. "Next time I come over, I will help you learn how to ride without training wheels. Then, you can always go with us. Deal?"

"Okay," I say through my tears.

He wraps one of my curls in his finger and tugs. "Don't cry. We will have lots of time to spend together now that we live just down the street. I promise."

"Cross your heart?"

"Cross my heart." He slashes his fingers over his heart and winks at me as he follows Nicco out the back door.

I think he might be my prince, just like Cinderella. Prince Cross.

CHAPTER
One

Brie

Present

As I step off the plane into the hustle and bustle of LAX Airport, anxiety kicks in. This is real. I am doing this. I left everything and everyone behind to begin again three thousand miles away from home.

I follow the horde of rushing travelers through the packed airport and into a surprisingly empty restroom. I look in the mirror at the weary face staring back at me. My chestnut eyes are slightly bloodshot, and my long, dark locks are a tangled mess from sleeping over half the flight from JFK. I splash some cool water on my face and run my fingers through my unruly hair. I pinch my cheeks and add a quick swipe of gloss across my lips. I take one last moment to gather myself. It's as ready as I am going to get.

I give myself a pep talk as I walk down to baggage claim to collect my luggage. "You can do this. You are Brie Masters. You are a single girl from the big city, here to experience life outside of your hometown bubble while finishing your degree." I work hard to convince myself as I grab my bags from the belt and head out into the warm California sun.

I take a deep breath to calm myself. Calm is something I haven't felt in a very long time. I am not exactly sure what Los Angeles has to offer a broken soul like me, but it has to be better than what I walked away from. It just has to be. Starting over is not something I thought I would be doing at twenty-two years old, but here I am. I have lived a thousand lifetimes in those twenty-two years, and I have cried over the past long enough. Time to chase—and hopefully catch—a few new dreams. So, I gather myself and walk into my future.

"Jeez, Brie, how did you manage to pack your life into two suitcases? I don't think I have ever known a girl to travel on vacation this light, much less move across the country."

With an emphasis on the name I now choose to be called, my cousin, Daniel, ribs me as he lifts all the belongings I cared to carry with me into this new adventure into the bed of his pickup truck.

"I told you, I am taking this moving-on thing very seriously. New everything. New name. New home. New friends. Even new clothes."

So far, I am happy with my decision to move west and reconnect with my cousin. We were great friends when we were children—before his parents divorced, and he moved to Cali with his dad, Matthew Taylor. Uncle Matt had done well for himself as the premier Dentist to the Stars. I assume well-maintained teeth are a fairly lucrative commodity in Hollywood. Every single face aspiring to be on stage, screen, or print has to have them after all.

Daniel and I kept in touch through the years as much as possible. Sending each other birthday cards every year and placing the occasional telephone call when we were younger and seeing each other when he came to visit his mom, my mother's older sister, in the summers. Once we were old enough for social media accounts though, it was like he had never left. That is the thing about sites like Instagram and Twitter; you feel like you are actively participating in the lives of people you haven't set your eyes on in ten or more years. It is the best and the worst thing about social media. Disconnected connection.

It felt good to be in the same space as him now. He has grown into a handsome man, tall and broad-shouldered, like his dad. His dark hair is a little wild, and he still has the scar that runs through his left eyebrow from when he fell from the tire swing in my backyard when we were about six years old. He is sporting a five-o'clock shadow; actually, it looks more like a seven-o'clock shadow at this point. And, of course, he has a smile that could blind you, courtesy of his dad. He is all grown up and an aspiring musician, still living at home in his dad's pool house in Beverly Hills while he lives his dream. He is a talented guitar player and singer-songwriter. I just know he is going to be famous one day. I wanted freedom and a fresh start, but I longed for a familiar face that wasn't vetted to the past in a way that it would keep popping up on me. Daniel is that face.

"You have certainly come to the right place. A lot of miles between here and New York. They are two completely different worlds, but don't worry; I am sure you are going to fit right in. Dawn and Kelsey have already gotten your room ready, and they are excited to officially meet you."

Dawn Martin is Daniel's current girlfriend and his stepsister, Kelsey Green's, best friend and roommate. Uncle Matt married Kelsey's mom when Daniel and Kelsey were already temperamental teenagers, so their relationship was strained from the beginning. Her mom was a former dental client and a wilting flower of an actress who had found fame in the early nineties, playing the sexy villain on a popular network soap opera. Daniel didn't take too well to the two female drama queens coming into and taking over his and his dad's easy bachelor lives. However, once he started dating his new sister's best friend, much to her chagrin, they were forced into a tentative truce. According to Daniel though, they grew on each other and settled into a love/hate, familial relationship.

The girls' former roommate, Tonya, just vacated her room and moved out on her own. That left them with a room for rent and hopefully room in their inner circle for me. I could use some friends.

Daniel told me all about the two—the good, bad, and ugly—and I feel like I already know them. My favorite part about them is the ugly. I know that sounds insane, but maybe my ugly won't seem so bad next to theirs. I guess we all carry a bit of it with us, but I am here to try to shed mine for good.

We pull up to a gorgeous stucco building in Santa Monica about thirty minutes later. It is a well-maintained place with a quaint court-yard and gated parking. It is close to the beach and the Third Street Promenade and definitely something I would never have been able to afford on my own, but with my savings and the money Una tucked into my hand as I left, I should, hopefully, be able to cover one-third of the cost until I can find a decent-paying job.

Enrolling in classes is my first order of business though. I gradu-ated high school a few months early and then took time off to spend a couple of years in Paris with my mom's younger sister, Aunt Mitzi. It was a glorious time in my life. Paris is a dream, and Aunt Mitzi is one of my favorite people on the planet. She took a heartbroken teen in and showed her a whole new world full of culture, food, fashion, and excitement that only Paris could provide.

I started taking classes at NYU the semester following my return to New York, but a little more than a year in was when everything in my life went sideways. Looking back, I probably should have stayed in France and gone to university. I loved it there, but something—or better yet, someone—kept calling me back home. Him. No, he is not allowed here. No thoughts of him in my new life.

Daniel parks the truck and hops out. I gather my purse and phone and open the door. A wonderful aroma of salt and sea envelops me, and I instantly love it here. Fresh air. Fresh start.

"Apartment number is three-B, and the girls are waiting for you. Go on up and say hi, and I'll grab your things and be up in a minute," Daniel instructs me as he types away on his phone.

I turn toward the courtyard and take it in. The space is a good size with a few large shade trees sprinkled about. There are cobblestone sidewalks lined with flower beds bursting with purple salvia and bright yellow coreopsis along the path. A couple of people are seated on benches under the trees, reading or typing away on their laptops, and one girl is lying on a beach towel, soaking up a few late rays of sunshine. *Yes, I will definitely love it here.*

I make my way to the center building and climb the exterior staircase leading up to the third floor. It is insane how anxious I am to meet my new roommates. *Will they be able to tell by looking at me the hell I have been through this past year? Is my outside as tattered as my inside?* I know these are silly thoughts because my scars do not show on the outside. They are not physical scars, not all of them anyway.

I reach the third floor, and I see 3B right at the top of the stairs. A shadow is peeking out of the front window before my foot even hits the landing, so I assume Daniel texted to let them know we had arrived. As I raise my knuckles to knock, the door swings open, and a tall, slender girl my age with shoulder-length blonde hair that has bright pink tips comes barreling for me and wraps her arms around me.

Dawn, I think to myself. *This must be Dawn.*

"Brie, we are so glad you are finally here," she practically squeals.

She smells like coconut, and I allow myself to absorb some of her enthusiasm as I squeeze her back and look behind her into my new home. It's intimidating, but she hooks her arm in mine and leads me in like we have known each other for ages.

"We have your room all ready for you. The bed is made up with fresh linens, and it has been thoroughly cleaned. Tonya took everything with her that wasn't nailed down, but all of the furniture is still here, so we'll just have to go shopping to get you all the essentials, like pillows, blankets, and a lamp. Not that you need too many blankets here. It's always warm."

She is talking a mile a minute as she leads me through the apartment, past a nice-sized living space and down a hall. I instantly like her.

"This is your room. It's the smallest of the three, but it has the best view. The ocean is across the street and down a couple of blocks. You have your own bathroom—well, sort of. It is the one across the hall, and it is also the guest bathroom when we have company. Kelsey and I have a Jack and Jill bath between our rooms, and we share it. Come on; I will show you the rest."

I follow her and check out both their rooms and the large-closet-sized space they use as a makeshift office with a tiny desk and shared computer and printer.

"Now, we come to our favorite spot in the entire apartment," she informs me as we round the living room.

She swings her arms wide in a dramatic game-show-hostess fashion. "Ta-da. The kitchen. This is where all the magic happens. We don't have a table or anything, but this island is massive, and the barstools are very comfy. It is the reason we rented this place. It is just so big and open. We like to cook, and we absolutely love to eat. There is a small deck through those sliding glass doors. It has an outdoor table and umbrella with a matching couch and electric fire pit. We sometimes like to sit out there and have coffee in the morning or dinner if it is a nice, cool evening. Or wine. We like our wine almost as much as we like our food."

She laughs, and I can't help but smile with her.

Kelsey, a petite girl with long blonde hair, is behind the island, cutting up what looks like bleu cheese and adding it to a board with other varieties, grapes, and crackers. My stomach growls at the sight.

"Yes, we do. We aren't exactly winos, but let's just say, we do our part to keep Napa Valley thriving." She looks up and adds, "Wow, look at you. You look like some exotic creature with your dark hair and olive skin. We don't see many Italian beauties around here. It's all bleached-blonde Valley girls with spray tans and fake tits. Present company excluded, of course." She slides her eyes to Dawn, who obviously has enhanced assets.

Dawn playfully sticks her tongue out at her friend. I can't help but notice that Kelsey is a natural stunner. Makeup free with a smattering of freckles across her nose. Her long hair is pulled back into a ponytail, and she is dressed in yoga pants and a tight tee.

I wonder if every girl in LA really is blonde and beautiful. It's very different from home. New York is a melting pot of ethnicity and culture, and everyone always seems to be made up to the max and in a hurry to be somewhere.

"I have some snacks here because we assumed you would be peckish after that long flight. We figured we would just call out for dinner later tonight after you had time to get settled in."

We hear Daniel enter the kitchen as I thank them for the warm welcome.

"No problem. We are happy to have someone new in here. Tonya was ... well, she was ..."

"She was the devil," Daniel finishes Kelsey's thought from the doorway.

Dawn walks over to him for a quick kiss and then admits, "Yeah, she was. I don't want you to think we are difficult to live with or anything. She was just in a bad mood most of the time and a bit on the lazy side. I mean, really, you are a twenty-three-year-old adult; wash your own dishes and pick your own clothes up off of the bathroom floor every once in a while." She rolls her eyes. "When she started hitting on Kelsey's boyfriend right in front of us one night, it was the straw that broke the camel's back. Girl Code. You never, ever break Girl Code. She had to go."

I get it. I have four brothers. *Tidy* is not a word in their vocabulary, and it drove me and my mother nuts. And I, too, have felt the sharp sting of a friend's betrayal.

"You guys do not have to worry about me. I like a clean and neat environment, too, and I have zero time or desire to hit on anyone at all. I am focusing on me right now. Only me."

A look of relief passes between my new roomies, and I know—I just know—I am home.

Other Books

Cross My Heart Duet

Both of Me

Both of Us

Acknowledgments

First, I want to thank every single reader, blogger, and fellow author who took a chance on this book. Each message, text, e-mail, share, giveaway, and review has meant the world to me.

To my friends and family who not only encouraged me to chase my dream, but also supported me every step of the way—I love you all with my whole heart.

To the gracious and amusing members of the Stockman Message Board who patiently answered a million questions about cattle ranching the past few months—I thank you from the bottom of my heart. Jefferson and Braxton would have sounded like idiots if it wasn't for you guys.

Amanda White and Gloria Green, thank you for your encouragement and honest feedback. You're both priceless.

Autumn Gantz, you are an amazing and hard-working publicist, but most of all, you are a fabulous friend.

Jovana Shirley, you are invaluable. Thank you for making me look good. If the world saw the hot-mess first draft of this book, they would know how true that statement is. You are an angel, and commas are still the devil.

Judy Zweifel, Stacey Blake, Sommer Stein, and Michaela Mangum, thank you for your contributions to this book. You are all incredible at what you do, and I'm truly blessed to have you all be a part of this journey with me.

Last but not least, David Miller, you are the unicorn husband. I know how lucky I am.

About the Author

Amber Kelly is a romance author that calls North Carolina home. She has been a avid reader from a young age and you could always find her with her nose in a book completely enthralled in an adventure. With the support of her husband and family, in 2018, she decided to finally give a voice to the stories in her head and her debut novel, Both of Me was born. You can connect with Amber on Facebook at facebook. com/AuthorAmberKelly, on IG @authoramberkelly, on twitter @ AuthorAmberKel1 or via her website www.authoramberkelly.com.

Made in the USA
Middletown, DE
12 July 2021

44033631R00165